SAWMILL SPRINGS

GERRI HILL

BELLA
BOOKS

2017

Bella Books, Inc.
P.O. Box 10543
Tallahassee, FL 32302

Printed in the United States of America on acid-free paper.

First Bella Books Edition 2017

Editor: Medora MacDougall
Cover Designer: Sandy Knowles

ISBN: 978-1-59493-550-3

Other Bella Books by Gerri Hill

Angel Fire
Artist's Dream
At Seventeen
Behind the Pine Curtain
Chasing a Brighter Blue
The Cottage
Coyote Sky
Dawn of Change
Devil's Rock
Gulf Breeze
Hell's Highway
Hunter's Way
In the Name of the Father
Keepers of the Cave
The Killing Room
Love Waits
The Midnight Moon
No Strings
One Summer Night
Paradox Valley
Partners
Pelican's Landing
The Rainbow Cedar
The Roundabout
The Scorpion
Sierra City
Snow Falls
Storms
The Target
Weeping Walls

About the Author

Gerri Hill has thirty-one published works, including the 2014 GCLS winner *The Midnight Moon*, 2011, 2012 and 2013 winners *Devil's Rock*, *Hell's Highway* and *Snow Falls*, and the 2009 GCLS winner *Partners*, the last book in the popular Hunter Series, as well as the 2013 Lambda finalist *At Seventeen*. Gerri lives in south-central Texas, only a few hours from the Gulf Coast, a place that has inspired many of her books. With her partner, Diane, they share their life with two Australian shepherds—Casey and Cooper—and a couple of furry felines. For more, visit her website at gerrihill.com.

CHAPTER ONE

"So, Murphy, what are you doing here, anyway?"

Mandi Murphy raised the beer bottle to her lips, pausing before drinking. The last of the evening sun was still visible through the windows and in a corner, she noticed a crack running diagonally across the glass in one of the panes. "Here?"

"Not here at Cross Roads Tavern. Here…in town."

Murphy leaned her head back, staring at the ceiling. She'd been in town over a month already…here in tiny Sawmill Springs. Lori, Chief Dixon's admin—after spending the first several weeks asking subtle questions—had finally talked her into a drink at the local beer joint. Murphy had deflected both personal and professional questions, choosing instead to fade into the background as much as possible and just do her job. Of course, after a fifteen-year career in Houston—working in both vice and homicide—she was having a hard time adjusting to riding in a patrol vehicle all day. Lori, however, was staring at her questioningly, and Murphy knew she had to give her something.

"It…it had been a hell of a week," Murphy said. "A week that changed my life."

Lori leaned forward, resting her elbows on the table. "I'm a good listener."

Murphy lifted an eyebrow questioningly. "Why?"

Lori shrugged. "Because you've been so secretive. And so has Earl," she said, referring to Chief Dixon. "Nobody knows anything about you except that you came from Houston."

"Oh, I see. And you've been charged with finding out about me, huh?"

Lori smiled. "Well, I'm curious by nature and I'm a bit of a gossip. So yeah, they voted me in." She tipped her beer bottle at her. "You've been here five weeks and not a peep out of you. The only thing we've learned is not to call you Mandi or we get the death stare."

Murphy smiled slightly. "My mother is the only one who still dares to call me that."

"So? Why are you here?" Lori asked again. "Why did you leave an exciting job at Houston PD to come here, of all places?"

"Exciting? Is that what you think?"

"Compared to Sawmill Springs? Yeah. It's a big night here when someone gets arrested for assault. The guys get all jacked up over a burglary, which might happen once a month if they're lucky. But murder? No. Very, very rare." She leaned forward. "You worked in homicide, Earl says. I'm sure you've seen your share."

"More than my share," she admitted.

"So why leave?"

"Like I said, it was a bad week." She picked absently at the label on her beer bottle. "My grandmother lived with me. My dad's mom," she explained. "Had been with me about six months, I guess. I came home one night, found her sitting in her recliner, my cat in her lap—which really wasn't odd. That was the same position they were in when I left." She finished off the beer, wincing at the lukewarm temp of the last swallow. "There was this eerie stillness in the room though. It was too quiet."

"Oh, no. She was dead?" Lori asked in a near-whisper.

Murphy nodded. "She was only eighty-one. In relatively good health too."

"Why was she living with you if she was in good health?"

"She had a vision problem. Couldn't drive anymore. Had a hard time in the kitchen." She smiled. "It was weird having her there at first, you know. I guess I didn't think I'd miss having her around." She sighed. "That old cat missed her too, I guess. Four days after she died, I found Tuffy in his bed by the window, the sunlight on him, just like he loved."

Lori gasped. "Oh, no. Not your cat too?"

Murphy knew Lori loved cats. She had several pictures of them on her desk. She blew out her breath, hoping she looked properly sorrowful. "Yeah, my cat wasn't sleeping. He was dead."

Lori covered her mouth with her hand, her eyes nearly tearing up. "Oh, my God. That's so sad."

"Yeah. Bad week all around."

Lori frowned. "That's why you left Houston? Because your grandmother and your cat died?"

Murphy brushed at the dark hair on her forehead, pushing it out of her eyes. Couldn't she have come up with something better than that? She hated cats, for one thing. Hated the little monsters. And Nana would kill her if she knew she'd fabricated her death. As she pictured her beloved grandmother—with that old tabby cat of hers sitting in her lap—she couldn't help but smile. Lori punched her in the arm.

"You made that story up!" she accused.

Murphy laughed quietly. "What? You don't believe me?"

"That was *so* mean," she said. "I love cats. I love grand-mothers."

"I hate cats. I do love my grandmother though."

"Is that your way of saying it's none of our business why you left Houston?"

Murphy shrugged. "There were a lot of reasons," she said evasively. Nothing she wanted to talk about, especially not with a woman she barely knew. How could Lori possibly understand?

"Okay. Fair enough. But you could lighten up a little, you know. You keep everyone at arm's length."

"I'm sorry. I'll try to be a little more open."

"Good. Because we're like a family here. And I'd like to include you in that too."

Lori was probably a few years older than she was. Married, two kids. They had nothing in common, really, other than they were the only two women in the police department. It was a small town and they had a small staff. She was one of eight officers. Chief Dixon had her riding with Tim Beckman, a rather burly man who'd worked there since he was twenty-three—nearly eighteen years—and he was now pushing forty.

He'd taken her across town to the county sheriff's department a couple of times. They also had one female on patrol—Gloria Mendez. Gloria was young and not in the least bit shy. She'd asked her out to lunch the first time they met. Nothing fancy, just a quick meal at the Arby's near the interstate—it was Gloria's lunch break. Four days later, they had dinner. At Gloria's place. Chili con carne, Gloria's grandmother's recipe. It was delicious.

However, the conversation lagged and Murphy wondered if it was due to their nearly ten-year age difference. Even so, Gloria had made it no secret that she was interested in getting to know Murphy better…in a much more intimate way than simply dinner. Unfortunately, Murphy didn't have the same feelings. Six months from now, she might be feeling differently. Hell, even a month from now. Right now, though, she wasn't ready. She was still trying to ease into the town itself, which she'd found more difficult than she'd imagined.

Maybe because she was used to the city, used to the fast pace, used to being alone. When she and Sean—her partner—had ended their shift, he went home to his wife and she went home to an empty apartment. Or when she had the energy, she'd hit the local pub where most of the guys hung out. Friendly wagers on pool or darts was the norm. It got loud and rowdy sometimes, but it was all in fun…a bar full of cops trying to shake off the stress of their jobs for a few hours. Some of them, like her, were married to the job only and had no one to go home to. She'd found, though, that the job made a lousy spouse. She sighed. Maybe this time it would be different. Maybe this time, she wouldn't be juggling open homicide investigations. Maybe this time, she wouldn't be in the middle of an FBI sting operation. Maybe this time, no one would get killed. And who knows… maybe in a few months, she might take Gloria up on her offer of staying the night.

"I should get going," she said. "My shift starts at six."

"Earl still got you riding with Timmy?"

She smiled. "He's nearly forty years old and weighs two hundred and sixty pounds. Can't believe everyone calls him Timmy."

"Oh, he's a big teddy bear, that's all he is."

She nodded. "Yeah, he's okay. And I've got one more week with him, and then I switch to nights."

"I've been here six years now and I still have a hard time keeping up with the schedules," Lori said. "Ten-hour shifts, three days on then two off, then two on and three off. I finally get them down, then you switch to nights and I'm all mixed up again."

"Doesn't bother me," she said. "If I was married and had a family, it would probably suck." Lori eyed her for a second and Murphy knew what question was coming next.

"You ever been married?"

"Are you fishing for more gossip?"

"I suppose it's nobody's business, but we are a small staff." Lori smiled. "And we're family and family tends to gossip about one another."

"And what conclusion did we come up with?"

"Let's see…six votes for gay, three for straight and one— Jeff—is afraid of you and didn't want to vote."

She faked a smile. "Wow. I got three votes for straight. That hasn't happened in a while."

"Guys—what do they know? They all think you're too cute to be gay."

She stood up. "Yeah…haven't been called cute in a while either."

"There's also the rumor that you and Gloria Mendez went out," Lori continued, still fishing for information.

"Is that right?" She gave Lori a friendly nod. "I need to get going. Thanks for the beer."

She was conscious of the curious glances that followed her as she made her way to the door.

"Come back and see us."

She turned, nodding at the bartender as she left. She'd learned—after Lori had been greeted with a hug when they'd gotten there—that her cousin owned the place. It was a local dive, dark and shadowy along the edges, but a pool table with a bright light overhead made it seem welcoming. There was even an old-fashioned jukebox in the corner, one that had been playing outdated country songs for most of the night. She figured she'd come back sometime. The house she was renting was lonelier than her apartment had been. Who knows? Maybe she could make some friends here. She had a vision of leaning over the pool table with a cue stick, lining up a shot. The only person she knew in town besides her own staff was Gloria. For some reason, she couldn't picture Gloria at the Cross Roads Tavern.

She got into her truck and sat there for a few moments, wondering—once again—if she'd been too hasty leaving Houston. She started the engine. No. While it may have seemed to be an impulsive decision, she knew that it had been past time to leave.

Leon's death wasn't the only reason she'd fled Houston... but it was the main reason.

She stared off into the darkness, picturing his face. In her mind, she ignored the ugly scar on his cheek, the scar that split his lower lip in half, giving him a permanent crooked smile. It was his dark, compassionate eyes that she remembered the most. Soulful eyes...tender and kind.

She took a deep breath, then blew it out quickly as she pulled away, Leon's image fading from her mind as the warm summer breeze blew in through the opened windows.

CHAPTER TWO

"So, you sick of me yet, Murphy?"

"Sick of your constant chatter, yeah."

Tim laughed heartily, his bushy mustache lifting up as he smiled. "What can I say? I like to talk."

That was an understatement, but at least it helped pass the time. Like most everyone else in the department, Tim had been born and raised in Sawmill Springs. And he, like the others, knew nearly everyone in this town of forty-five hundred souls. He'd introduced her around everywhere they went, and while she was greeted with smiles and handshakes, she could tell they viewed her as an outsider.

He turned into the parking lot of Knott's Café. "You got a preference for lunch or is this okay?"

She looked at the nondescript, stone building situated between a car wash on one side and a self-storage building on the other. "The café again?"

"Thursday is meatloaf day," he said.

"And Wednesday was chicken-fried steak," she said, echoing his reasoning for stopping yesterday.

"It was damn good, wasn't it?"

"It was. Would have been better for dinner. I'm not used to eating that big of a meal at lunch."

"That's how I keep my figure. Eat a big meal at lunch then skip dinner." His bushy mustache lifted up as he grinned. "Kidding, of course. I never miss dinner."

They were greeted at the door by the same woman who had welcomed them yesterday—Paula.

"There you are," Paula said. "I was thinking you wouldn't be able to pass up Brenda's meatloaf."

"Of course, I wouldn't miss it. Her meatloaf is better than my momma's and that's sayin' something."

"I see you brought your friend back with you," Paula said with a smile.

Murphy cringed at her statement but returned her smile. "Officer Murphy, ma'am. Good to see you again." She deliberately adjusted her duty belt, placing her hand on the butt of her weapon. Maybe Paula failed to recognize her uniform, but surely the presence of her weapon told her that she wasn't Tim's *friend*. Perhaps she should have whipped out her handcuffs and spun them around on her finger.

"Lighten up. She didn't mean anything," Tim said after they'd scooted into a booth.

"So how long do I have to be here before they treat me like a cop? Or is it because I'm a woman?"

"You're a stranger and a woman. Two strikes against you," he said as he sipped from a glass of water. "If they have a choice of vegetables, get the green beans. There's chunks of bacon *and* ham in there. And if you ask, they'll put a pat of butter on top too."

She stared at him for a second, then shook her head. "That is so not good for you."

"Oh, man. That's some good stuff right there."

They weren't given a menu when they came in and she wondered if she dared to request something other than the meatloaf. She glanced around them, noting a few curious glances, but for the most part, the café patrons were enjoying lunch and quiet conversations.

"Hey, y'all," the waitress said. Murphy couldn't remember her name from yesterday so she simply smiled at her.

"Hey, Sherry," Tim greeted.

Oh, yeah. Sherry.

"Y'all both want the special today?"

"Sure do. You got green beans on the menu?"

"Sorry Timmy, not today. Brenda's got squash instead."

"That's fine. I like her squash too."

"Actually, I don't think I want meatloaf," Murphy said, causing both Sherry and Tim to stare at her as if she was talking gibberish. "Do you have something like a...a club sandwich? Turkey?"

"Got some ham left from breakfast. Will that do?"

"That'd be great. Lettuce? Tomato?"

"I'll get her to fix up a sandwich for you."

"Thank you."

"Sweet tea?"

"I'll just have water," she said.

When Sherry left, Tim looked at her disapprovingly. "If you want to fit in, eat the daily special. Look around," he said with a wave of his hand. "Nobody's eating a sandwich."

"Sorry. I'm not crazy about meatloaf. And like I said, I'm not used to eating such a heavy meal at lunch."

"Tomorrow is burger day," he said.

"I remember. We came here last Friday." She leaned back against the bench seat. "How about, next week, I pick lunch places."

"Don't drag me to any of those fast-food chain places over by the interstate," he warned.

"If those are off your list, there's not much left."

"Got the Dairy Mart. Or we could run out to Cross Roads. They make a mean burger. Sometimes they have fried chicken too."

"Went to Cross Roads the other night."

He nodded. "Yeah, with Lori. What'd you think?"

"Typical beer joint. Reminded me of some of the places around my hometown."

"Oh, yeah? Where's that?"

"Eagle Lake. It's out west of Houston, a town a little smaller than Sawmill Springs."

"Smaller than us? It must be small then." He nodded at Sherry who brought his tea. He took a sip, and then reached for a sugar packet. "You heard about Earl's daughter?"

"Didn't know he had a daughter. What's up?"

"She's coming back."

She shrugged. "Okay. And?"

"She's a cop."

"Oh, yeah?"

"Started out here in the department, way back when," he said. "She used to do dispatch."

"And did she knit like Shirley does?" she asked, referring to one of the ladies who manned the call center. She didn't recall a time she'd ever seen her without knitting needles and yarn in her hands.

"Nah, she left here right after high school. Married Kevin Lade. You know, his family has the Ford place in town."

She nodded. "Right."

"Anyway, they married and moved to Austin. She went to college and he got a job. Wasn't but a year later they divorced and he moved on back home."

"And now she's a cop?"

"FBI," he said. "Earl's kept a spot open for her, hoping she'd come back one day. Now it looks like she finally is."

She frowned. "What do you mean, kept a spot?"

"Harvey Fisher retired, oh, six or seven years ago now. Earl never filled his spot. Told us he was keeping it open for his daughter."

"So whose spot did I take?"

"Larry Bostic's. He transferred down to Huntsville." He stirred his tea slowly. "Anyway, we're all kinda wondering how that's going to work out with her."

"What do you mean?"

"Well, she's FBI."

"That doesn't mean anything. Maybe she had a desk job."

"No, no. She was out in the field. She even did some undercover work one time too. She was in Miami for a while. Then New Orleans. Last few years, up in Dallas."

"So what are you worried about?"

"New officer comes in, they're low man on the totem pole, you know? Like you. Even though you were a detective and you've likely got more experience than all of us put together, you're still low man on the pole."

"Right. I understood that coming in."

"Exactly. But what about her? She was damn FBI."

"You speak of the FBI as if they're godlike. Trust me, they're not. My last assignment in Houston, I was teamed with them. And they can fuck up as well as anybody."

Tim's eyes widened. "Damn, Murphy. You got issues with them?"

"You might say."

"Well, I can't say that we're looking forward to Kayla being here, that's for sure. I mean, she's nice enough when she comes by to visit Earl, but still, she's FBI."

"Kayla? That's her name? So when's she coming?"

"I don't know. In case you haven't noticed, Earl doesn't talk much."

"I thought he just didn't like me."

"No, no. He's a man of few words, as they say. Lori processed the paperwork though. That's how we found out. Guess he's going to spring her on us one day."

"So she'll be out on patrol?"

"Who knows what he'll have her do. Makes no sense to me. Why would you leave the FBI to come here?" He must have realized what he'd said as he stared at her. "Of course, you were a homicide detective in Houston. Why in the hell would you leave that and come to Sawmill Springs?"

She lifted one corner of her mouth in a smile. "Well, you see, my grandmother was living with me."

"Oh, hell, Murphy, don't give me that shit. Lori's already told us the story about your grandmother and the cat."

She laughed, not surprised that Lori—a self-proclaimed gossip—shared her story with them. She was spared having to answer as their plates were brought out. A huge platter of meatloaf, mashed potatoes and gravy and a heap of squash with, yes, chunks of bacon, was placed in front of Tim. He grabbed a fork and took a scoopful even before her plate was slid over to her. On it sat a nice, thick ham sandwich, bulging with lettuce and tomato, with creamy mayo escaping at the edges.

"Didn't know if you wanted mustard, so I brought the bottle." She also placed a small bag of potato chips beside her plate.

"This looks great, Sherry. Thank you."

"Well, it ain't meatloaf, that's for sure." She turned to Tim. "How is it?"

His mouth was full, so he nodded and smiled.

"Good." She leaned down. "I had Brenda put a little extra on there for you," she said quietly before walking away.

Murphy lifted the bread and squirted a little mustard on top. "She's flirting with you. She did that yesterday too."

Tim blushed. "Sherry? No way."

"She married?"

"Not anymore. Been divorced several years already, I guess."

She took a bite of her sandwich, glad she'd requested it instead of settling for the meatloaf. "So, back to Earl's daughter. How old is she?"

"Kayla? Oh, gosh, I don't know. In school, I think she was a year ahead of Kent. Kent's my younger brother," he explained as he stabbed into the pile of squash. "So she's probably thirty-two or thereabouts. What did you say you were? Thirty-five?"

"In a few months I will be."

"Yeah, so, y'all are about the same age, I guess."

"Kinda young to be quitting the FBI, don't you think?"

"Maybe something happened." He looked at her and smiled. "Thirty-four's kinda young to be quitting the Houston PD, isn't it?"

Murphy met his gaze. "Yeah. Maybe something happened."

CHAPTER THREE

Kayla felt her stress slip away little by little, as each mile took her closer to Sawmill Springs. Even though she'd resigned from the FBI almost two weeks ago, she felt like she hadn't had a minute to relax. Coordinating the move had been harder than she'd imagined, especially when she couldn't find a house to rent. Her mother, of course, had offered up her old room, but that was absolutely *not* an option. Well, maybe as a last resort, but certainly not up front. The very real possibility of her having to stay with them loomed large, however, as Mr. Foster at the local real estate office continued to come up empty on acceptable rental properties. Her move date was already scheduled and she'd gone so far as to rent a storage building to store her stuff when a duplex had finally opened up. She'd sent her mother over to check it out and she'd given it her approval, but with a warning—tiny, tiny kitchen. As much as she loved to cook, a tiny kitchen still won out over moving into her parents' house.

She looked in the mirror, seeing the movers she'd hired following behind her in their large truck. She was excited to be moving, and that excitement helped to temper the fatigue she felt. The last week had been filled with goodbye lunches and dinners, and last night, she'd been surprised by a group of seven coming over with pizza and beer for an impromptu goodbye party. Conspicuously absent from last night's group was Jennifer, the only one of their team not accounted for. Kayla wasn't sure if she was happy Jennifer had skipped or if she was angry that she didn't bother to say goodbye. A little of both, she supposed. After all, the main reason she was leaving was because of Jennifer.

Oh, that wasn't entirely true. Their breakup had simply complicated things more, that was all. She'd had the urge to move on from the FBI long before that. Knowing she had a place to go to, knowing her father had an opening, made the decision easy…once she'd finally decided it was time. These last few months, with her and Jennifer trying to avoid each other as much as possible, had made their working conditions nearly unbearable—not only for them but their team as well. Avoiding Jennifer had nothing whatsoever to do with Jennifer starting to date again. She'd been asked out plenty of times herself. She could also have been dating. She simply chose not to.

"You're the one who broke things off," she reminded herself as she slapped at the steering wheel. Yeah, she'd been the one to end it, but that didn't mean that she didn't miss Jennifer—at least at first. She'd found that Jennifer was a bit spiteful, though, as if Kayla had simply crushed her with the breakup. Truth was, Jennifer knew as well as she did that their romance was far from perfect. Kayla also knew that it had run its course. She just didn't realize how vindictive Jennifer would be. More than one person had shared some of the hurtful stories Jennifer was spreading.

With her already waning exuberance for the job, that had simply pushed her over the edge. A phone call to her father had set things in motion, and now here she was, heading back to her hometown, about to join her father's squad. From FBI agent in a big city, to patrol officer in a small country town—all in a matter of weeks.

She pushed her sunglasses on top of her head, meeting her eyes in the mirror. The eyes that looked back at her were no longer shrouded in stress. No, they were nearly dancing with anticipation…and a little bit of nervousness as well.

She had no idea how the other officers on her father's staff would treat her. She had no idea if she'd even fit in. Added to that fear was another: would she be bored out of her mind?

CHAPTER FOUR

Murphy stood with the others, smiling as Tim covered his mouth to stifle a yawn. It was six a.m. and shift change. This would be the last day she rode with Tim. Then, after her two days off, she'd be out on her own. She thought six weeks of orientation was a little excessive, considering her experience, but she didn't protest. At least Tim let her drive occasionally.

Everyone was there, including Jeff and Ivan, who were off duty today. Well, everyone except for the two still out on patrol. There were nine officers sharing ten-hour and twelve-hour shifts, so there was always an overlap.

She elbowed Tim as he yawned again. "Guess I'll be driving today since you look like you're still half asleep."

"Hell, I stayed up and watched a damn movie last night."

Chief Dixon walked to the front of the room and the quiet conversation came to a halt. She'd been told it was a rare occasion that he assembled everyone like this. She assumed, as did Tim, that Earl was about to brief them on his daughter joining the staff.

"First off…Ivan, Jeff…thank you for coming in. This won't take long." He cleared his throat and got right to the point. "Adding a new officer to the group. Kayla Dixon, my daughter. She'll officially start on Monday, but she'll probably be around here the next couple of days."

The only sound in the room was some idle shifting of feet, and Earl raised his eyebrows.

"Questions?"

Ivan raised his hand. "Is she going to be like…squad leader or something?"

The chief wasn't an overly tall man, but his jet-black mustache and dark eyes made him a little intimidating. That, and his ever-present white Stetson hat gave him a rakish look that would have served him well in the Wild West days. He tilted his head slightly and arched one eyebrow up into the shadow of his hat.

"Squad leader? Do we have any squad leaders? Hell, do we even have enough here to be broken up into squads?"

Light laughter filled the room.

"Well, I mean, she's FBI and all," Ivan said, as if that explained everything.

"Yeah. But she ain't coming in here as an agent or a detective. We ain't got no damn detectives." He glanced over at her. "No offense, Murphy."

"So what's her title?" This question coming from Tim.

"Title? Well, Timmy, I think we already got our pecking order here, don't we? I'm the chief, Wilson here is the sergeant and the rest of you are the rest of you. She'll be the rest of you." His mustache lifted up in one corner. "Until I say otherwise, that is."

He left the room leaving them all standing there. Murphy nudged Tim. "Title?"

"Hell, I thought maybe he'd make her a captain right off the bat." He glanced over at Wilson. "Nothing against you, Pete."

"Did you know about this, Pete?" Jeff asked.

"He told me yesterday. Of course, Lori's been whispering about it for a week now."

"So, is she going to be assigned to someone, like Murphy was?"

"I'd imagine so. You volunteering, Ivan?"

Ivan shook his head. "No sir. I mean, I've met Kayla a few times, but I don't think I want to be riding with the chief's daughter."

"I just got through training one," Tim said, motioning at her. "I've done my deed."

"Training?" Murphy said. "Is that what you call it?"

The others laughed, including Tim. "Hey, I showed you all the best places to eat, didn't I?"

"I'll let the chief decide who she rides with. Tim, you've been here the longest. That's why I put Murphy with you. He might want to do the same with Kayla."

"How the hell am I supposed to train an FBI agent? She's going to probably think she knows it all already," he complained.

"Yeah, and she probably does." Wilson motioned to the door. "Hit the streets, guys." He paused as he glanced at Murphy. "And gal, of course."

She smiled quickly. "I'm good at being lumped with the guys, Sergeant. The FBI agent might not appreciate it though."

She and Tim walked out to the patrol car, and she beat him to the driver's side, reaching for the door handle seconds before he did. "Don't want you falling asleep while you're driving."

"This is our last day together, Murphy. You sure you don't want me to take the wheel?"

"I got it."

She pulled out onto the street, cruising slowly toward the downtown area. When Tim drove, he usually waited until eight before hitting Main Street.

"Ain't nothing happening down here yet. Why you cruising this way?"

"If you're going to break into one of the stores, you're going to do it before hours, don't you think?"

"If you're going to break in, you'll do it before daylight."

"So maybe we'll catch somebody on their way out."

"Some fool kid tried to break into Allen's Appliances one night," he said. She'd heard this story twice already, but she kept quiet as he continued. "Used a baseball bat to break the window. Jeff was cruising by and saw the kid hung up in the glass. Hell, he's lucky it didn't chop his damn head off when the glass fell."

She smiled. "And that was four years ago and the last time someone tried to break into one of the stores downtown."

He laughed. "See? You're learning. If you're going to burglarize something, you try a store off by itself. There's too many buildings here and no alleys. No place to run to, no place to hide."

"So you say."

"Yeah. I know this town, Murphy. Now, when you switch shifts and go to nights, then you'll cruise out on the edges. You might scare up some action then."

She nodded. "I'll keep that in mind."

"So…what do you think?"

She shrugged, knowing who his question was referring to. "Not much to think, really. I guess we'll find out on Monday."

"I can already see it. Everyone's going to be walking on eggshells around her, trying not to say something wrong. I mean, we all love Earl, but sometimes, you just got to vent about things. Now, we got to watch our mouth."

Murphy wasn't looking forward to Kayla Dixon joining the staff any more than the rest of them, but for completely different reasons. She had no love for the FBI and she didn't trust them. They were secretive and manipulative to the extreme. She had no reason to think Kayla Dixon would be any different.

"So, is she moving here with a family? Got kids?"

Tim shook his head. "No, after she and Kevin divorced, she didn't remarry. That's kinda weird too. From what I hear, she and Kevin are still friends."

"Well, not all divorce has to be a war, you know." She glanced over at him. "Why didn't you ever marry?"

"Momma's boy," he said. He patted his belly. "Couldn't no one match up to my momma's cooking."

"That an excuse or the reason?"

He sighed. "Just an excuse. Never fell in love, I guess. What about you?"

"What about me?"

"Well, Lori…well, she told us, you know."

She nodded. "Okay. You got a problem with it?"

"No, I'm cool with it. But, you know, you ever been in love?"

She shook her head. "Can't say that I have. Can't say that I really tried either. Too busy with the job."

"Yeah…well, Gloria Mendez, I hear—"

"What? You trying to play matchmaker?"

He laughed. "Just sayin'. You might hit it off."

"Yeah, well, maybe you and Kayla might hit it off. Then your worries will be over with."

He laughed again. "You obviously have never seen Kayla Dixon. She's a blond-haired beauty. Got these gorgeous blue eyes that you could just drown in." He shook his head. "No. A woman like that doesn't look twice at a man like me. Even so, you can't help but look at her. She's like…you know that saying, where a man is lured to a woman and he can't help himself, no matter what?"

"Lured? What are you talking about? A siren?"

"Yeah, yeah, that's it. A siren."

She laughed at him. "You need to start dating more, man. She's just a woman. I doubt she's going to lure you to your death."

"Yeah, well, we'll talk after you're around her for a while. You'll be all tongue-tied like the rest of us. Besides, you know, FBI and all, she kinda intimidates me."

"No reason to be scared of the FBI."

"Yeah, we'll see, Murphy."

CHAPTER FIVE

"I don't know why you want to do this. Even at shift change, you still won't meet everyone," he said. "Why can't you show up on Monday morning, ready for work, just like everybody does?"

"Because I'm not like everyone else," Kayla said. "You've already said they were questioning my role here. I don't want them to treat me differently because I'm your daughter."

"They're going to anyway."

"Maybe at first, but I want to be just one of the guys. I think it's best that I talk to everyone informally first. Besides, I already know most of them anyway."

"Yeah. Got a new one though Murphy."

She nodded. "You mentioned him one time. How long has he been here?"

"Six weeks. And he's a she."

"A woman? That's a first. What's gotten into you?"

"Oh, hell, I can't say I'm crazy about her though."

"If you don't like her, why did you hire her?"

"Because she was the most qualified. Her lieutenant from down in Houston said she was top-notch."

"Houston?"

"Yeah. She was a detective down there. Homicide."

"How in the world did a detective from Houston find her way to Sawmill Springs?"

"Don't know. Didn't ask," he said.

She looked at him suspiciously. "So why don't you like her?"

He turned into the station parking lot, pulling into his reserved spot. "No particular reason."

"Oh, no. Are you kidding me?"

"What?"

"She's gay?" she guessed.

His mustache twitched. "Rumor has it."

She shook her head. "Wow. What a double-edged sword for you, huh."

"Meaning?"

"Meaning you hired her because she was the most qualified, yet you don't like her, simply because she's gay."

"You know me better than that," he said. "I ain't got nothing against gay people. If that was the case, I wouldn't still love you."

She smiled at him. "That's because you don't think I'm really gay."

"You can't blame me for holding out hope."

She sighed. "Dad…we've talked about this."

"Oh, honey…but Kevin…he was the best. He—"

"Yes, he's a good guy. We dated all through high school, so I know him very well."

"He still pines for you. He—"

"Oh, God…he's not *pining* for me," she said with a roll of her eyes.

"Of course he is. Everyone can see it."

"He's married. He's got three kids," she reminded him as she got out.

He looked at her across the top of the car. "Then how come you two always get together whenever you come home to visit?"

"We don't *always* get together. Besides, we were best friends in high school."

"You weren't best friends. You were boyfriend and girlfriend," he said, slamming his door a bit harder than was necessary.

"Dad…why do you think our divorce was so amicable? We both knew being married wasn't the right thing for us."

"You hardly gave it long enough to work out. What? Nine, ten months?"

"It was a very long ten months. And because we were smart enough and mature enough to end it when we did, we're still friends." She walked closer and squeezed his arm. "That was so many years ago, Dad. You've got to let it go. Kevin's moved on, he's got a great family now. Why can't you just let it go?"

"Is it wrong for me to want you to get married, to have kids someday? Wouldn't mind a couple of grandkids to bounce on my knee."

She tried not to be short with him, but she was so weary of this same discussion they seemed to have whenever she came back to Sawmill Springs.

"I can get married now, if I want to. I can have kids too. I choose not to." She looked at him pointedly. "And Jason has given you three grandchildren already."

"They live way over in Alabama. It's not the same."

"Look. I love you. I know you're getting old and crotchety, but this has got to stop, Dad. Mom never has these conversations with me. Why do you feel the need to constantly question my sexuality?"

She was surprised that he actually blushed, his face turning bright red. "I ain't talking nothing about sex now," he said. "Besides, you started this conversation, not me."

She nodded. "You're right. I did. Because apparently the only reason you don't like this Murphy person is because she's gay."

"Well, don't be too quick to judge. You may not like her either. According to Lori, she's a little standoffish. Hasn't shared much about her personal life to them."

"Lori is the world's biggest gossip. If you don't dish out your life story to her, she considers you rude and unsociable."

He paused at the door. "I thought you liked Lori."

"I like her fine. She's just one of those people who are *too* friendly. Not everyone wants to be an open book. Like me, for instance."

"If you're worried that they...well, that they know, then don't be."

"Know? Know that I'm gay?"

"Yeah. That. I've never said anything."

"Really? You mean all these years I've been living in the closet and didn't know it?" she teased.

He didn't return her smile. "Ain't nobody's business."

She didn't reply as she followed him inside. That wasn't the reason, and they both knew it. The real reason was because he was embarrassed to have a gay daughter. He'd never come right out and said it and he didn't have to. She loved him, regardless, and she knew he loved her. Thankfully, her mother had no such issues and they talked openly about it. In fact, her mother knew all the sordid details of her breakup with Jennifer and the aftermath. She doubted her father even knew Jennifer existed.

Which again begged the question: Why would he hire a lesbian? She tried to envision the woman—Murphy: Older, most likely, unattractive and maybe a little overweight. Probably overly butch with very short hair. In her father's eyes, that's what lesbians were supposed to look like. They weren't supposed to look like his daughter.

* * *

"Oh, my God! Look at you!" Lori explained as she pulled Kayla into a hug. "I swear, you get prettier every time I see you."

Kayla accepted Lori's enthusiastic hug with a smile. "Good to see you again. How's Rusty and the kids?"

"They're good. Sara's in high school, if you can believe that."

"Wow. Has it been that long since I've seen you?"

"Probably two or three years," Lori said. "We need to get lunch and catch up."

"I know," she said, although that wasn't very high on her list. She always felt like Lori was more interested in learning information that she could pass on rather than being genuinely interested in her. "Let me get settled in first. I don't even know my schedule yet."

Lori leaned forward. "Rumor has it, you'll be riding with Timmy. He just got through taking Murphy through her first six weeks." Her voice lowered. "Have you met Murphy?"

Kayla shook her head. "No, not yet. I understand she's new."

"She's a little on the quiet side, but nice enough, I guess."

"Quiet?"

"Keeps to herself, kinda guarded about her private life."

Kayla shrugged. "Well, some don't like to broadcast their business to everyone."

Lori grasped her arm and pulled her even closer. "She's gay," she whispered.

"Really?" she replied, trying to keep a smile from forming. "Well, in law enforcement, that's not a big shock. Or is she not welcome because of that?" she asked, fishing for her own information.

"Oh, no, nothing like that. I'm just sayin'."

Just passing on gossip, in other words, but she smiled nonetheless. "What's her first name?"

"Oh, it's Mandi—with an 'i'—but I don't recommend you calling her that. She gives what I call the 'death stare' when you do."

"I see. Well, I'll keep that in mind." She made a show of looking at her watch. "I came by hoping to meet everyone. Or at least those changing shifts at four. If I'm going to be riding with Tim, I'd like to visit with him a little. I haven't seen him in a few years."

"Yes, he and Murphy end their shift at four. Kimbro and Wade are in the back. They go on at four," she said.

"Kimbro?"

"Kim Nguyen," she said. "Everyone calls him Kimbro."

"Okay, yes, I've heard my father mention him, but we've not met. I know Wade. It's Wade Washington, right? He was a year ahead of me in school."

"Yes, I thought y'all were close in age."

She smiled, remembering the tall boy who'd been the star of the basketball team. She wondered if he was still as quiet as he'd been back then.

"Jeff and Ivan are off today," Lori continued. "Ricky and Carlos are on midday shift.

"So they end at eight?"

"Yes, ten to eight. There's two ten-hour shifts and two twelve-hour shifts. I can't keep up with all their schedules without a chart."

"Oh, I'm sure." She motioned to the closed door that would take her into the back of the station. "I guess I'll go meet the guys. We'll catch up later," she said as she opened the door.

Little had changed in the squad room over the years. She didn't remember a time in her life that her father didn't work here. He'd been chief for at least fifteen years now and sergeant before that. She'd come by here often, listening to stories with rapt attention. Even as a young child, she'd wanted to be a cop. Her mother, however, discouraged her, saying she needed to go to college for something that would land her a *normal* job. She started out doing just that, but after she and Kevin ended their marriage, she knew in her heart what she wanted to do and she switched majors to criminal justice. Her father was pleased, she knew, and her mother's disapproval was tempered after the enthusiasm Kayla showed, something she never did while contemplating a business degree.

She found Wade Washington and a man who she assumed to be Kim Nguyen in the breakroom, filling travel mugs with coffee. Wade's eyes widened and he smiled, his even white teeth a contrast with his dark skin.

"Kayla Dixon…it's been a long time," he said, holding his hand out.

She shook it firmly and returned his smile. "How are you, Wade?"

"Doing great. Been working for your father about four years now."

"Late bloomer?"

"No. After I got married, we lived up in Madisonville. Started my career there." He turned and pointed at a nervous-looking man beside him. "This is Kim Nguyen. Kimbro, meet Kayla Dixon, Earl's daughter."

Kayla shook his hand as well. "Nice to meet you."

"Yes, you too. I…I thought you were starting on Monday."

"I am. But I had some time, thought I'd swing by and introduce myself."

"If you don't mind my asking, why would you leave the FBI for this job?" Wade asked.

She knew she'd get this question, of course, but she still hadn't settled on an answer. She shrugged. "I was ready for a change." That much was true, at least.

Wade nodded, then glanced at his watch. "Well, we should get at it," he said. "Good to see you again."

"Nice to meet you," Kim added as he hurried after Wade.

She sighed as they left. Two down, six to go—of the officers, anyway. Sergeant Wilson—Pete—she'd known since she was a kid. Her father promoted him to sergeant as soon as he became the chief. She would stop in and say hello to him, however. It had been a few years since she'd been around the station.

She went back to the main room where the desks were. There were four of them, two facing each other, the other two against a wall. Each held a computer and a phone, but they were all exceptionally neat, as if they were rarely used. She heard laughter through the hallway that led out to the door where the patrol cars were parked at the back of the station . She waited as two officers came in. Tim Beckman looked as familiar as always, his bushy mustache hiding his upper lip. The woman next to him, however, nearly took her breath away. She was the same height as Tim but much leaner. Dark hair, cut in layers, feathered around her face, just brushing the collar of her uniform. As dark eyes met hers, she had an almost overwhelming itch to brush away the hair that hid the woman's eyebrows. Surely to God this wasn't the woman her father had hired. Surely to God this wasn't *Murphy*. No. She was supposed to be older. She was supposed to be overweight. She was supposed to be *ugly*.

"Well, hey there, Kayla. Didn't expect to see you today," Tim said with a hesitant smile. He jerked a thumb at the woman. "This here is Murphy. She just finished a six-week tour with me."

Kayla stared at the woman, finally noticing that she was holding her hand out. Kayla reached out and clasped hands with her briefly.

"Nice to meet you," she said.

The woman paused an almost awkward beat before replying. "Yes. Same here."

"You starting early or…" Tim asked.

"No, no," she said. "Just wanted to come by and meet everyone. Rumor has it I'll be riding with you on Monday."

"I heard that rumor too."

Kayla didn't miss the guarded look in his eyes. Of everyone, she thought that Tim Beckman would be the most open to having her here. He was several years older than she was, but besides Mr. Wilson, he'd been with her father the longest. Maybe her father was right. Maybe she should have just shown up on Monday morning.

"I'm going to take off," Murphy said, her words directed at Tim and not her. "Have a good weekend."

"Yeah. And hey, you be careful next week. I won't have your back."

Murphy smiled and slapped his shoulder. "I'll try to stay out of trouble." She turned then, and nodded at Kayla. "Nice to meet you."

"See you around," Kayla replied as she watched her walk away. She turned to Tim, her desire to visit with him before their shift on Monday vanishing. "I'm sure you've had a long day. I guess I'll see you on Monday."

"Yeah, well, it's good to have you here," he said, and she knew he was lying. "See you Monday."

She stepped aside, letting him pass by. She took a deep breath. So this transition from the FBI to Sawmill Springs Police Department wasn't going to be as smooth as she'd hoped. The one person she'd assumed would be her ally was as cool to her as the rest of them.

Speaking of cool, Murphy had been downright frosty. What was up with that? Had the others already influenced her? And God, she was *so* not what she'd been expecting. No woman should possibly look that good in a uniform. So much for the preconceived image she'd had in her mind.

Oh, well, even though she knew most of them—some only in passing—had she really expected everyone to welcome her with open arms? Not only was she coming from the FBI, but her father was the chief. What did she expect? Knowing her as an FBI agent who popped in from time to time to visit her father was different than working alongside her as a peer.

She shrugged. She wasn't going to spend the weekend worrying about it. She wanted to get completely unpacked and settled into her new, albeit small, duplex before Monday morning. At least she didn't have to worry about dinner. Her mother already had the weekend meals planned…all childhood favorites of hers, starting with chicken and dumplings. The thought of tonight's meal was almost enough to make her forget about the chilly reception she'd received.

Almost.

CHAPTER SIX

After yet another uneventful two days off—in which she'd very nearly called Gloria Mendez—Murphy stood in front of the mirror in her bedroom and adjusted the collar of her uniform. She still wasn't used to seeing herself like this. It had been many years since her patrol days in Houston. Once she made detective, she never thought she'd one day go back on the streets and wear a damn Sam Browne again. She shifted the duty belt around her waist to a more comfortable position.

While she was looking forward to riding on her own, she knew she'd miss Tim's constant chatter. She'd never tell him that, of course. She wondered if Tim was looking forward to his new riding partner.

She had to admit she'd been a little rude to Kayla Dixon. It wasn't intentional, she told herself, even though she'd thought of the exchange several times over the weekend. So she was an FBI agent? That didn't mean she was anything like the two pricks she'd worked with in Houston. Still, she'd been a little short with her, and she wondered if it was because of Tim and the guys' apprehension about having her on board. Or maybe she'd simply been shocked when she saw her. Even though Tim had called Kayla a blond-haired beauty, she wasn't really expecting such a...well, such an attractive woman.

What? Did you think she'd have a dark mustache like her father? she thought with a smile. And what about those blue eyes? Tim had been right...you wanted to just fall right in and drown.

She shook her head and looked away from the mirror. Maybe it was time to take Gloria up on her offer. She couldn't remember the last time—if ever—that she'd found a straight woman this attractive...and all from a two-minute meeting.

A straight woman, an ex-FBI agent and the chief's daughter, she reminded herself. Everything about that combination screamed trouble. So yeah, maybe she'd invite Gloria out for dinner the next time their schedules meshed.

She glanced once more in the mirror, pausing to brush the hair away from her eyes. She needed a trim, but she'd been too scared to go to the local shop in town—the Tan and Curl. She'd been spoiled having James cut her hair for the last ten years. When she'd decided to move, worrying about a hairdresser hadn't even crossed her mind.

No...worrying about her sanity had been her only priority. Why else would she have ended up in Sawmill Springs of all places?

She locked up her house and backed her truck out of the driveway. She'd lucked out when she found this place. Smack in the so-called historical district of Sawmill Springs, it was a stately old house, way too big for her. The lot was huge—not like the tiny city lots you find today. Ancient oaks—four of them—were in the front, and the backyard sported a giant magnolia tree. She was told she'd missed the spring display of the flowering shrubs and she looked forward to next year's season. The owner of the house had been an avid gardener and long-standing member of the Garden Club. She'd passed away six months before Murphy had come to town and the house was sitting vacant. The lady's daughter wasn't ready to sell it, but she'd never considered renting it out. Lance Foster, the real estate guru in town, had set up a meeting for her, and after an hour's visit, Murphy was handed over the keys without even signing a lease. Apparently, being a cop in town had its advantages.

She pulled into the back of the station at five thirty, surprised that Tim's red car wasn't there. Surely he didn't end his shift early on his first day with Kayla Dixon. She'd just gotten out when Ivan pulled up in his patrol car, the one she'd be using for her shift. She gave him a wave before going inside. She was shocked to find Kayla sitting at one of the desks. Kayla turned and gave her a smile, and she returned it involuntarily. How could she not? The woman was simply too cute to ignore.

"Hi."

"Hey," Murphy said with a nod, hoping she appeared more nonchalant than she felt. "Tim end your shift early?"

"Oh, no. Change of plans. Tim was scheduled to go to nights this week anyway, so Sergeant Wilson wanted to keep the shifts the same."

"Lucky you. You'll be spared lunch every day at Knott's Café," she said without thinking. "Unless, of course, you like that sort of thing."

Kayla laughed and Murphy had to pull her eyes away from her. *Damn*. She *really* needed to call Gloria Mendez!

"I like Knott's Café in small doses," Kayla said. "The food's great. There's just nothing healthy about it."

"Yeah, nothing like a plate full of chicken fried steak and mashed potatoes drowning in gravy for a noon meal." She decided—for whatever reason—that she owed Kayla Dixon an apology. She tapped an index finger on the desk nervously. "Listen…the other day, I…well, I wasn't exactly friendly to you."

"That's okay. No one was," Kayla said.

Murphy shrugged. "Well, their reason was completely different than mine."

"How so?"

"I'm not scared of you."

"Then why?"

Murphy lifted one shoulder in an apologetic shrug. "I'm not really fond of the FBI. Bad blood."

"I see." Kayla smiled at her again. "Well, you're in luck. I no longer work for the FBI." The smile faded slightly. "But the others…why are they scared of me?"

"Partly the FBI thing and partly because you're the chief's daughter."

"Ah. Well, I guess that's to be expected. They assume everything I hear, I'll run and tell my father."

"Yeah, something like that." She arched an eyebrow. "Will you?"

Again, the smile that nearly caused her heart to race lit on Kayla's face. "I hadn't planned on it. I suppose it depends on what it is. I mean, if there's going to be a mutiny or a coup or something, I'd probably warn him."

Murphy found herself returning that smile—like an idiot. She finally shook herself and moved away.

"Well, I should get ready to head out," she said as Ivan came inside and tossed her the keys. "Hope it goes smoothly tonight."

Kayla nodded. "Yes, let's hope."

Murphy grabbed a water bottle from the fridge and left without looking back at the woman who made her feel like the nerdy boy in the band getting flustered by being around the beautiful head cheerleader.

"You're friggin' thirty-four years old," she murmured to herself as she went outside. She met Tim on his way in. "You're late."

His bushy mustache lifted in a smile. "Still got time. I'll let you keep the streets safe until I get out there."

"I thought they were going to keep you on days since you've got more training to do."

"So did I," he said with a shrug. "Man, I'm not looking forward to this one bit. What in the world are we going to talk about?"

"Knowing you, I don't think that'll be a problem," she said with a quick laugh. "You talked my ear off for six weeks."

"Yeah, but riding with you and riding with Kayla Dixon are two completely different things. I get all tongue-tied around her. Add to that, she's the chief's daughter...damn."

Murphy nodded and slapped him on the shoulder. "Better you than me, big guy."

She got in the patrol car and adjusted the seat and mirrors, then radioed dispatch—Shirley was working the call center until seven—to let her know that she was on duty. Their shifts weren't nearly as regimented as they'd be if she were in a large city with a beat to patrol. Here, they had certain areas to cruise through more often than others but for the most part, they were free to choose their routes. Kimbro was the only one on midday so they'd have three cars out until eight, then she and Tim—and of course, Kayla Dixon—would be the only police presence during the night. Depending on shift change and vacations, there were occasionally four out at once but usually only three. A town of forty-five hundred people, she thought they needed more cars out at night, but this apparently worked for them. As Tim had told her on numerous occasions, nothing much exciting happens in Sawmill Springs—especially now that school had started up again and kids couldn't get into as much "mischief," using Tim's word.

That's why, a mere fifteen minutes later, she was shocked to hear Shirley's frantic voice on the radio.

"All units...get to Kirby's. Something's happened to Guy Woodard," she said, her voice crackling with nervousness. "Repeat...Guy Woodard. Kirby said he was...he thought he was dead. Oh, my goodness."

Where the hell was Kirby's again? And who was Guy Woodard?

Oh, yeah—the Shell station near the old downtown area. And "*Oh, my goodness*"? Whatever happened to radio protocol? she thought with a shake of her head.

"Ten-four," she responded as she flipped on her lights and siren with a smile. She was sorry for whoever Guy Woodard was but finally...some police work.

When she pulled to a stop in front of Kirby's, there was already a crowd gathered. She slammed the car door, wishing

Tim was with her. She didn't know these people, and most of them glanced at her suspiciously.

"Step back," she said as she moved between the eight or ten folks who were gathered at the pumps.

"Where's Timmy?" someone asked.

"He'll be along," she said without looking. Her eyes were on the body. An older man, perhaps mid-sixties, was lying between the gas pumps and a dark gray Lincoln. Blood oozed from the back of his head.

"Everyone, get back," Murphy said as she held her arms out, trying to push the gawkers away. Not a one of them moved an inch.

"Dropped right where he stood pumping gas," someone said. "I thought he had a heart attack or something."

"Get the hell back," she said loudly. "Right now."

They finally moved back, most of them mumbling under their breath.

"I done called Brett Newberry." The man who had spoken held his hand out to Murphy. "I'm Kirby, by the way. This is my place."

"Who's Brett Newberry?"

"Funeral home."

"That's a bit premature, don't you think?"

He looked at her blankly. "He's dead. Who else am I gonna call?"

Murphy squatted down beside Guy Woodard, who was indeed very dead. She didn't need to feel for a pulse to know that. She turned his head slightly, hearing gasps from the onlookers. The back of his skull was missing. She stood up quickly.

"Mr. Kirby, will you please help me get everyone back? This is a crime scene."

"Actually, Kirby is my first name. My last name is—"

"Yeah, whatever. Get them back, please."

He nodded. "Okay, everyone. Y'all heard her. Get back now. Go on," he said with a wave of his hand, the crowd finally dispersing a few feet away. Murphy saw several of them on their phones and no doubt the news was traveling all over town.

Traffic had slowed to a crawl along Oak. One truck stopped and a man stuck his head out of the window.

"Kirby? What the hell's going on? I heard on the scanner that Guy Woodard was down."

"Jesus…are you kidding me?" she murmured.

"That'd be Ray Beckman, Timmy's uncle," Kirby explained as he walked over to the truck.

A siren blaring and tires squealing signaled Tim's arrival. Everyone seemed to be talking at once as Tim pushed his way through the gathering crowd with Kayla following behind.

"Murphy? What the hell happened?"

"Gunshot to the head," she said quietly, although apparently not quiet enough.

"Shot? No, no. We didn't hear any shots," someone said. "He just fell."

She grabbed Tim's arm. "These are your people. Get them the hell away from here." However, Kayla had already stepped up.

"Mr. Arnold…you must get back. This is a crime scene." She held her hands out wide. "Everyone…please, get back. Let us do our job."

"Kayla? What are you doing here? I didn't hear you were coming back."

"Are you kidding me?" she whispered to Tim, who shrugged.

"Small town, what can I say?"

Kayla walked over to them. "What we got?"

"Judging by the damage, I'd say it was a high-powered rifle. Sniper maybe."

Kayla nodded, but Tim gave a nervous laugh. "Sniper? In Sawmill Springs? No way, Murphy."

"No one heard shots. He's obviously been shot."

Tim was still shaking his head. "Not here. We don't have *snipers* here."

The man called Kirby came out of the crowd and nodded at Tim, then held his hand out to Kayla. "Good to see you again, Kayla. I heard a rumor you were back in town."

Kayla shook his hand firmly. "Kirby. Did you see what happened?"

"Like they said, he just fell." Kirby tilted his head as another siren was heard coming toward them. "That'd be Earl. I tracked him down over at the Cross Roads. They usually go over there for burgers on Monday evenings."

Murphy shook her head. *Unbelievable.* She'd been on the job six weeks, and she and Tim hadn't had anything more than a traffic accident to handle. She wasn't counting the day they helped out the sheriff's department when Joe Duffy's cattle got out on the highway. Even so, surely there was some sort of protocol to follow, some set procedures that they followed. Surely the owner of the local Shell station didn't summon the police chief at will.

Chief Dixon silenced his siren as he pulled into Kirby's gas station. As he stepped from his car, his white Stetson stood out above the crowd, making him appear taller than he was. He was intimidating with his jet-black mustache and narrowed eyes as he walked up. The crowd parted for him, all taking several steps away as he passed by.

"Kirby, get these people the hell out of here," he said with a jerk of his head.

"Come on now," Kirby said to the onlookers. "You heard the chief. Go on about your business."

"Timmy…is it true? He was shot?"

"It appears that way, Chief. Murphy was first on the scene."

"Gunshot to the back of the head," Murphy said. "Witnesses heard nothing. I'm going to guess a sniper rifle with a silencer, most likely shot from a distance."

Earl Dixon stared at her several seconds without blinking. "Silencer. Sniper rifle." He slowly shook his head, his dark eyes never leaving hers. "Well, I'm going to guess that you're wrong. This is Sawmill Springs, Murphy. This ain't Houston. We ain't got goddamn snipers here."

She stepped aside as he bent over Guy Woodard's body. Tim shuffled nervously beside her and the smell of gasoline wafted in the air. She followed the length of the hose, which was still stuck in Guy Woodard's gas tank. She looked over at Kayla, who was watching her father. As if feeling eyes on her, she turned, meeting Murphy's gaze.

Murphy pulled her eyes from Kayla and glanced down at the chief instead. He was staring intently at the body, his head moving slowly from side to side. By all accounts, Earl Dixon was an honest, fair man, and he was well-respected in the community. He'd been a cop in Sawmill Springs for thirty years, the chief for the last fifteen. When she'd interviewed with him the first time, she got the impression that he'd taken an instant dislike to her for some reason. She had no hopes of getting hired. Turned out, however, that Earl Dixon knew her lieutenant and apparently, her lieutenant had given her a glowing recommendation. Earl called her up and offered her the job. Still, they hadn't exactly hit it off. At all. She could count on one hand the number of times they'd spoken.

"Well…I'll be a son of a bitch," Earl finally muttered. He stood back up, his gaze meeting hers. "I forget this ain't your first rodeo, Murphy. This is probably right up your alley." He turned and looked at Kayla. "What are your thoughts?"

Murphy watched as Kayla bent over the body and moved his head to the side revealing the wound in the back. She looked back up at her father. "Judging by the damage, it was a high-powered rifle. I concur with Murphy. Rifle with a silencer."

He took his hat off and scratched his head. "Well, then… unless we think this was an accidental shooting, it looks like we got us a murder on our hands. The goddamn president of the bank." He turned to Tim as he put his Stetson back on. "Get some crime scene tape up, for God's sake. Find out who was out here when he was pumping gas. We need to interview anyone who saw it."

"I'm on it, Chief."

The chief turned to Kirby. "You called Brett?"

Kirby nodded. "Yep. Thought he'd be here by now."

"Shouldn't we process the scene first? I mean, I know there's no M.E. to call but—"

"Doesn't take a medical examiner or a goddamn autopsy to determine the cause of death, Murphy," Chief Dixon said harshly.

Unbelievable.

Then he surprised her by apologizing. "Sorry. I forget that you're used to having forensic specialists and coroners and medical examiners at your beck and call." He pointed at Kayla. "You too, I suppose, up in your fancy FBI offices. No, Brett Newberry is coming to collect the…the body," he explained, glancing down at Guy Woodard. "He'll transport it down past Huntsville. We use the Montgomery County coroner's office there." He looked back at the body. "I'll be goddamned," he murmured. "Guy Woodard."

Murphy took a step back. "I'll go help Tim," she said and turned without waiting for a reply.

Well, so much for processing the scene. The chief apparently didn't deem it necessary. She paused to glance up into the evening sky, absently noting that the puffy white clouds floating by were tinged with a bit of color from the approaching sunset. It was still breezy, the wind making the late summer evening seem a little cooler than it actually was. She took a deep breath, reminding herself that it was her choice to come here, her choice to leave the city…her choice to want to move to a small, backwoods town where crime was minimal and murder was rare.

Yep. Murder was rare in Sawmill Springs.

Yeah…tell that to Guy Woodard.

CHAPTER SEVEN

The chief had pulled Murphy off patrol and called in Jeff on his night off to take over for her. She had been as shocked as anyone when he'd said she was to take the lead on the investigation. It made sense, of course. She was a homicide detective. Who else was he going to put on lead? His daughter? Other than her, Kayla was obviously the most qualified, but she'd only been on the job a few hours. She could imagine the uproar that would cause. She sighed. It didn't really matter, did it? It wasn't like there were any leads to go over or evidence to ponder. She leaned back in the chair, staring at the monitor. She'd chosen one of the two desks that faced each other. There were four workstations that were shared between the eight officers. This was the one she normally used when she needed a desk. It also faced the doors to the breakroom and the main office.

She reached for her cup of coffee and took a sip, pleased that it was still warm. She flipped through the notes once again, reading the same thing over and over. Dottie Reynolds from the Tan and Curl beauty salon said that Guy Woodard had been facing east, toward Rooters Drug. Harry Larson swore that Guy had been looking north, up toward downtown where the bank was. And Kirby himself said that Guy had been turned to the south, facing the station and the pumps. That seemed to be the most plausible scenario. If you're pumping gas, you're most likely watching the gallons and dollars spin by.

Trouble was, he'd landed on his back, away from the pump and nozzle. He wasn't shot directly from the back. If he had been, he would have most likely landed on his face. Her theory was he'd been shot more from the side and as he fell, his shoulder had hit the pump, pushing him onto his back.

This meant the shot had to have come from the downtown area on a rooftop. However, by the time they'd interviewed the few witnesses, it was already dark. All of the stores had closed, too, so they'd have to wait until morning to search the roofs.

That brought her to the next line of questioning. Who had a beef with Guy Woodard? Depending on who you spoke with, he was either a saint or the devil himself. Guy Woodard's name and the bank had been synonymous for the last thirty years, according to Chief Dixon. No doubt he'd made his share of enemies. And if it wasn't an enemy who killed him, then who? Family? Was there a disagreement? Was someone jealous of his position? Obviously they would need to go to the bank to get some answers.

The office door opened and she expected it to be Yolanda, who worked dispatch during the late night hours. She was surprised to see Chief Dixon come in instead.

"Murphy? What the hell are you still doing here?"

She shrugged. "Working."

He glanced at her monitor. "Going over the notes for a hundred times is not going to make evidence materialize. You should go home and get some sleep. Gonna be a long day tomorrow," he said as he walked into the breakroom.

She glanced at the clock on the wall. It was one thirty-seven a.m. and she had nothing. He was right. She should get some sleep and start over in the morning…in daylight. He came back out with a cup of coffee in his hands.

"You're sending me home, but you're planning on staying a while?"

He pulled out a chair and sat down at the desk facing hers. "Couldn't sleep. Known Guy Woodard my whole life."

She nodded. "He was sixty-two. Older than you."

"I'm fifty-six, so no, we weren't close in school or anything. He's been at the bank since he got out of college. His daddy was president before him."

"I imagine he's made enemies over the years."

"Sure. Can't think of anyone in this town who would be angry enough to kill him though," he said as he sipped his coffee.

"We need to consider that it could have been random. Maybe he wasn't a target."

"I think that'd be worse, Murphy. A sniper in our little town targeting people at random?" He shook his head. "Don't see that happening."

"Probably not."

He leaned on his desk, his cup cradled between his hands. "You've met my daughter."

She nodded. "Yes."

"The guys, they all feel threatened by her, don't they?"

Murphy shrugged.

"Oh, hell, you don't have to say it. I can see it for myself. Hell, Pete told me what their reaction was."

"Can't blame them."

"No? What about you?"

"Do I feel threatened?" She wondered at his line of questioning. She also wondered why he was in here talking to her. She'd been here over six weeks, and this was the first time they'd actually had a sit-down conversation.

"I learned from your lieutenant that you and the FBI weren't exactly on good terms."

Murphy lifted an eyebrow. "I was under the impression that your daughter had resigned from the FBI."

Earl smiled. "So she did."

"But to answer your question, no, I don't feel threatened. I haven't been here long enough to worry about the pecking order, as you called it."

He nodded. "I ain't one to show favoritism. Of course, I've never had my daughter working for me before either."

"I thought she used to do dispatch," she said, remembering her conversation with Tim.

"She was in high school. Thought she was tough shit," he said with a laugh. "Ain't the same as being an officer though." He put his coffee cup down. "Got me a dilemma here. We haven't had a murder in this town in seven years. And that didn't require any investigation. Bubba Wright shot Lawrence Tapper over on the east side of town. Seems old Lawrence was tapping Bubba's wife, if you know what I mean. Damn shame all the way around." Earl shook his head. "Ex-wife, to be fair, but they were both drunk as Cooter Brown. Had a dozen witnesses to boot."

She nodded. Tim had already told her the story.

"So my problem is, do I put my two most qualified officers on this case or do I worry about upsetting the apple cart and getting everyone's tighty-whities in a pinch?"

"You think Kayla and I should work this investigation together?"

He nodded. "It goes against my better judgment for a number of reasons. However, it makes the most sense."

"She's been on the job a few hours," she said, repeating her thoughts of earlier. "That'll cause a stir."

"Oh, I know. But you need somebody partnering with you. My other choice would be Timmy. He's the most experienced and you and him have been together for six weeks. But if I do that, then Tim's gonna want to take the lead, not you. Besides, Tim's a good old boy. He's not going to be suspicious of anyone in town. You and Kayla? You won't have any prejudices."

Of course it made sense. She wasn't really crazy about the idea though. Besides Kayla being FBI—whom she loathed—there was the whole fumbling schoolboy-head cheerleader scenario she'd fallen into earlier.

"What do you think, Murphy?"

"I think you're right on all accounts," she said, despite her personal misgivings.

He stood up and nodded at her. "I'll talk to Kayla first. Get her take." He turned to go, then stopped. "And get your ass to bed. I'll need you fresh tomorrow. We'll start early."

* * *

Kayla was surprised to see a patrol car pull up beside them. She was even more surprised to see her father behind the wheel. He rolled his window down and she did the same. However, he looked past her to Tim.

"Timmy…you finish the shift alone. I need to talk to Kayla."

"Ah…sure, Chief." Tim looked at her with raised eyebrows and shrugged. He pulled away as soon as she got out.

"What's up?"

"Get in."

He didn't say anything as he turned around and headed in the direction of the station. She sat there quietly, knowing he would talk in his own good time. It was a tactic that she found more annoying than endearing, but he'd been that way her whole life.

When they pulled into the station, he killed the engine but didn't get out. She stayed quiet, waiting on him to talk.

"How do you feel about…well, about working this case with Murphy?"

"Wow. You're really trying to get the whole squad pissed off, aren't you?"

"I'm trying to solve a goddamn murder. You and Murphy are the most qualified. Who else should I put on it?"

"You're right. I suppose we are the most qualified. Especially in a case like this where there is little to no evidence."

"Little? We got nothing, Kayla. Let's be honest here. We got nothing but a body. And I need something. Guy Woodard was one of the most prominent men in town. He gets shot and killed in broad daylight and I don't find the killer…I'll be run out of town," he said.

"I doubt you'll be run out of town. I'm sure the news of what happened has already spread by now."

"You know it has."

"Okay. So what's the plan?"

"Go home. Get a few hours' sleep. We'll start first thing in the morning."

"What about Murphy?"

"Yeah, I already talked to her. Sent her home too. We'll go over a plan of action in the morning."

She got out, and then leaned in through the open window. "You know the guys aren't going to be happy about this."

"Can't worry about that."

She watched her father drive away. Guy Woodard. She shook her head slowly. She remembered sitting across from him at his desk at the bank when she was eighteen, applying for a car loan. And she remembered him sitting in the front of the church when she and Kevin had gotten married. Everyone in town knew Guy Woodard. That's not to say that everyone loved him. He was too powerful for that. Still, she couldn't imagine someone in Sawmill Springs being the killer.

She stared up into the night sky with a sigh. And here she thought she was leaving the FBI for a slower, more peaceful career in her old hometown. Nothing like starting out with a murder investigation after one of the town's most prominent citizens is gunned down.

And nothing like alienating the rest of the squad by being assigned to the case. She wondered if Murphy was feeling the apprehension too. She was just starting her seventh week. How did she feel about being thrust into the lead? She'd questioned Tim—as subtly as she could—but he'd remained noncommittal on Murphy, simply saying that she was a detective in her former life and she probably knew what she was doing. It wasn't really a ringing endorsement, but she didn't get the impression that Tim felt slighted. Maybe that was only because Murphy was the first on the scene.

What would his reaction be when he found out that she, too, had been assigned to the case?

CHAPTER EIGHT

"No offense to you, Kayla," Sergeant Wilson said before looking back at her father. "But Earl, I think this is a bad decision." He pointed at Murphy. "Half the town doesn't even know who she is yet. And Kayla? She's been on the job less than twenty-four hours. How's that gonna look, Earl, you putting your daughter on a case like this?"

"She's not my daughter right now, Pete. She's a former FBI agent. Aren't we trying to solve the goddamn murder? Hell, we'd be fumbling around in the dark with our pants down. Who's got experience with this kind of stuff? Do you? I sure as hell don't." He pointed over at them. "One's FBI, the other's a homicide detective from Houston. I say we lucked out having them here." Her father leaned back in his chair. "Is that what you're really worried about, Pete, or is it the guys?"

"There'll be some grumblings, I'm sure."

"Well, I don't give a goddamn," he said. "I don't care if I hurt some feelings or bruise some egos. Guy Woodard, president of the goddamn bank, was shot dead in the middle of town." He pounded his fist on his desk. "That's all I'm worried about."

Kayla glanced over at Murphy, who was standing beside her. Her face was expressionless, and she wondered what she was thinking. Murphy turned then and met her gaze. She had really dark, really intense brown eyes. Hard to read, yes, but there was a flicker of something there…something she couldn't quite put her finger on.

"Now, if you have no more objections, let's get to it." He motioned for them to sit, then looked pointedly at Pete Wilson. "You want to stay or…"

"I've got some paperwork to do."

"Fine. I'll let you know if we need your help with anything."

Kayla watched him leave, and he quietly closed the door behind him. She turned to her father.

"Of everyone here, Pete was the one who I thought would welcome me the most," she said. "He's been less than friendly."

Her father glanced over at Murphy. "He's looking out for the guys, that's all. What's your take on it?"

"Are you asking me to tell you what the vibe is in the locker room?"

"If you want to call the little closet we have a locker room, sure."

Kayla could tell Murphy was hesitant to speak out as she looked between the two of them. The fastest way to lose trust was to tell tales to the upper brass.

"The guys are probably more nervous than anything," Murphy finally said. "Nervous about screwing up something, you know, in front of a big shot FBI agent." She tempered her words with a smile, and Kayla couldn't help but return it. "I don't think that they're going to feel like they were passed over with this case. Like everyone else, they know my background, they know Kayla's." She shrugged. "To be honest with you, Chief, I'm not sure they would even know where to start."

He nodded. "Good enough. So…where *do* we start?"

The question was directed at Murphy, not her, so Kayla kept quiet, even though she had a few suggestions herself. Murphy stood up, pacing slowly behind the desk. Apparently, she thought better while moving so Kayla adjusted her chair so that she could see her.

"We need to see if there are any surveillance cameras. Kirby has one at the pumps, but he says it's not working."

"Hasn't been for years."

"I would assume the drugstore has one at the drive-thru window," Murphy continued.

"I believe they do."

"We need to get to the bank and interview them there." Murphy stopped pacing, looking at the chief. "I think they might be more receptive to questions from you than either me or Kayla."

Her father nodded. "I was planning on swinging by there as soon as we're done here. That snotty-nosed VP can't stand me. It'll be fun to grill him."

"Who is it?" Kayla asked.

"Ronnie Polach. The bastard wouldn't sign off on a new car loan for your mom a couple of years ago. I had to go over his head to Guy."

"I don't know the politics around here," Murphy said, "but did he stand to move up if Mr. Woodard was no longer president?"

"The bank's hierarchy is a mystery to most of us," he said. "They made Herbert Miller chairman of the board, for God's sake—a ninety-year-old man who can barely still drive."

"If this VP won't cooperate, make him a person of interest," Murphy said. "That ought to pickle his ass."

Her father laughed heartily. "Damn, Murphy, hadn't heard that saying since my daddy died."

Murphy smiled. "One of my grandmother's favorite expressions."

Her father sobered up. "Okay. What else?"

"We'll need to canvas the rooftops. I'd like to go back to Kirby's and try to determine the trajectory of the bullet." She shrugged. "Of course, we'll have to do without lasers and such, seeing as how we don't have a fancy crime scene unit or a forensic team at our beck and call," Murphy said, repeating her father's words from last night. She looked over at Kayla. "Something else we need to think about. Guy Woodard was pumping gas.

If he was indeed a target and it wasn't random, how would our killer know he'd be there at that exact time?"

"A pattern," she said. "He probably took the same route to the bank each day. Probably took his lunch break at the exact same time every day. So maybe Monday was his normal day to get gas."

"Check with Kirby on that," her father said as he leaned back in his chair and sighed. "So we really don't have anything, do we?"

Murphy shook her head. "No sir. Not a thing. Not yet."

"All right. I'll go to the bank and see what I can stir up." He stood. "If you need help with anything—like crawling around on the rooftops—let Sergeant Wilson know. He can get one of the guys up there to help."

"If we're going to get the guys to help with anything, it probably shouldn't be grunt work," Kayla said, but Murphy contradicted her.

"They wouldn't consider it grunt work. None of them have ever been involved in a murder investigation. Just to be a part of something as mundane as combing the rooftops for shell casings would at least make them feel included."

"I suppose you're right. You have a better feel for them than I do, obviously."

"There's one more thing," her father said. "Kayla, you know how gossip runs in this town. I'd like to keep everything we're doing between the three of us. Let's use our cell phones for communication, not your radio."

"I don't suppose we could pretend we're detectives and go to plainclothes?" Murphy asked.

Her father's mustache lifted at one corner. "How about we just stick to the uniforms for now?"

While Kayla wasn't particularly fond of wearing one, she thought Murphy looked sensational in hers. She pulled her eyes away quickly when Murphy glanced at her.

"So? Drugstore first? Then Kirby's?"

She nodded. "You're lead detective. I'm just your sidekick."

"We'll see how long that lasts," her father muttered. "She's a little bossy," he warned Murphy. "She gets that from her mother."

CHAPTER NINE

It was going to be another hot, dry day, it seemed, but that didn't prevent her from driving with her window open. After being in the city so long, she couldn't seem to get enough of the fresh air that living in the country afforded her.

Kayla sat quietly in the passenger's seat as they drove the short distance over to Rooters Drugstore. Murphy was still a little apprehensive about the situation she found herself in. The last time she'd partnered with an FBI agent, all kinds of wrong happened and Leon was caught in the middle…literally. It cost him his life. She gripped the wheel a little tighter as images from that fateful night flashed through her mind.

"So, Mandi, I understand you're from Houston."

Mandi? She turned her head and glared. "Just Murphy… that'll be fine."

That statement was met with a smile. "Is that the death stare that Lori warned me about?"

She turned into the drugstore parking lot and parked in the shade of the big oak in front. "Mandi is not a cop's name," she said by way of explanation.

"Well, I'm sure your mother had no idea what your profession would be when you were a baby. Or is your given name Amanda?"

"No. I could probably deal with Amanda. Mandi Murphy sounds like a porn star," she said, causing Kayla to laugh.

"Yeah, yeah, laugh it up. It's not your name."

"That's true. So who did she name you after?"

"I don't think anybody. She was hoping for a cheerleader when she named me."

"I take it she didn't get her wish?"

Murphy got out, remembering how hard her mother had tried to get her—and keep her—in a dress. No amount of dance lessons or piano lessons could squash the tomboy out of her. By the time she was in high school, her mother had thankfully given up. She glanced over at Kayla, wondering if Lori had already shared the gay gossip with her. She figured she had. And if she hadn't, the sooner Kayla found out, the better.

"Well, I did become quite friendly with one of the cheerleaders, but I'm fairly certain that's not what my mother had in mind."

Kayla laughed. "Oh, my. My father would have killed me if that had been me."

Murphy stopped walking. "What?"

"I was a cheerleader. He would have killed me if someone like you…you know, got *friendly* with me."

"I imagine so. No doubt your boyfriend would have been a bit upset too."

Kayla frowned. "Just how much do you know about me?"

She shrugged. "I rode with Tim for six weeks. He likes to talk," she said as she started walking again.

Kayla caught up to her. "Why was I the subject of a discussion?"

"It was just the one time. He mentioned that you were coming back. I didn't even know that Earl had a daughter." She held the door open for Kayla and let her precede her into the store.

"Thanks, but that's not necessary," Kayla said as she passed by her. "I've worked in a man's world for a long time. I don't expect gallantry, especially from another woman."

"Well, I wasn't exactly shooting for gallantry. I figured they knew you here. They're more likely to hand their video over to you than to me…a stranger."

"Oh."

"And I'll let you get the door for me on the way out." She smiled quickly. "I don't mind gallantry."

Kayla paused, matching her smile. "I don't mind it either, actually. I just said I wasn't expecting it."

Kayla walked through the store and Murphy followed a few steps behind, trying to keep her eyes from locking on Kayla's backside. Some women looked really, really good in a uniform, and others…well, not so much. Kayla definitely was in the former group, not the latter. Kayla bypassed the checkout, pausing to say hello to a Mrs. Wilson before continuing to the back of the store. Murphy also smiled and nodded at Mrs. Wilson, but all she got in return was a suspicious look.

At the pharmacy, Kayla knocked on the counter and a woman came around the side, her face breaking out into a smile.

"Hi, Dorothy."

"Kayla Dixon! Why, I'd just heard from your Aunt Charlotte that you were coming back to town." Murphy watched as Kayla was enveloped in a tight hug by the older woman. "You look so pretty, as always." She leaned closer, her voice teasing. "My David is single again. Should I tell him you're back?"

Kayla laughed. "You've been trying to get me and David together since I was ten. How have you been?"

"Oh, good, good. Nothing much changes around here." Then her smile faded. "Of course, with what happened with Guy…" Her voice drifted away as her glance went out the window and Murphy assumed she was looking across the street at Kirby's. "Terrible, isn't it?"

"Yes, it is."

"Who would have done such a thing? Why, I can't even imagine that someone from town, someone we may even have as a customer here, would have done that."

"I know." Kayla stepped back. "Have you met Officer Murphy?" she asked.

Dorothy turned her attention to her, and Murphy offered a quick smile and extended her hand.

"Pleased to meet you."

While Dorothy's smile appeared genuine, her handshake was brief. "I've not met you before, no. Where are you from?"

"I'm from Houston, ma'am," she said.

"Houston?"

Before Dorothy could question her further, Kayla stepped forward. "We're lucky to have her. She was a detective there."

"Lucky to have an FBI agent too, I'd say."

"Thank you, but I'm in uniform. My dad finally talked me into joining his staff," Kayla said.

"Well, that is good news." She leaned forward, her voice again quiet and conspiring. "No offense to your daddy, but I think most people in town are going to love having the FBI here. I don't believe they even have a suspect yet."

Murphy wanted to roll her eyes, but she kept her face as expressionless as she could. Kayla glanced quickly at her, and Murphy could tell she was trying to hide a smile. "I'm not with the FBI anymore, Dorothy. However, Officer Murphy and I will be handling this case." She cleared her throat. "Which brings me to the reason we're here. Mr. Rooter has a surveillance camera outside, doesn't he?"

"On the side at the drive-thru, yes," Dorothy said.

"We're wondering if we could take a look at the footage from yesterday," Kayla continued.

"Well, I don't see why not. I'm not sure how far they range though."

"Even if it doesn't reach as far as Kirby's, sometimes things reflect off glass, off windows and such," Murphy offered. "We'd just like to take a look."

She nodded. "Okay. Let me go tell Roger. I'll be right back."

Murphy raised her eyebrows and smiled. "Roger Rooter? Really?"

"Afraid so," Kayla whispered.

"So who's David?"

"Dorothy's son. He's a few years older than me. If he's single again, then I imagine his third marriage hasn't worked out." Kayla eyed her. "What about you?"

"What about me?"

"You move here from Houston alone or do you have a...a partner or something?"

Murphy raised an eyebrow. "What? Lori got you fishing for gossip?"

Kayla laughed. "She does like to gossip, doesn't she? But no, I was just making conversation."

"You move here alone or is there a...a boyfriend or something?"

"A boyfriend?" Kayla seemed surprised by her question. "No, no boyfriend."

"Husband then?"

Kayla laughed again. "No, there's definitely no husband."

Dorothy stuck her head back out. "Roger says for you to come on back."

CHAPTER TEN

The upper right corner of the frame showed Kirby's station and they could make out Guy Woodard's gray Lincoln. Kayla nodded at Murphy.

"You were right. The shot came from the downtown area."

"Rewind that again, please."

Kayla did and they watched for the third time as Guy Woodard fell against the pump, then down onto his back. She could see no flash of gunfire, nothing else out of the ordinary.

"Doesn't help us much," Murphy said.

"No, it doesn't. I'll get Mr. Rooter's permission to take this though. There's no need for anyone else to see this."

Murphy nodded. "Okay. Rooftops?"

"Let's go across the street to Kirby's first, see if we can get an idea of where to start," she suggested. "And see about Guy Woodard's habits, see if Monday was his usual day to stop for gas."

"Okay. I guess I'll call Tim, see if he wants to climb on some rooftops with us." Murphy paused. "Or would you rather not involve them?"

"No, I think you were right. We'll only alienate them if we keep them in the dark."

Three hours later, they were standing out in the hot sun, surveying the view of downtown from one of the rooftops. Some of the old buildings didn't have roof access any longer, but of those that did, there was only one with a good view of Kirby's. Murphy felt pretty certain that the one they were standing on was the one used by the shooter. Kayla had to agree with her as they leaned on the ledge, both pretending to hold rifles. It was a clear, clean line of sight to Kirby's.

"Seems kinda far," Tim offered as he peered over their shoulders.

"Three hundred yards, tops," Murphy said. "You deer hunt, Tim?"

"Yeah…and about two hundred yards would be my max attempt."

Murphy nodded. "So maybe we're dealing with an expert marksman." She moved away from the ledge. "Anyone in town fit that description?"

"Got a lot of hunters in town, sure, and a lot would tell you they could make that shot, but they'd be lying."

"What about ex-military?" Kayla asked.

"Yeah, there's a few. Wesley Barker comes to mind. He did at least three tours in Iraq." Tim shook his head. "Wesley's a good guy. He's working for the feed store. You know, they do plumbing on the side."

Murphy raised her eyebrows questioningly. "Plumbing?"

"Yeah, his daddy is a plumber."

"So Wesley Barker and his father work for Myer's Feed as plumbers?" Kayla asked, just to clarify.

Tim nodded. "Yeah, but just because he's ex-military, that don't mean he's a killer."

"Of course not," she said. "I wasn't suggesting that he was a suspect."

"But when you have no evidence and no suspects, you have to start somewhere," Murphy said. "This wasn't just a lucky shot. This was made by someone who knows what they're doing."

"So what now? You want to round up everyone in town who's got a hunting rifle?" he asked defensively. "Because that'd be my whole family too."

Kayla held her hands up. "We're not suggesting that at all, Tim. What Murphy said is true. When you have no evidence and no suspects, then you've got to poke around and hope to stir up something."

"So you want to question Wesley Barker?"

"No," Murphy said. "We do some research first and find out what he did in the military. Maybe he was a mechanic and not a marksman. Let's don't jump the gun here. Just because we have no suspects, that doesn't mean that everyone is a suspect."

"Well, I know Wesley. He and my brother are friends. And I'm telling you, he didn't do this."

Kayla wondered if Murphy was second-guessing her decision to include Tim after all. Her father had been right to assign her and Murphy to this case. While she knew a lot of people in town—and was still considered a local—she wasn't as close to them as the guys were. She could not say emphatically who was and was not capable of killing Guy Woodard. Neither could Murphy. Tim, on the other hand, already had his mind made up as to who wasn't guilty and that was probably most, if not all, of the town.

"Let's forget about Wesley Barker," Murphy said. She spread her hands out. "We don't have any shell casings up here, no shoe prints...nothing." She glanced at Kayla. "This wasn't an amateur."

"I agree." Which, of course, ruled out most—if not all—of the townspeople. "Unless it *was* a lucky shot."

Tim looked between the two of them. "Okay, so what does that mean? Where do we start?"

Kayla noticed the twitch of a smile that Murphy hid, presumably because of Tim's use of "we."

"We already know they don't have surveillance cameras downstairs so we need to question whoever was working yesterday. See who was in the store."

"The store closes at five," Tim said, referring to the old Sears store that now housed the local quilting and hobby shop. "He was shot right about six."

"There's no other access to the roof except through the stairwell in the attic," she said. "Whoever shot him had to have come into the store at some point."

"And had to know where the access was," Murphy said. "And he had to get back out again." She turned to Tim. "See if you can find out who came in yesterday. Maybe they saw a stranger in the store."

Tim nodded quickly. "Yeah, yeah. I can do that. I know Miss Bernice."

"Our shooter is most likely male," she said. "I would assume most of Bernice's customers are female. Shouldn't be hard for her to remember a guy coming in here."

"All right. I'll go down right now," he said, then he paused, glancing over at Murphy. "Unless there's something else. Chief said you were the lead on this."

"No, go ahead. We'll be down in a bit." He turned to leave but Murphy stopped him. "And Tim, just because I'm the lead, that doesn't mean you don't still have seniority, you know."

Kayla had to admit that she was impressed with Murphy's people skills. Tim was nearly beaming.

"Yeah...and don't you forget that," he said as he nearly jogged to the roof access door.

"Well played," she said as soon as he was out of sight.

Murphy shrugged. "He's a good guy."

Kayla nodded. "You do know that after he questions Bernice, she'll tell the very next customer she has. It won't take long before it'll spread around town."

"Yeah, no doubt. I guess we should be thankful there's only a weekly edition of the paper instead of daily."

"And it comes out on Thursday, if my memory is correct," she said.

"And Guy Woodard's picture will be on the front page, probably taking up the whole top of the page."

"And there'll be a side article noting that the police department has no motive and no suspects," she added.

Murphy smiled. "And in the gossip section, Bernice will have a starring role as she recounts the questions of little Timmy Beckman."

Kayla laughed. "So you're familiar with small towns."

Murphy nodded. "I grew up in one."

"Not Houston?"

"No. Eagle Lake. West of Houston. We moved to the city when I was ten," she said as she started walking toward the door. "Still got family there. My parents recently moved back."

"So why here?" she asked. "Why not closer to home?"

"Closer to home didn't have a job opening," Murphy said as she disappeared into the stairwell.

Kayla had more questions—namely, why did she leave Houston in the first place—but Murphy was hurrying down the stairs. Kayla followed, deciding to save her questions for later. Back inside the store, they spotted Tim talking to Bernice near the counter. Bernice Nichols had to be pushing seventy-five by now, she thought. She could remember when her mother would drag her into the store back when she was a kid. Her mother had gone through a sewing stage where she wanted to sew all of Kayla's clothes. They'd made numerous trips to Bernice's shop for fabric. Fortunately for her, her mother's newfound love of sewing didn't last long.

When Tim saw them, he waved them over. Bernice's eyes lit up when she saw her and Kayla found herself engulfed in a tight hug.

"Oh, my goodness! You're as beautiful as the day is young," Bernice said. "So good to see you again, Kayla."

"Bernice, how have you been?"

"Oh, can't complain." She looked around her empty store. "Business isn't what it used to be, that's for sure. Not many people still take the time for handmade things anymore." Bernice turned her attention to Murphy. "You must be the new one I've been hearing about."

"Officer Murphy, ma'am," she said. "Nice to meet you."

"Well, Tim here seems to think that someone snuck up my stairwell to the roof and shot Guy Woodard. Is that true?"

Kayla cringed at that statement and she noticed that Murphy's jaw clenched as well.

"No, ma'am, we're just covering all our bases," Murphy said with a quick glare at Tim.

"Well, Tim said—"

"We're checking all the rooftops, Bernice," Kayla said. "Not just yours."

"She said she didn't see anyone in here yesterday," Tim supplied. "No men, in other words."

"Marcie Perkins and her daughter came by after school. They were in here until almost closing," Bernice said. "They were my last customers. Oh…and your Aunt Charlotte came by earlier in the day. I didn't know she even still sewed, but she bought some fabric."

"Do you close for lunch?" Murphy asked.

"No, no. I always bring my lunch and eat it in the back room."

"Were you the only one here? Did you have help?" she asked.

"Janice only works two days a week," Bernice said, pointing to the lady who had greeted them earlier. "Oh, I can handle the place by myself now. I'm not exactly run over with customers, you know, but it's nice to have the company."

"I understand," she said with a smile. "Well, I guess we've taken up enough of your time."

"So what about my roof? Should I be concerned?"

"No, ma'am, nothing to worry about," Murphy said. Then, "Do you keep the door to the attic locked?"

"No. There's no need to. But I rarely go up there." Bernice turned to Tim. "You think someone was hiding in there? He got out this morning after I opened up?"

"Just speculation, Bernice," Kayla said quickly. "Nothing for you to worry about."

"Well…okay, if you say so. Still…"

Despite that, Kayla knew that she'd be on the phone as soon as they left, telling whoever would listen that Tim thought the shooter had been on her rooftop. When the three of them got outside, Murphy turned to him, her dark eyes glaring.

"What the hell were you thinking?"

Tim seemed surprised by her question. "What are you talking about? You said to question her."

"Yeah…question her. Not give her information. Jesus Christ, Tim. You ask her point-blank questions, that's all. Did you see anyone in the store? Was there a stranger? Was there a man you didn't recognize?" Murphy ran a hand through her hair. "You don't tell her that we think someone might have come into her store and gained roof access to shoot Guy Woodard. You ask questions, Tim. That's all," she said forcefully.

"Well, excuse me for not knowing all the damn steps to follow," he said. "I've known Miss Bernice my whole life. I'm not going to question her like she's a suspect or something."

Kayla stepped between them. "What's done is done." She looked at Tim. "Unfortunately, whatever you insinuated to her will be all over town by morning."

But Tim was looking at Murphy. He tapped his chest. "I've got seniority here. You said so yourself."

"Yeah…and we've got lead on this," Murphy said. "Don't complicate things. We're not in the news business, Tim. We don't have to broadcast every bit of information that we have or that we may *think* we have. We're gathering information now, that's all we're doing. We're not feeding the gossip pipeline. You ask direct questions, that's all."

She didn't know if Tim's feelings were hurt or if his ego was bruised…or perhaps both. Regardless, he finally nodded, backing down a bit.

"Okay. You're right. I was too eager to share what we knew."

Murphy touched his arm. "The problem is, Tim, we don't really know anything yet. Whatever we were discussing up there on the roof was just that…discussing, tossing out ideas. That's what you do when you don't have any leads."

He nodded. "I understand. Sorry." He motioned to his patrol car. "I guess I should get back on the street."

"Yeah, we'll probably head back to the station and go over our notes and see if we can come up with anything."

Tim fiddled with his mustache nervously, as if he wanted to say more, but he turned around without another word.

"Unbelievable," Murphy murmured as she headed to their car.

"Well, in fairness to him, questioning people in a case like this is a learned trait. As we know, he's had zero experience with a homicide investigation."

Murphy got behind the wheel and slammed the door. "Some things should be common sense." She pulled out onto the street, then glanced over at her. "Don't get me wrong. I like Tim. He's a nice guy, but I guess I should have known. He's a chatterbox and loves to talk. I rode with him for six weeks and I don't think there's much about this town that he doesn't know."

"Maybe the chief found out something at the bank," Kayla offered.

Murphy raised an eyebrow and smiled. "The *chief?*"

She had a really pretty smile, Kayla noted as she returned it. "Calling him Dad while on the job doesn't seem like the proper thing to do."

CHAPTER ELEVEN

Kayla plopped down on her sofa, cradling a bowl of ice cream on her stomach. She couldn't decide if she liked the sofa against the wall or if she wanted to move it into the middle of the room and make a more intimate TV area. She wasn't really a big TV watcher, but that was mostly due to her job and her lack of time. Now that she was back home in sleepy little Sawmill Springs, she figured to have more down time. That is, as soon as they wrapped up Guy Woodard's murder, which was going nowhere fast. Her father had gotten exactly nothing from the bank. The snot-nosed VP—his words—was acting like it was an inconvenience to even talk to him and had told him to get Judge Peters involved if he wanted information. Kayla shook her head. If she and Murphy would have been questioning him, they'd have probably hauled his ass to the station. Then he'd really know what inconvenience was.

Her thoughts drifted to Murphy. She grinned as she remembered her assertion that Mandi Murphy sounded like a porn star. Yes, she had to agree that Mandi did not fit her in the least, regardless if she was a cop or not. The woman didn't talk a whole lot, though, which was fine. Idle chitchat normally bored her to tears. Murphy's silence, though, seemed a little forced. She hoped Murphy wasn't being guarded because of Kayla's FBI connection. She'd said there was bad blood but hopefully Kayla wouldn't be lumped in with whoever had pissed her off. Or maybe Murphy simply didn't like her. She stared off into space for a moment. No, she really didn't get that impression from her. Maybe she was naturally a quiet person.

She hoped that was the case because it would be nice if they could become friends. The guys were the guys and Lori was Lori—a married woman seven years her senior. She and Lori were on friendly terms, and yes, they'd had lunch on occasion when Kayla had come to town, but they didn't have enough in common to constitute a close friendship.

Murphy? Lori had already checked her personnel file. She was two years older than Kayla, but Lori didn't know anything about her personal life. Maybe there was someone in Houston. She wouldn't be surprised if there was. Murphy was attractive with a very nice body that appeared—at least as far as she could tell with clothes on—to be very fit. Murphy was a little taller than her own five foot six inches and her dark hair was cut shorter than Kayla wore hers.

Kayla ran a hand over her hair now, the ends pulled back in a ponytail. She'd been letting it grow for the last year, and it finally was long enough to pull back. Her mother said it made her look like a teenager, which, at thirty-two, she took to be a compliment.

She finished off the last of the chocolate chip ice cream and dropped the spoon into the bowl with a clank. She *really* needed to slow down on the ice cream. Unless she joined the local fitness club, she would get nowhere near the workout she was used to getting. Her father's version of a fitness room for the staff was a used treadmill he'd gotten off the Swap Shop on the radio and an assorted collection of dumbbells of various weights. She'd stuck her head into the converted closet and found a layer of dust on both the treadmill and the weights.

She rubbed her full stomach, thinking back to the fried chicken and mashed potatoes and gravy she'd stuffed it with earlier at her parents' house. It was delicious, but as she'd told her mother, she could not afford—calorie-wise—to eat with them every night. Oh, but it was so much easier than cooking for herself.

Especially here. It was a nice duplex and she'd been lucky to find it. There wasn't a whole lot of rental property to be found in Sawmill Springs. Still, the kitchen was painfully small. There would be no elaborate meals created there.

"Right…like you're a gourmet chef," she murmured.

With a sigh, she picked up her empty bowl and walked barefoot into the tiny kitchen. She put the bowl in the sink and filled it with water. There was no dishwasher, which would take some getting used to. Not that she'd had a lot of dirty dishes. So far, she'd had dinner with her parents every night and despite her protests to her mother, she imagined she would eat there again tomorrow. Her mother had casually mentioned that she would be making her homemade enchiladas for dinner. And Kayla *loved* her enchiladas.

The ringing of her phone pushed images of her getting as fat as a house out of her mind. It was her dad's ringtone and she wondered what he'd forgotten to tell her. They'd already talked the case to death over dinner.

"Hey, Dad…what's up?"

"Kayla…you're not going to believe this."

"What? Did someone confess to the murder?"

"If it were only that easy," he said. "But it's much worse. Found Lance Foster dead."

She gasped as she pictured the man she'd been chatting with for the last month when she was trying to find rental property. "Lance Foster Real Estate?"

"Yeah, he didn't make it home for dinner. His wife got worried."

"Please say it was natural causes."

"Wish I could."

She sat down heavily on the sofa. "What the hell is happening here?"

"Ferguson took the call. He found him at his office. I'm on my way over there."

She stood up quickly. "You want me to come?"

"Wouldn't mind a professional eye taking a look."

"I'll be right there," she said, already heading to her bedroom. "I don't remember where his office is."

"Over on the other side of town—before you get to the interstate. Built him a fancy office suite there. Shares it with Bobby Lott."

She stripped off her shorts and found a pair of jeans. "And Bobby Lott is?"

"He's a goddamn lawyer, that's who he is."

The call ended before she could reply, her father's disdain for attorneys still evident. She was in her car and heading out when she remembered Murphy. She should really call her too. She fumbled with her phone, finding the number she'd put in that morning. It was answered after only two rings.

"Yeah…Murphy here."

"It's me. Kayla," she said. "What are you doing?"

"Sitting in my recliner, drinking a beer."

"Well, put the beer down. Meet me at Foster's Real Estate."

"We buying a house or what?"

Kayla smiled. "I wish. The house I'm renting has no kitchen to speak of."

"I have a huge kitchen," Murphy said. "I don't cook."

"Figures," she murmured. "Do you know where the office is?"

"Yeah, he's the one who found me this place. What's going on?"

"He's dead."

"Jesus. Dead, as in 'dead'? Or dead…like—"

"Don't know details." She slowed as she saw the flashing lights of the patrol cars. "I'm here now."

"Okay. On my way."

Kayla parked beside her father's car. The newer brick building appeared to be designed to look more like a house than an office. There was even a small, well-manicured lawn between the parking lot and the covered porch in front. Several men were standing out in the parking lot, probably curious about the police lights. She recognized Ray Beckman, Tim's uncle. Ray knew everything that went on in town. His hardware store was the main gathering place for the retired or idle men in town. She wondered how many pots of coffee they went through each morning as they sat around and told tales while playing dominoes or checkers. Or what was discussed in the afternoons at closing time when they passed around beer before all heading home to their wives and dinner. Of course, gossip he learned at the store wasn't his sole source of information. Like a lot of the locals, he had a police scanner.

"Kayla, can you believe it?" Tim Beckman said as he left the circle of men with his uncle and walked over to her. "First Guy Woodard, now Lance Foster. The town hasn't had this much excitement in…well, ever."

She counted three patrol cars, not including her father's. That meant that no one was actually out on patrol. Well, she couldn't blame them, really. Never in their careers had they had this much activity in one week.

"What happened?" she asked Tim.

"Jeff found him slumped over his desk. Shot in the chest, looks like."

"How many people are in there contaminating the crime scene?" she asked as she brushed by him.

There were four people in the outer office, two of them on their phones. Inside Mr. Foster's office, there were six more, including Wade and Kimbro. She walked over to where her father was talking to Jeff Ferguson.

"Shouldn't we be clearing everyone out of here?" she asked quietly.

Her father glanced around, as if just now noticing the number of people inside. He motioned to Jeff.

"You know Jeff Ferguson, Kayla. He found Lance."

"Hello, Kayla. Good to see you again."

"Jeff," she said with a nod. "And not to get all technical on everyone here, but this *is* a crime scene. Please tell me that no one's touched anything."

"Oh, hell, everyone's just curious," her father said. "But yeah, Jeff, you should probably clear everyone out."

Kayla rubbed her forehead. "Any evidence we might find is going to be pretty worthless," she said. "Not a single person in this room has gloves on. One of the guys was *sitting* on the edge of the desk, for God's sake!"

"Calm down, Kayla. They know enough not to touch anything."

She turned to the body. Lance Foster was covered with a black suit jacket, probably his own. "Is this how he was found?"

"No. Ferguson found him slumped over. He moved him back in the chair like that."

"And the jacket?" she asked tersely.

"Hell, I covered him up. As much as Lance Foster was a jackass, didn't seem right for everyone to see him like this."

She shook her head. "That's why you don't let anyone in here until it's been processed. Please tell me you took pictures of everything before his body was moved and covered?"

"Listen here, young lady. You may have FBI experience, but this is still my gig and this is my town. This isn't some stranger you come upon in a crime scene. Like Guy, I've known Lance my whole damn life. And while I didn't necessarily like his ways, the man deserves some goddamn respect."

"What the man deserves is for us to catch his goddamn killer!"

They stood staring at each other, neither wanting to back down.

"I swear, does anything happen in this town without the masses knowing about it? It's like Grand Central Station out there."

Kayla turned, glancing at Murphy. "Yeah, well it was Grand Central Station in *here* a second ago."

"What the hell are you doing here, Murphy?"

"I called her," Kayla told her father. "Thought you were looking for a professional eye."

"That's what I got you for, although your mouth's gotten a little too smart for your britches," he said.

Murphy removed the jacket that covered Lance Foster's face and torso. Kayla walked over to her, staring at the bright red stain on his once pristine white shirt.

"Close. Point blank," Murphy said quietly. She pointed at the shirt. "Powder burns."

Kayla nodded, then turned to her father. "Any evidence of a forced entry?" By the look on her father's face, they hadn't even checked.

"Let me get with Jeff."

She sighed. "I love the man to death, but I swear, he and his team are not equipped for a murder investigation. I don't know how much we're helping though. We have absolutely zero evidence so far. Unless someone confesses to Mr. Woodard's killing, we're pretty much screwed on that one."

Her father came back in with Jeff and Tim in tow. "Jeff says the front door was ajar when he got here."

"And Mr. Foster's office door was closed," Jeff added with a quick glance at Murphy.

"So he probably knew his killer," Kayla said.

"Or it was a customer," Murphy said. "We need to check his appointment schedule. Maybe he had a late appointment."

Her father held up his hands. "What are you two doing?"

"Discussing, bouncing ideas, speculating," Kayla said.

He shook his head. "No. You have your hands full with Guy's investigation. I'll assign someone else for this one. Maybe Jeff and Tim here."

"Excuse me, Chief Dixon, but two murders in two days? I think it's pretty obvious that they're linked," Murphy said.

"There's nothing obvious about it," he said. "Two completely different killings."

"No offense, but…while I don't even pretend to know the pulse of this town, there's no way that these two murders aren't related. It's not a coincidence."

He stared at her, a stare that Kayla had seen plenty of times in her life, but Murphy never blinked. Kayla stepped forward before her father could speak. "I agree with Murphy. These aren't two random murders."

Tim fidgeted with his mustache, a habit Kayla was beginning to recognize. "Well, it's been a few years since I did my initial training and all but I'm pretty sure serial killers use the same M.O., don't they? Here, we got one using a rifle, long distance, then another shot with a handgun, up close and personal. Can't be the same killer."

"This isn't a serial killer," Murphy said.

Tim laughed. "Well, what? Doesn't two make a serial? Or do we need three?"

"Murphy's right," Kayla said. "Serial killers pick their victims randomly. The only thing they might have in common is a physical description or their age, things like that. They don't normally know their victims."

"Unless it's their very first one," Murphy added.

"True. Sometimes that's what triggers their obsession to kill, that's what feeds it." She stopped talking, noticing that the three men in the room were staring at them silently. She shrugged. "This isn't a serial killer. This has the feel of some kind of vendetta."

"Someone is exacting revenge for something," Murphy agreed.

"Okay, look," her father said. "All of this sounds great. Textbook, in fact. But this here is Sawmill Springs. If somebody's got a problem with somebody else, they talk about it. Or else they don't talk at all. Like old man Carthage. He and Sammy Breaker haven't spoken in forty years because of some damn dispute that probably neither of them could tell you what it was about anymore. That's how things are handled. Not by murder. Not in this town."

Murphy turned to her, ignoring her father. "What about a foreclosure? Bank forecloses on something—a farm, a ranch, a house—and Lance Foster has it up for sale."

"That's great, but Lance Foster would have to buy it first. Foreclosures are first offered at public auction," she said. "If that was the case, then perhaps you have something. The disgruntled owner would have it in for both the bank and the real estate office," she said with a nod. "It's a place to start."

"Did neither of you hear me?" her father demanded. "I said—"

"That kinda makes sense, Earl," Tim said. "I mean, you know, if I lost my house and then I saw it up for sale, I'd be a little pissed too."

"Enough to kill?"

"Well, no, I wouldn't. But, you never know. It could set someone off."

Her father sighed. "Foreclosures are public record. They're filed at the County clerk's office. I guess that's a good place to start."

Kayla smiled at him. "What a great idea. And what about this attorney who shares office space here?"

"Bobby Lott," her father said. "Got his office on the other side, around back, like sleazy lawyers should have."

"I take it the chief is not real fond of Bobby Lott," Murphy murmured.

"It's lawyers in general, I'm afraid." She turned to Tim. "It's been a while since I've done my own fingerprint dusting. Who's the expert?"

"Ivan's a whiz with fingerprints, but he's on days."

"Wake his ass up if you have to," her father said. "All hands on deck."

CHAPTER TWELVE

Murphy rubbed her eyes, the words on the screen beginning to blur. She should have taken Earl's advice. She should have gone home and grabbed a few hours' sleep. Whatever fingerprints Ivan had pulled were still being processed. There had been no witnesses to interview. Jeff had gone over to Bobby Lott's home. Bobby had left the office at three that afternoon to attend his son's baseball game, and no, he had no idea if Lance Foster had a late appointment. Earl himself had called Lou Ann Riley, Foster's secretary. As far as she knew, his last appointment had been a showing of a house at noon. She left at five, like always, and he was still in his office, alone.

She sighed. According to the wife, Lance was always home by six. If he was going to be late, he would call. She'd started calling him at six-fifteen. By seven, with still no word, she'd called Yolanda at dispatch, asking to have someone check the office. Jeff Ferguson found him at seven-thirteen p.m.

"Hey."

She turned, surprised to find Kayla standing beside her. She'd not heard the door open. "What time is it?"

"Nearly four." Kayla headed into the breakroom. "I couldn't sleep."

"Bring me a cup," she called.

"Black?"

"Toss in a little sugar."

Kayla came back out with two cups. She placed one on the desk beside Murphy, pulled out the neighboring chair with her foot and sat down.

"Perfect," Murphy said as she took a sip.

"You sleep?"

"No, I haven't been home."

"Fingerprints?"

She shook her head. "They've been scanned. Ivan said he'd let me know when he had results."

"He estimated that there were ten or twelve different prints that he pulled," Kayla said.

"Yeah, he said he was going to run them in 'every database known to man.' It'll be blind luck if we get a hit."

Kayla leaned back in the chair and sipped from her coffee. "He was killed between five and six, most likely. Or six-fifteen, to be more precise, since that's when his wife first called and got no answer," she said. "It's August. At six p.m., it's still daylight. It's still daylight at seven. A town this size, where everybody knows everybody, who is going to chance being seen like that?"

"Are you thinking it might not be someone from town?"

"I don't know. I've been in the business long enough to be skeptical of everyone, but I do tend to agree with my dad. It's a close-knit community, for the most part."

"But if it's a local, they would blend in. No one would think twice about a local coming out of Lance Foster's office. Probably wouldn't even notice him. A stranger? They would tend to stick out more."

"True."

Murphy watched as Kayla took a sip of coffee. Even at this ungodly hour, she looked beautiful. She knew she should keep the conversation on the case, but she was curious about her. "How long have you been in the business, anyway?" she asked.

"Right out of college. After a couple of years muddling through a business degree, I switched to criminal justice, much to my father's delight. He anticipated me coming back home and working with him right away."

"But you had grander aspirations of the FBI?"

Kayla shook her head. "Not really. I only applied with them on a whim. The first few years were rather dull, actually."

"Not like TV, huh."

"No. Mostly desk duty and background checks. I worked in Miami for a while, then in New Orleans. That city is wild and I don't mean that in a good way. Been in Dallas the last three years."

"What prompted you to quit?"

Kayla leaned forward, an eyebrow raised. "What prompted you to leave Houston?"

She shrugged, trying to ignore the blue eyes that were staring at her. "A lot of things," she said vaguely.

A smile played on Kayla's mouth. "Like the death of your grandmother and a cat?"

Murphy fought the urge to return her smile but failed. "Something like that, yeah."

"Small town like this, people are curious when strangers move here," Kayla said as way of explanation. "I get to avoid that since I'm still considered a local."

"Tim tells me your ex-husband still lives here."

Kayla seemed surprised by the statement, but she nodded. "And like any small town, people like to gossip. But yes, Kevin lives here. He moved back right away."

"Are you on friendly terms, or is that forbidden?"

Kayla laughed. "We're still friends, if that's what you mean. I get along quite well with his wife too. And they have three cute kids who call me Aunt Kayla."

She shook her head. "There's something wrong with that picture."

"I'm sure it seems that way to most people, but we were good friends in high school. Neither of us wanted to let a little thing like a failed marriage ruin that," she said with a smile. "So what's your thought?" Kayla asked as she motioned to the notes, signaling an end to the personal questions.

"My thoughts are the same as they were last night. It's someone he knew, someone he let into his office, maybe even someone he was expecting."

"His wife said he always called if he was going to be late," Kayla reminded her.

"Maybe he wasn't planning on being late. Maybe they came right at five when the secretary left."

"Was it a secret meeting? Lou Ann said he had no appointments scheduled."

"You know more about him than I do," she said. "I met him only the one time when he showed me the house I'm renting. Seemed like a straightforward guy."

"Well, rumor and speculation being what it is in a town this size, he's made a few shady business deals. And he's been known to buy up houses and land from people down on their luck and turn around and sell them for a nice profit."

"So a foreclosure wouldn't be out of the question?"

"From what I know of Mr. Foster, I don't think he'd have any qualms of bidding on his neighbor's foreclosed property, no. He didn't get to where he was by being a nice guy."

"I guess we should go to the courthouse later this morning, see what's been filed recently."

Kayla nodded. "As we said last night, it's a place to start."

Murphy covered her mouth as she yawned. "Sorry."

"Why don't you go home, sleep for a few hours? We can meet at the courthouse at nine," Kayla suggested.

Murphy glanced at the monitor, noting the time. It was barely four thirty. She figured she could squeeze in four hours and still be at the courthouse on time. She nodded.

"Yeah, I think I'll take you up on the offer," she said. "See you about nine."

"I'll meet you out front."

She paused at the door, turning back to Kayla. "I anticipated being bored out of my mind when I took this job." She smiled. "I was *hoping* to be bored out of my mind."

"I know what you mean. I was actually looking forward to being on patrol and writing traffic citations," Kayla said. "I was ready for things to slow down."

"Me too." She shrugged. "Guess it'll have to wait."

CHAPTER THIRTEEN

The courthouse trip had been futile. There were only eight foreclosures in the entire county going back five months. Only two of the eight had been sold, but neither by Lance Foster. Only one of the eight properties had been financed by the Sawmill Springs State Bank. As far as they could tell, Lance Foster had never bid on the property nor ever listed it for sale. It was several miles outside of town, but, after getting Subway sandwiches for lunch, they decided to drive out there anyway. A five-acre lot with a double-wide mobile home—it had seen better days. Kayla understood why it had never sold. Weeds nearly obscured the stepping stone walkway and the remnants of an old rusted-out car sat nearby. A dead oak tree leaned over the house and limbs had fallen from the tree, most of them still littering the roof of the house. The property appeared to have been abandoned years before the foreclosure claimed it.

So, they'd shelved that angle for the moment and had instead called Lou Ann Riley, Mr. Foster's secretary, and asked her to meet them at his office. As Murphy had said to her earlier, they didn't really snoop around last night. Kayla knew the reason why and she didn't need Murphy to say it out loud. Her father was being respectful, as he'd called it. "His body ain't even cold yet." Well, out of respect for *him*, she hadn't disagreed with him in front of his officers but she intended to have a talk tonight at dinner. She'd at least gotten him to request a search warrant from Judge Peters. And in spite of his assertion that he'd be run out of town if he didn't produce a suspect—and soon—he didn't seem to have much urgency to solve the murders. The look on Murphy's face last night told her she was thinking the same thing. That, of course, contradicted everything he'd said and done after Guy Woodard had been killed. Something was going on with him and she hoped to find out what at dinner.

She turned to look at Murphy as she drove them back toward town. Still a little on the quiet side, Murphy had yet to offer a single bit of personal information about herself. Not that Kayla was prone to pry into other peoples' lives. She wasn't, especially on the job. Still, there was something about Murphy's silence that piqued her curiosity. For one, she had yet to explain her issue with the FBI. Nonetheless, she wasn't going to come right out and ask her point-blank questions. No…she'd pry another way.

"Where do you live? When I was looking for a place, there wasn't anything suitable to rent."

"Oh, I know," Murphy said. "Mr. Foster showed me about four places that were…well, let's just say not in the best part of town. The house I'm in, it was vacant. Somebody died and they hadn't decided on what to do with it."

"Who's house?"

"Lancaster, I think."

"Oh, yeah. Lucille Lancaster. I know where that house is. It's a nice one."

"Her daughter lives in town. After I met with her, she decided to let me rent it," Murphy said. "It worked out great. It still had furniture and stuff. All I brought with me was my bed."

"Well, I brought all my furniture down, but the duplex I'm renting is a little small—especially the kitchen. But really, I was lucky to get it. I thought I was going to have to move in with my parents," she said with a laugh. "That *may* have lasted a week."

"I noticed you and your father do bicker a little."

"A lot," Kayla corrected. "He's stubborn and set in his ways, and he drives me crazy sometimes."

"Like last night?"

"Could you tell?"

"Yeah."

Murphy looked at her as if waiting for her to elaborate. For some reason, discussing her father's police tactics didn't seem like the proper thing to do, even though they most likely felt the same way about them. Instead, she steered the conversation back to Murphy.

"It's going on ninety degrees, yet you drive with your window down."

"Sorry. Are you hot?" Murphy asked.

"No, the AC is working fine. But I am wondering why."

Murphy drove with her elbow sticking out of the opened window, and she gave Kayla a quick smile. "Making up for lost time."

"What does that mean?"

"It means there's not a damn skyscraper in sight. It means there's fresh air and I'm not stuck in six lanes of traffic."

"Ah…I see. You said you moved to the city when you were ten. I guess you still have fond memories of country living."

"I do. I regret I didn't get back home more often."

Murphy slowed as they came into town and the speed limit changed. Kayla had to bite her lip to keep from asking more questions. She would let Murphy tell her in her own time, if she was inclined to do so. She didn't want to alienate her by peppering her with personal questions. No, she hoped they could become friends. One of her reservations about moving back home was whether she could develop friendships. Oh, she knew plenty of people and a lot of the ones she'd gone through school with were still in town. However, she couldn't think of a single one of them that she'd want to hang out with. Kevin had been her best friend all throughout school. They'd mucked that up by dating and, even worse, by getting married. And as much as she still enjoyed his company, her vision of hanging out with friends didn't include him and his wife.

And making friends was all she was interested in at the moment. She had no aspirations for anything deeper than that. Not after the fiasco with Jennifer. God, what a disaster that had been. No, she was perfectly happy being single for the time being.

Her glance drifted back to Murphy. Was she single? Could that be something they could share? Did she have a bad breakup? Maybe that's why she left Houston for tiny Sawmill Springs. They would certainly have something in common then. And they had their work in common. Although as attractive as Murphy was, she wouldn't imagine she'd be single for long. Someone in town would latch onto her. Wasn't there a lesbian who worked for the sheriff's department? She wondered if Murphy had already met her. For all she knew, maybe they were dating.

"What?"

Kayla blinked. "What?"

"You were staring."

"Oh. Sorry. I was…never mind."

Murphy turned into the parking lot at Lance Foster's office. "You want to ask me a bunch of questions, don't you?"

Kayla smiled. "Is that what you think? Do you want to ask me a bunch?"

They got out of the car and Murphy looked at her over the top. "Why did you leave the FBI?"

"Why did you leave Houston?" she countered once again. They both smiled though neither answered.

A patrol car was parked in the front, the only other vehicle in the lot. Kim Nguyen stood at the door, seemingly on duty. Murphy walked up to him with both eyebrows raised.

"What's going on?"

"It's locked up. Chief told me not to let anyone inside."

"I'm pretty sure he didn't mean *us*," Kayla said.

"He was pretty adamant. He said *no one* gets inside."

Murphy put her hands on her hips. "Unlock the damn door, Kimbro."

Kayla was surprised when Kim quickly fumbled for the keys to unlock the door. Was he afraid of Murphy? Regardless, he pushed the door open for them and stepped aside.

"Lou Ann Riley is meeting us here," she said. "Please let her in."

"Okay. But I should probably run that by the chief."

"Fine. We're going over Mr. Foster's appointment schedule with her."

Murphy was at Lou Ann's desk, snooping in drawers. The drawers appeared to be as tidy and organized as the top of the desk. Nothing appeared out of place.

"Not much paperwork," Murphy said as she handed her a pair of latex gloves.

"Maybe they were a paperless office." She slipped the gloves on, embarrassed that she'd not thought to bring any.

Murphy lifted a corner of her mouth doubtfully. "In this town? Have you seen the stacks of paper on Pete Wilson's desk?"

"I know. My father's too. We're a little behind the times." She adjusted the focus on the camera and snapped a couple of pictures of the desk. "How did I get camera duty, anyway?"

"I have seniority," Murphy said as she walked over to a door. It was locked. "Wonder where this goes?"

"A supply closet or something?"

"Maybe a file room."

Murphy then pushed open the door to Mr. Foster's office. It appeared to be in the same condition as when they'd left it last night, minus the body, of course. Nothing else looked disturbed. She watched as Murphy walked near the wall, studying the various paintings that hung there. She moved one to the side, then went to another. Looking for a safe, perhaps?

She pointed the camera at his desk, snapping three shots. She was about to open his desk drawer when she noticed the portrait Murphy had just moved. It was a close-up of a young child dressed in a red velvet dress. Nothing about the painting was spectacular, but something wasn't right. Murphy stared at it too, then moved it again.

"Got scratch marks on the wall, as if this gets moved to the side quite often," she said. "But there's no safe back here."

Kayla stared at the child's face, then the eyes. One eye was dull, the other shiny. "I'll be damned," she murmured.

"What?"

"Look here," she said, reaching out to touch the eyes. The dull one wasn't an eye at all but only a tiny piece of fabric.

Murphy took the painting off the wall and flipped it over. On the back of the painting was a cutout, about three inches wide.

"A camera," Kayla said.

"Where?"

"No, I mean there was one here," she clarified. "It's been removed."

"How do you know that's what it was?"

"Because I've seen this before. The images are stored on it and you plug it in to a USB port."

"So it's not a live feed?"

"Well, it could be, sure, depending on what he used. I mean, if you want to put a tiny surveillance camera up, the choices are endless. But something small like this, concealed in a painting… you're obviously going for secrecy. If Mr. Foster is the one with the camera, why do a live feed? He's in the room. It's probably just something that is recording things so that he can review them later, if he chooses."

Murphy shrugged. "Makes sense. I'm not an expert on surveillance."

"It's pointing directly at his desk. Maybe he was paranoid and filmed his meetings with clients."

"Or maybe he didn't trust Lou Ann and he turned it on when he was gone," Murphy suggested.

"From what I understand, Lou Ann has been with him forever. I don't think that's the case."

Murphy hung the painting back up and went on to look at the rest. None of the others had been altered like the portrait had. She turned to look at her, head tilted.

"So who took the camera?"

"Better question is who knew about it?" Then she shrugged. "Of course, we're assuming it was operational. Maybe there hadn't really been a camera there in years."

"Maybe the killer took it."

"How would the killer know it was there?"

"If not the killer, then who? The killer was the last one in the office."

Kayla's phone interrupted them. She sighed. "The chief," she said before answering. "What's up?"

"Where are you?"

"You know very well where I am."

"Yeah, so what are you doing there?"

Murphy was blatantly listening, and Kayla met her gaze, holding it. "We *are* investigating a murder, right?"

"I thought you went over everything last night."

She raised her eyebrows. "You're kidding, right?" She hesitated, wondering if she should be discussing this with him in front of Murphy. "You were being respectful last night, remember? We did nothing more than collect fingerprints." She paused. "Judge Peters *did* sign off on the search warrant, didn't he?"

"Yes, of course. I think maybe I should be there while you're snooping through his things though. And what's this about Lou Ann meeting you there? I talked to her myself last night."

She blew out her breath, trying not to lose patience with him. "We're following up, that's all. Now, I'll see you at dinner. I'll let you know if we find anything."

"Is that your way of saying you don't need me there?"

"I think Murphy and I can handle it. If not, I'll be sure to give you a call." She disconnected before he could say more.

"I may be out of line here, but I get the feeling he's no longer keen on us taking the lead on this case. I think he'd rather have two less-experienced officers on it."

Kayla didn't know Murphy well enough to air her own concerns, but she'd hit on the very thing she herself had thought. But was that really true? He was the one who had been adamant about her and Murphy taking the lead on Guy Woodard's murder. Yes, but that was before Lance Foster had met with the same fate. Now, it seemed—as Murphy had suggested—that he was having second thoughts.

"You may be right. Something's going on with him and I don't have a clue what it is." Before Murphy could comment, the outer door opened. "I suppose that's Lou Ann."

Murphy gave a quick nod, then pushed open the office door. "Ms. Riley?"

"Yes."

"I'm Detective...I mean, Officer Murphy. I met with Mr. Foster about renting a house a while back."

"Yes, I thought you looked familiar."

Murphy held the door open. "Please, come in. I've got Officer Dixon here. I think you know her."

Lou Ann Riley came into the office, and a look of relief passed across her face. "Kayla, it's you. So glad you're back in town."

"Hi, Lou Ann. I wish we could be meeting under different circumstances."

"I still haven't..." she said, shaking her head. "I still can't believe it."

"I know. It's quite a shock. I spoke with him on the phone quite a bit when I was looking for a place."

Lou Ann's gaze slid to the desk. "Hard to believe I won't ever see him sitting there again." She brought a hand to her chest. "Who would have done such a thing?"

"We're hoping you can help us," Murphy said. "We want to take a look at his appointments."

Lou Ann dismissed Murphy and turned to her instead. "Like I told your daddy last night, I left here at five. He didn't have any appointments scheduled. None since noon." She paused. "Unless..."

"Unless what?"

"Well, Mr. Foster wasn't always diligent about keeping the calendar up-to-date. He wasn't exactly crazy about the computer and he preferred to keep a paper schedule." She was already walking over to his desk. "He was meticulous, though, about record keeping. He always had me log in his appointments, even after the fact."

"There's no computer. Did he use a laptop?" Murphy asked.

"Yes." Lou Ann's gaze went to a spot on the desk that was now vacant, and Kayla assumed the killer took it.

From the very bottom drawer on the right side of his desk, Lou Ann pulled out a spiral-bound calendar. She opened it up and flipped through the pages, finding yesterday's entry.

"Oh," she said, almost to herself.

Kayla took the book from her. "Who is Mr. X?"

Lou Ann shook her head. "I don't know. He comes once a month maybe."

Murphy took the book, then flipped back through the pages. "Got a handful of them. All at five thirty."

Kayla pulled Lou Ann from around the desk and gently nudged her toward the leather sofa. "Okay, walk us through this. He meets with a Mr. X, but it's not on your calendar. The next day, he has you log in the meeting, correct?"

"Yes."

"And you have no idea who this is?" Murphy said.

"No." Lou Ann was fidgeting nervously with her hands. "This entry started showing up about, oh, I don't know…six or eight months ago—maybe longer. It could have been late last year even."

"Did you ever ask who it was?"

"Yes. One time. And Mr. Foster told me it wasn't any of my business and I should never ask again. And of course, I didn't."

"Was he agitated?"

"A little, yes. But Mr. Foster had a bit of a temper. I've learned how to read him over the years and knew when to steer clear," she said.

Kayla looked at Murphy with raised eyebrows. They hadn't worked together before and she had no clue as to what Murphy was thinking. Murphy motioned with her head toward the portrait. Kayla nodded.

"Lou Ann, do you know if Mr. Foster kept a surveillance camera in the office?"

Lou Ann's gaze immediately went to the portrait too. "Yes! Yes, he did. Maybe the camera—"

"It's missing," Murphy said.

"Missing? But how? Mr. Foster always recorded his meetings. Why, I don't recall a time when he didn't."

Murphy took the portrait off the wall and showed it to Lou Ann. "Is this where he kept it?"

"Yes, for the last few years, anyway. Before, he had one in the corner, but he said he felt that it made his clients nervous to see the camera."

"Was it a wireless camera, by chance?" Kayla asked. "Did the images automatically download to his computer?"

"No, no. It had a memory card. He was talking about upgrading to a wireless one so he wouldn't have to mess with the cards." She sighed. "Now…well…"

"Do you know where he kept them?" Murphy asked. "The cards?"

"Yes, in the safe." Again, her hands twisted together nervously. "He didn't keep them all in one place though. Some…he kept in a secret place." She smiled quickly. "He thought I didn't know about it."

Kayla smiled too. "Can we see?"

Lou Ann unlocked the door that Murphy had tried earlier. It was indeed the file room. It was also much, much larger than a closet. Upon first glance, she would guess there were twenty-five or thirty 4-drawer filing cabinets.

"I know," Lou Ann said, as if reading her mind. "Mr. Foster was meticulous about keeping a record of everything. I've worked for him seventeen years and a lot of this predates me."

The file cabinets appeared to all be the thick-walled, fireproof kind. Each one had a combination lock on the top drawer. Lou Ann went to one and spun the dial expertly, opening the drawer in a matter of seconds. She pulled out a flat, metal container and brought it to the table.

"These are all clients, both buyers and sellers," she explained as she opened the lid. Row after row of small memory cards, all neatly labeled with what Kayla recognized as mostly local names, filled the case. Probably clients. Kayla took several shots of it before Lou Ann slid it to the side. "There are several of these cases." She then went to another file cabinet.

"Are all the combinations the same?" Murphy asked.

"No, but there is a pattern. So it wasn't that hard to learn."

Kayla walked over to her, watching as she slid file folders out of the way.

"This one has a false bottom," Lou Ann explained. "I found it by accident one day. Of course, curiosity got the best of me."

She lifted the bottom panel as both she and Murphy peered over her shoulder. However, the secret compartment was empty.

"It's gone. It…it was just like the other one."

"When did you last see it?" Murphy asked.

Lou Ann stepped back, a frown marring her features. "I'm not sure. It wasn't like I kept tabs on it or anything. Like I said, Mr. Foster thought he was hiding it from me."

"But you opened it up?" Kayla said. "Can you remember what was inside?"

Lou Ann nodded. "Yes, memory cards, labeled just like that one. Of course, there weren't nearly as many."

"Do you remember any of the names?"

Lou Ann looked at her. "Your Uncle Ned was on some of them."

"Uncle Ned?"

"Yes. And even Billy N was on a few."

"Billy N?"

"Floyd Niemeyer," Lou Ann said. "Everybody still calls him 'Billy N.'"

"Mr. Niemeyer? The mayor?" she asked.

"Yes."

"Who else?" Murphy asked.

"Guy Woodard. There were a couple of names I didn't recognize so I don't believe they were locals. I don't remember them. One was a Julio or something like that." Her eyes widened. "Oh…then of course Mr. X."

"Did you watch them?"

"Oh, gosh, no. I wouldn't dream of it."

Murphy moved away from them, pacing slowly in the file room. "As far as you know, did anyone else know about the camera or the memory cards here?"

Lou Ann shook her head. "I think only me and Mr. Foster."

Murphy glanced at her, and Kayla knew Murphy was ready to talk about it without Lou Ann present. She smiled at the woman and led her away from the file cabinets.

"Thank you for coming in, Lou Ann. We appreciate it."

"I don't mind at all. Anything to help."

"We're going to need to keep his appointment book," Murphy said.

"And if you could print out his appointments from your calendar, that would be helpful," Kayla added. "If you could go back, say, ten months to a year?"

"Yes, I keep all of that archived. Like I said, Mr. Foster was—"

"Meticulous about record keeping," Murphy finished for her. "Hopefully, that will turn out to be helpful for us."

They walked back out to Lou Ann's desk, but Murphy went on into Mr. Foster's office, leaving her alone with Lou Ann. As she waited for her to log into her computer, Kayla glanced at the pictures she had on her desk.

"Is that Clifford?" she asked, pointing to one. "I haven't seen him in years."

"Yes, he's still so handsome, isn't he?" she said, referring to her youngest son. "And not married yet," she added with a wink.

"He doesn't live in town anymore, does he?"

"No, he's up near Lufkin. He doesn't make it back home much anymore," she said sadly. "Holidays, mostly."

Kayla nodded in understanding but didn't reply. Before long, the printer buzzed to life and pages were spitting out.

"Would it be too much trouble for you to email this to me as well?" she asked.

"Of course not."

Kayla jotted down her email address, then took the pages from the printer, glancing through them as Lou Ann finished up with the email.

"Do you know when I'll be allowed back to get my personal things? I've spoken with his wife and she said, for the time being, the office is going to stay closed." Lou Ann sighed. "I can't imagine what she's going to do with this. Who's going to take over?"

"I don't know, Lou Ann, but you can't take anything out just yet. I'm sorry."

"Well, I don't know who's going to water the plants," Lou Ann said a bit dejectedly. "Mr. Foster thought having living, green plants made the office…well, more inviting."

"Hopefully it won't be too long."

"Okay. Well…" Lou Ann stood and ran her hand across her neat desk, as if telling it goodbye. Kayla nearly felt sorry for her. Lou Ann clutched her purse against her side and went toward the door. She paused. "If you need anything else…"

"Thank you. We'll be in touch."

As soon as she left, Kayla went into Mr. Foster's office, finding Murphy studying the portrait.

"Do you suppose a bug sweep could have found it?" she asked, referring to the camera.

"Yes. But with this type of camera, if you turn the lights off and use a flashlight, you'd be able to find it," she said. "The lens of the camera would have reflected back at the light."

Murphy hung the portrait back on the wall, then walked over to his desk. "So…do you know everybody in town?"

She shrugged. "Well, my dad's the chief of police and my mother's a schoolteacher. It's more that everyone knows *me*."

Murphy walked closer to her, eyebrows raised. "What's your theory on the secret tapes? Especially with your uncle being one of the names she mentioned."

She really had no theory. Not yet. And Uncle Ned? She had no idea why Uncle Ned would need to meet with Lance Foster. Unless he was expanding at the concrete plant and needed more land. But why would that require a recorded meeting, one that was being stored in a locked, fireproof cabinet in a secret hiding place. She rubbed her forehead absently, different scenarios running through her mind, plenty of them involving illegal activities.

"Kayla?"

Kayla dropped her hand and stared at her. It was the first time Murphy had said her name. For some reason, she liked the way it sounded.

"I...I don't know," she said finally. "Uncle Ned, that's my dad's older brother. I have no idea why he and Lance Foster would be meeting."

"What does your uncle do?"

"He's...he's got a concrete business," she said.

"Concrete?"

"You know, the big concrete trucks. They pour slabs for new houses, sidewalks, pools, that sort of thing."

"Was he a builder too? Maybe he and Foster—"

"No, not a builder. In fact, Uncle Ned and Lance Foster ran in completely different social circles." She laughed lightly. "If that's even appropriate to say in Sawmill Springs. There are no fancy restaurants where only the higher-ups in town hang out, but you know what I mean."

"Different friends, in other words."

"Yes. And I should really let my dad know about the tapes. This whole situation...he's been acting weird."

"So maybe he knows what's going on."

Kayla bristled at her tone. "Are you insinuating he knows something about the murders?"

"I'm insinuating that perhaps he suspects something, yes. He didn't want us rummaging through the office last night. Frankly, I'm surprised he followed up on the warrant."

"Look, my father is by the book." As soon as she spoke the words, she wanted to take them back. Her father was *so* not by the book. "Okay, that may be stretching it. But in a murder case, there's no way he'd do something to jack with it. No way."

"We've already discussed that. They haven't had a murder here in seven years and even then, it wasn't like they had any investigating to do. One guy shot the other after an argument. They had a dozen witnesses." Murphy motioned around the office. "This case is completely different. You and I, this is what we do. The rest of them? They're in over their heads."

Kayla wanted to be offended by her words, but they were the truth. Her father had been a cop for thirty years. He'd never even fired his weapon. Half the time, he didn't even carry one. The guys? Tim had the most experience. But his experience, like the others, was just what it was—a small-town cop who broke up the occasional fight, investigated a break-in here and there and, on occasion, worked an assault case that, more often than not started with a lover's quarrel. So yes, they were in over their heads.

"Yes, you're right," she conceded. "But I have another concern."

"What's that?"

"There's very little secrecy in town, even within our department. Professionalism only goes so far. Everybody knows everybody."

"So you're saying if we discuss anything in front of the guys, then it would be all over town by evening?"

She nodded. "Gossip is what it is. Tim's Uncle Ray, for instance. He'll know everything. There are no secrets," she said again.

Murphy arched an eyebrow. "Obviously there are secrets. Secret video recordings, secret hiding place. Two men dead."

"The secret recordings are now missing," she added. "Which tells us maybe they weren't so secret after all." She pointed to the empty spot. "And a missing laptop."

"I searched his desk." Murphy shook her head. "Nothing much at all in his desk drawers."

"Guy Woodard was on the tapes. He's dead." She met Murphy's gaze. "My uncle is on the tapes. I need to let my dad know."

Murphy nodded. "Okay. But when you tell him, tell him as a cop and not as a daughter. Read his expression."

"You still think he knows something?" Kayla shook her head. "He's my *father*. And I've already agreed with you that he was acting strange, but if he knows anything, he wouldn't keep it from me."

Murphy shrugged. "Okay. Your call."

She glanced at her watch. It was going on five already. "Look, how about we talk to him together—at dinner."

"Dinner?"

"Yeah, my mom is making enchiladas." She wiggled her eyebrows. "White chicken enchiladas. They're to die for."

"White chicken?"

"Meaning a cheesy, white sour cream sauce—not a red sauce. You'll love them."

"Well, yeah, they sound good, but...I don't know about crashing your parents' dinner." Murphy gave an apologetic shrug. "I'm not sure your father really likes me all that much, you know."

"It's because you're gay, that's all," she said without thinking.

Murphy's eyebrows rose. "*That's* the reason? God, I haven't had to deal with that in more years than I can remember."

Kayla sighed. "It really has nothing to do with you. It's more about—" Her phone interrupted and she smiled before answering. It was Kevin. "Hey there."

"Hey. I heard a rumor you got into town last week and not even a call yet?"

"Sorry." She glanced at Murphy and smiled. "Been kinda busy. I'm actually at Mr. Foster's office right now."

"Oh, I'm sorry. I guess Earl put you to work right away, huh? Crazy happenings in town."

"Yeah. Listen, can I call you later? Maybe we can get together for lunch or something," she suggested.

"Sure. But Cheryl and the kids would be mad if I got to see you and they didn't. Maybe next weekend we can grill out, do burgers or something. You free?"

"Hard to say right now, Kevin. Let me get back to you."

"Okay, sure. Give me a call when you can."

She looked at Murphy, wondering why she felt the need to explain. "That was—"

"The ex-husband," Murphy supplied with a shake of her head. "A lunch date?"

She smiled. "Actually, he invited me over to their house. Over the weekend," she clarified. "So...dinner? We talk to Dad?"

"Okay. If you think he won't throw me out."

"He won't throw you out. And you'll love my mom. She's the complete opposite of him. She's very nice, very friendly." Then she laughed. "Not that I'm saying my dad isn't nice, mind you."

"Right."

Kimbro was still guarding the front door and dutifully locked it when they came out.

"You going to get relieved soon?" Murphy asked him.

"Yes, ma'am. Jeff's gonna take over for me at six."

When they got back into the patrol car, she couldn't help but laugh. "'Yes, ma'am'? I think he's scared of you. What did you do to him?"

"Nothing. I hardly talk to him."

"I think that's it. Lori said you were kinda…well, standoffish with everyone."

"That's what she said, huh?" Murphy said as she pulled out of the parking lot.

"What did you think of Cross Roads?"

"The beer joint? Wouldn't mind shooting pool there sometime. Got a lot of stares though."

"Well, not too many strangers pop in, you know. But I'm not too bad at pool. We should go one night, have a beer and play."

"You're not worried about your reputation getting soiled?"

"How so?"

"Well, your dad apparently doesn't like me because I'm gay. I'm sure he's not the only one in town who feels that way." Murphy glanced at her and smiled. "You need to be careful who you associate with, you know."

Kayla laughed. "Of the people who hang out at Cross Roads Tavern, we would be the two most upstanding citizens there. I don't think we'll need to worry about our reputations."

CHAPTER FOURTEEN

"You be nice to her," Kayla said, pointing her finger at her father.

"Anything we need to discuss, we could have done it at the station."

"I already explained why," she said as she went to the door. She hated to admit that Murphy was right, but she got the feeling that her father definitely was hiding something.

She opened the door, finding Murphy standing there, looking a tad nervous. Kayla couldn't hold back her laugh. "You look like you're picking me up for a date, and you're scared of my father," she teased.

Murphy smiled at her. "If I was picking you up for a date, I'd be honking my horn from the curb. No way I'd come inside. Your father has a gun."

Kayla grinned too, then grabbed Murphy's hand and tugged her in, closing the door behind her. "I'll warn you; he's a little cranky tonight."

"Oh, well, there's something new."

She laughed again, then her smile faded a little as her father stood watching them from the dining room. She ignored his glare. "Come into the kitchen. I'll introduce you to my mother."

Murphy, too, ignored her father, giving him only a slight nod as they passed by him. Her mother was at the stove, tending to the Mexican rice she'd decided to make at the last minute.

"Mom, meet Mandi Murphy." She heard Murphy's groan and she laughed quickly. "Sorry, but I refuse to introduce you as just Murphy."

"So you're the mysterious Murphy I've been hearing about," her mother said. She wiped her hands on a towel, then reached out and shook Murphy's hand heartily. "You're much cuter than I would have thought. The way Earl made you sound; you had two heads or something."

"Mother!"

"Oh, I'm sure she knows how your father is by now."

"Yes, ma'am, I do," Murphy said with a smile. "Pleased to meet you. I hope you don't mind me popping over for dinner."

"Of course not. I know y'all are going to want to talk police business, but I'll have none of it until after dinner." She turned toward the dining room "Earl? Come mind your manners and help set the table. Dinner's ready." She turned back to Murphy. "Don't let him scare you off. He's more bark than bite."

Kayla hid her smile as her father came in, mumbling under his breath as he took four plates from the cabinet. She couldn't tell if Murphy was amused or frightened by him.

"Oh, and I made up a fresh pitcher of sweet tea. Would you fill the glasses, Kayla?"

Kayla elbowed Murphy. "You get the ice. I'll get the tea."

It was a rather quiet affair as her mother loaded their plates with enchiladas and rice. She patiently waited as her mother said grace before picking up her fork. She was only barely able to stifle a moan at her first bite. Murphy, however, wasn't shy.

"Wow, this is incredible," she said as she chewed. "I wish I cooked. I'd steal the recipe from you."

"Thank you, Mandi. It's one of Kayla's favorites. I've given her the recipe several times, but I doubt she's even tried it yet."

"I tried it once," she said. "And it tasted nothing like this. Besides, in the tiny kitchen I have now, I wouldn't even attempt it."

"Well, I'll volunteer my kitchen," Murphy said. "It's huge. But if you cook it there, you'll have to leave half of it with me."

"Maybe I will. I like to cook, but making dinner for one is not much fun."

"No need for you to cook," her father said. "You can eat here every night if you want."

"If I ate Mom's cooking every night, I hate to even think about how much weight I'd gain."

"I eat it every night and I ain't gained a pound."

Her mother laughed. "Oh, Earl...are you blaming that belly of yours on beer then?"

"Same belly I had when you married me."

"Hardly. You were as thin as a rail." Her mother looked at Murphy. "Jason, our son, took after me, poor thing. Kayla can be thankful she's got her daddy's build. The only thing I gave her was her blond hair and blue eyes. That's from my side of the family."

Her mother was short and a little on the plump side, but Kayla would never call her fat. And her father, despite the beer belly he'd sported for the last ten years or so, was still tall and thin. She didn't get his height, but neither did Jason. Jason was only an inch taller than she was and at least sixty pounds heavier.

"Speaking of Jason, have you talked to him lately? I emailed him a couple of weeks ago—to let him know I was moving back here—but I never heard back from him."

"I called him and let him know about Guy Woodard," her mother said. "He was as shocked as everyone else. Why, I still have a hard time believing it." She shook her head dramatically. "And I heard from Margie—her sister is a teller—that the bank is in total disarray now."

"Don't know why," her father said. "He was only the president. Not like they don't have a whole slew of people to make decisions. Course they're saddled with Herbert Miller as chairman of the board. Hell, everybody knows he doesn't do a damn thing."

"I heard they were going to have his funeral on Saturday," her mother said.

"So you've gotten the coroner's report back?" she asked her dad, wondering why he hadn't shared that with them.

He snorted. "Yeah, I got a report. Like I need a damn doctor to tell me his whole goddamn head was practically blown off."

"Earl! We have company!" her mother protested.

"Yeah, and like she hasn't heard that word before," he muttered. "Hell, your daughter hasn't even been back a week yet and I've heard her use it three or four times already."

"I learned it from you." Kayla reached across Murphy for the rice. Murphy pushed the bowl in her direction but not before scooping out some for herself first. "Thanks."

"More enchiladas, Mandi?" her mother asked.

"Just a little, if I may. And…you can call me Murphy, Mrs. Dixon. I'm not too keen on answering to Mandi."

Kayla laughed. "Her mother wanted a cheerleader."

"Bet she was surprised," her father drawled.

"If that's what you wish, then Murphy it is," her mother said. "But there'll be no ma'am or Mrs. Dixon. I get enough of that at school. You may call me Bobbie."

Murphy nodded. "Thank you. I will."

The rest of the meal was passed with idle chatter about the weather—her mother couldn't remember the last time they'd had such a rainy summer—and stories about the new school year which had just gotten started. As promised, there was no mention of police work and, thankfully, her mother had not showered Murphy with personal questions. When everyone had finally pushed their plates away, her father was the one to initiate the move from the table.

"You said you had something to discuss. Let's go on back to the den."

Kayla nodded and shoved her chair back. Murphy stood and started gathering plates, but her mother stopped her.

"I got this. Y'all go on back and get it over with. I picked up an apple pie at the bakery. We can have dessert later."

"That meal was delicious, Bobbie. Thank you."

"Yes, Mom. Very good."

"Thank you, girls. Oh, and there's enough left for me to send some home with you, Murphy."

"That'd be great. Thanks."

"That's it. This is the last time I invite you to dinner," she teased. "You're stealing my leftovers."

"You had three helpings," her mother said. "I think that's plenty." She waved them away. "Now go with your father before he starts bellowing for you."

"I like your mom," Murphy said as they went in search of her father.

"Yeah, she's nice."

Her father was standing with his back to them, and he turned when they entered the den. He didn't take the time for idle chitchat.

"So what's so important that it couldn't wait until morning at the station?"

"Found a few things at Foster's office," Murphy started. "First, he did have a late appointment. It was at five thirty."

Her father shook his head. "Lou Ann told me he didn't. Why do you think he did?"

"He kept a separate appointment book," Murphy said. "Lou Ann would update their master calendar after the fact."

"What the hell does that mean?"

"Dad, he didn't always tell her when he was meeting with clients after five, but he was meticulous—her word—about keeping a record of things."

"Mr. X."

"Mr. X? What the hell? Are we in some kind of a spy movie?" Murphy smiled. "Maybe."

"He had a secret camera hidden behind one of the portraits on the wall," she said. "The camera was missing, but Lou Ann knew where he kept the recordings. They're all on memory cards."

"There were two sets," Murphy said. "One was of clients— buyers and sellers. The other, which he'd kept hidden in a secret drawer, was something else entirely."

Kayla watched as her father twisted the corner of his mustache, an unconscious gesture on his part but one she knew well.

"Secret camera? Secret drawer? Secret meetings? Hell, Murphy, you make it sound like Lance Foster was a goddamn secret agent or something."

"Dad, there was a false bottom in one of the file cabinets. Lou Ann found it by accident. But when she went to show it to us, the drawer was empty. Someone had taken the memory cards."

"I don't guess I understand what all the hoopla is about then."

"Lou Ann remembered the names on some of the cards," Murphy said.

"Uncle Ned was on several, she said."

He stared at her. "Ned?"

She could tell by his voice that he wasn't really surprised, even though he pretended to be. Murphy's intuition was correct. Her father knew more than he let on. "What would Uncle Ned and Lance Foster need to meet about?"

He looked over at Murphy. "Whatever it was, I don't think it has anything to do with this case, so it doesn't need to be discussed in front of a stranger. This is a family matter."

"The hell it is! This is a police matter, Dad. It's no longer about good old boys having each other's backs, even if one of them is your brother. Two men have been killed."

He ran his hand over his hair several times but said nothing.

"What in the hell is wrong with you?" she demanded. "You know what's going on, don't you?"

"I've got two men dead. Two men I've known my whole life. If I knew something, don't you think I'd tell you?"

She wanted to think that he would, but suddenly she wasn't so sure. "She listed off some names on the tapes besides Uncle Ned. The mayor, Floyd Niemeyer and Guy Woodard. And this Mr. X. And there were others she couldn't remember, others not from town."

"Julio, she said," Murphy added.

"You said these tapes were missing. How does this help?"

Kayla wondered if he really didn't see the connection or if he was pretending to ignore the link. She assumed the latter.

"I think we need to question Floyd Niemeyer and your brother," Murphy said.

"Question the mayor? Question *Ned*?" Her father shook his head sharply. "You'll do no such thing."

"Dad...there's a reason these memory cards were kept separate and hidden from the others. Whether it was shady business dealings or whatever, Lance Foster felt the need for secrecy."

"Shady business dealings?" Her father gave a humorless laugh. "Well, we are talking about Lance Foster. That'd be a given."

"Murphy's right. We need to question the mayor and Uncle Ned. We need to—"

"I'm the goddamn police chief," he said loudly. "And you two take orders from me!"

"Then act like the goddamn police chief!" she shot back. "If you didn't want competent officers working for you, you shouldn't have hired Murphy. You shouldn't have asked me to come back." She walked over to him. "Something's going on, Dad. If you don't know what it is, then surely you suspect something. Two prominent members of our community have been shot and killed. And don't say they're not linked."

He sighed. "I swear, you always did talk back to me. Should've washed your mouth out with soap when you were a kid."

She smiled slightly. "The first time I cursed, Mom threatened to...'til I told her I learned it from you."

He sat down heavily on the sofa. "Yeah, Ned's mixed up in something. Only I don't know what it is. But he's been acting weird lately. Secretive. And we've been having a family barbeque on Memorial Day every year for as long as I can remember. He canceled on me this year." He shook his head. "And he missed the goddamn Fourth of July picnic and softball tournament and even Charlotte didn't know where he was."

"Have you asked him?"

"I asked enough questions to know he ain't going to tell me anything. I saw him and Lance Foster coming out of the bank one day a couple of weeks ago. Didn't occur to me at the time that it was anything more than an accidental meeting. But now, the more I think about it, they were in a serious discussion. It ended in a handshake." He stood up and paced across the room. "Now you know Ned as well as I do. Him and Lance never did see eye to eye. Why, when they were in high school, they couldn't stand the sight of one another. I should have known something was up right then. I asked him about it. He told me to mind my own goddamn business."

"So maybe we should try to call him."

"I already did. He ain't answering his cell. I called Charlotte. She said he was in the shower and she'd have him call me back." He looked at his watch. "That was a couple of hours ago."

"So let's go out to the plant first thing in the morning," she suggested.

"If anybody's going to question Ned, it'll be me, not you two," he said loudly.

"It won't be you," she contradicted. "At least not alone."

He wanted to protest, she could tell, but he nodded as he blew out a heavy breath. "I suppose you're right. It's just… well, hell; you know how this town is. People find out we're questioning Ned, questioning Billy N, hell, it'll be all over town within an hour."

"Why's he called Billy N?"

"Floyd William Niemeyer," he said. "He and Billy Grable were in the same grade in school. Still can't believe that fool got elected mayor." He glanced over at Murphy. "I don't mean to be so gruff with you. I know you're plenty competent. So is my daughter. But this thing with Ned's got me worried."

Murphy shoved her hands in the pockets of her jeans, but said nothing.

"Pie's ready," her mother called from the other room.

Kayla knew she'd most likely heard every word they'd said. As loud as they'd been talking to each other, she was surprised that her mother hadn't come in to intervene. Of course, her mother was used to them arguing. It was a common occurrence when she'd lived at home.

"I think I'm going to have to pass on the pie," Murphy said. "I couldn't possibly eat another bite."

Kayla wondered if she was lying and was just anxious to get out of there. There was enough tension in the room to fill it.

"I'll walk you out," she offered.

Murphy nodded. "Let me say goodbye to your mother."

As soon as Murphy walked out, her father turned to her. "You think I need to apologize, don't you?"

"To me or to Murphy?"

"Well, I ain't going to apologize. You just need to keep in mind that I am still the boss around here."

"That's fine. You need to keep in mind that Murphy and I know right from wrong. And you, of all people, should know that you questioning Ned without a witness present is asking for trouble. You can't let this get personal."

He didn't comment on her statement, which meant that he knew it was the truth. Instead, he motioned to the door. "Now, you want to tell me why you feel the need to walk her out?"

Kayla smiled. "Well, it's the polite thing to do. Besides, she's pretty cute," she said as she wiggled her eyebrows. "You should have warned me that she was attractive."

CHAPTER FIFTEEN

Murphy leaned against her truck, her gaze drawn to the Dixon house.

"I noticed that she gave you a piece of pie."

"She did. She said I was too skinny."

"She thinks everyone is too skinny. But since you don't cook, what *do* you eat?"

"I eat a lot of sandwiches," she said.

"Sandwiches? Like bologna and white bread?"

Murphy shook her head. "No, no. I buy different kinds of fancy bread in the bakery. Toast it sometimes; sometimes not. Lots of different veggies too. I usually have turkey, sometimes roasted chicken." She held her hands about a foot apart. "They're huge."

"So like Subway but at home."

"Yeah."

Kayla leaned beside her against the truck. "So why did you leave Houston?"

"Why did you leave the FBI?" she countered.

"I asked first."

"So why don't you tell first."

Kayla sighed. "It's no big deal, really. I was ready for a change. Past ready." She shifted beside her. "I was in a relationship with another agent. And it became too…complicated," Kayla said. "It didn't work out and things were horribly stressful."

"Were you partners?"

"No, thankfully. But that's not the sole reason I wanted out. I told you before; I was ready for things to slow down. Coming back home seemed like the logical thing to do. I missed my family, I missed walking into stores and greeting people by name. I missed the family get-togethers and cookouts and a bonfire on a cool fall evening out in the woods." She turned to her. "I missed all those slow things, you know. I always felt like I was in a race. A race against time, as they say, but it's so true." The wind blew Kayla's hair and Murphy stared as she tucked it behind her ears. "Honestly, I was exhausted. Mentally. Physically. And when the affair ended…well, things at work were, well, like I said, horribly stressful. I needed a change."

"So you quit and came home?"

"I didn't quit right away, no. I managed another seven months, but my heart wasn't in it anymore. I just kinda felt disconnected from the whole thing. I knew it was time to get out. And I knew my dad had a spot for me, so I thought, what the hell, just do it."

"So you missed Sawmill Springs that much, huh?"

Kayla smiled. "I did. I even missed high school football games." She elbowed her playfully. "I *love* football, by the way."

"You do, huh. Cowboys fan, no doubt."

"Absolutely. What? You're not?"

"I'm from Houston."

"Oh, God. Texans? Really?"

"Really."

"Well, maybe this season we can watch games together. I may be able to tolerate the Texans for a game or two."

"And I may be able to tolerate the arrogance of the Cowboys."

Kayla laughed. "Well, they *are* America's team, you know." She shoved off the truck. "I should let you get going. See you at what? About eight?"

"Maybe we should get there earlier and make sure your dad doesn't take off without us."

"Good idea." Kayla touched her arm lightly. "Goodnight, Murphy."

"Goodnight."

Murphy watched her walk up the sidewalk and onto the porch, the light illuminating her face as she turned to wave. Murphy got inside her truck, pausing to run her hand over the dash. She'd bought the truck—brand new—when she left Houston. It was the first new vehicle she'd ever owned. It was also the first truck. Her thought was, moving to a small town where trucks outnumbered cars two to one, she'd be much more likely to fit in. Her previous car, a very fast, red Camaro, wouldn't exactly help her fade into the background, which was just what she wanted to do. So, the white Ford F150 was her choice. She didn't skimp on the inside though. It was fully loaded with leather seats and a moonroof.

She opened it now as she pulled away from the Dixon residence. It was another warm, humid evening, but she didn't mind. The wind blowing inside, stirring her hair, made her feel…alive. She hung one arm out the window and drove slowly down the street, her thoughts going to Kayla Dixon. So she liked football, huh? And she wanted to watch games together.

Well, that could be fun. She supposed she liked her okay, even if she did have FBI ties. Maybe they would become friends. After being in town for over six weeks, seven now, she'd been wondering if she'd ever meet someone she could connect with. She and Kayla had some things in common and not just their work. She, too, loved football. And shooting pool. And Mexican food. She imagined spending time with Kayla would be enjoyable. When—if—things settled down in Sawmill Springs, maybe she and Kayla could do dinner one night or hang out at Cross Roads Tavern. Kayla wouldn't be the first straight woman she'd made friends with.

Of course, if Kayla started dating someone, that'd probably put an end to that. When Monica had started dating—what was the jerk's name? Dustin?—he had all but put an end to their friendship. Apparently he was threatened by a lesbian being friends with his girlfriend. Although Kayla seemed pretty strong-willed, judging by how she stood up to her father. She couldn't see some guy telling her who she could and could not be friends with.

Oh, well, nothing to worry about. Right now, their focus was on two murders and a missing box full of cryptic tapes. She had half a mind to go by the station and pore over all the notes again, but she wasn't sure what good that would do. Not alone, not without someone there to bounce ideas off of. If she'd been in Houston, though, with two high-profile murders, there's no way they'd save a brainstorming session until morning. No, they'd be at it all night, tossing ideas back and forth. They wouldn't take time for a home-cooked meal and apple pie for dessert. She wouldn't be heading to bed at ten o'clock.

Again, she reminded herself she wasn't in Houston any longer. She was in peaceful little Sawmill Springs, where murder was as rare as a winter blizzard. She figured people were locking doors that hadn't been locked in years. Porch lights that seldom came on now burned brightly all night long. And if she had to guess, there were rifles and shotguns and handguns being taken out of their hiding places and placed within arm's reach. No, peaceful Sawmill Springs wasn't quite as peaceful as it once was.

CHAPTER SIXTEEN

The ride out to the concrete plant was made in near silence and Kayla gave up trying to carry the conversation. Her father offered nothing more than grunts to her questions. Murphy was in the back and she could see her amused expression in the mirror. Her father was in rare form this morning.

It had been years since she'd been out to the plant, and she very nearly missed the turnoff. Her father grabbed the dash dramatically as she took the corner way too fast.

"Sorry."

"I'd like to get there in one piece," he mumbled.

The plant was several miles outside of town, and she took the time to enjoy the scenery on the way out. The rolling hills were still green after the unusually wet summer they'd had. The days were no longer blistering hot, but summer was still hanging on, even as the calendar crept closer to fall. It was a lovely sight, as oaks and the occasional pine dotted the rolling landscape. She was already looking forward to next spring when the rains would cause the earth to explode in lush colors of green. Soon after, the wildflowers would cover the pastures in blues and yellows and reds. It was her favorite time of year, when there was so much color at once; it was almost too much to take in. When she was telling Murphy all the things she'd missed, she failed to mention springtime.

She looked in the mirror, finding Murphy watching her. She smiled slightly, then turned her attention back to the road. There were a lot of months left before spring rolled around again—a lot of months, and now a murder investigation. She glanced over at her father who was staring straight ahead. She only hoped Uncle Ned wasn't involved in any way. Sure, he had been in Lance Foster's office, and sure, the visit had most likely been recorded without his knowledge or consent…but that didn't mean he was linked in any way to Guy Woodard or Lance Foster. He could have been trying to buy some property, for all they knew.

The plant entrance was on the right and she slowed as she turned. The plant was a little larger than she remembered. In fact, the place was bustling with activity. Concrete trucks were lined up, waiting their turn to be loaded with cement. She pulled out of the way as one was backing up into the plant's loading dock, its loud beeping signaling a warning to her.

"Has it grown?" she asked as she headed toward the office.

"Yeah, he's got six crews now…five or six guys to a crew."

"What's over there?" A section was fenced off, and inside were rows and rows of birdbaths and statues, all different shapes and sizes.

"A statuary, he calls it. Been doing it a few years now." He motioned to a spot next to the sidewalk. "Stop here. I don't see his truck around. Let me go see where he is."

He got out and slammed the door, and she turned in the seat, glancing at Murphy. "You ever handled a murder investigation quite this way?"

Murphy smiled. "Can't say that I have. You?"

"No. And I miss having resources. I'm sure we would have fingerprint results back by now."

"That just means we haven't gotten a hit yet. We likely won't."

She motioned out the window with her head to where her father stood—cell phone to his ear. "That must mean Uncle Ned's not here."

"Are you close to him?"

"Ned? Growing up, our families were always together. My cousins are all older than I am, but we still got along. Like my dad said last night, lots of family gatherings over the years."

"Are they still around? The cousins?"

"Two still live in town, yes. The boys. The girls both married right after college. One lives in the Houston area and the other in San Antonio." She hadn't thought of them in years though. When they were younger, yes, they'd been close. She was the last to move away. After her marriage to Kevin ended, she'd intentionally stayed away from Sawmill Springs during family holidays to avoid questions. Over the years they'd simply drifted apart. She couldn't recall the last time she'd even seen them. She looked at Murphy and shrugged. "I guess to answer your question, not really close, no."

"I know what you mean. When I was growing up—"

Her dad got back inside the car, interrupting Murphy with a slam of the door. "Not here and not answering his cell. Charlotte says she doesn't know where he is, but I don't believe her."

"Charlotte? She's your aunt, right?"

Kayla nodded at Murphy's question, but her attention was on her father. "What are you thinking?"

"I'm thinking he's mixed up in something and now two men are dead and he's hiding."

"Hiding because he had something to do with the killings?" Murphy asked.

"Oh, hell no. That's my goddamn brother we're talking about. He didn't kill anyone. Hiding because he's scared."

Kayla looked at Murphy. "And if we had resources, we could track his cell phone."

"We don't need to track his damn cell phone," her father said. "I know where he is."

"Then why the hell didn't you say so?"

"Because I'm still contemplating whether I want you two to go along with me or not."

She put the car into reverse and pulled away from the office. "That's not an option and you know it."

He turned and looked over his shoulder at Murphy. "When we find him, you let me do the talking. Don't need to get him spooked, having a stranger asking questions."

Murphy nodded. "Yes, sir. You're the boss."

"Yeah." He glanced at Kayla. "About time somebody recognized that fact."

"Put your seat belt on," she interjected, the incessant beeping getting to her.

"Bossy like your mother," he murmured.

She sighed. Maybe she should have stayed with the FBI. Everything was structured. There was procedure to follow, and it was hardly ever deviated from. She should have known going to work for her father wasn't going to be as smooth as he'd said it would be. She stopped the car at the entrance to the plant, not knowing which direction to go.

"So are you going to tell us where he is?"

He pointed to the right. "I'd bet a hundred bucks he's up at the hunting cabin."

"The old hunting cabin way back off Zimmerman Road? Where the pond is?"

"Yeah, but he's got it fixed up. That's where we've been having the family barbeques the last few years. It's way back in the woods. Got to get through a locked gate to get on the property. That's where I think he is."

Kayla pulled out onto the road, then glanced in the mirror, meeting Murphy's gaze. She couldn't tell if Murphy was annoyed or amused by her father. As their eyes held, Kayla wondered what she was thinking. She wondered if she, too, was having second thoughts about leaving her job and coming to Sawmill Springs.

* * *

"Well, I'll be damned," Earl muttered as he jerked on the chain. "He changed the lock on me." He pocketed his keys, then jerked his head toward the car. "Get me the goddamn bolt cutters."

Kayla popped the trunk for her and Murphy opened up the toolbox, pulling out the bolt cutters like he'd requested. He easily snapped the chain in two, and then opened the gate.

"Let's close it behind us. Just in case someone comes around," he said.

She held the gate open while Kayla drove through, then she closed it, slipping the broken chain between the fence and the gate.

"I hardly remember this," Kayla said as she drove along the narrow road.

"Yeah, he's let the woods grow up along the road."

"How much land does he have?" she asked.

"Three hundred acres. He bought it years ago, just for hunting," Earl said. "Fixed up that old cabin though," he said to Kayla. "Even got AC in it now."

The lane turned sharply, disappearing into the woods. From the main road, you wouldn't even know it existed, it was so well hidden. After a few minutes, they came to a fork, one road more used than the other.

"I'm assuming we go left," Kayla said.

"Yeah. That way takes you back to the pond and where he's got his deer blinds."

"Does anyone fish it anymore?" Kayla asked, referring to the pond. "That used to be one of my favorite things to do when we'd come out here."

"His boys still come out some, I think, but it's not like it used to be. They've both got little kids now. Seems nobody's got time anymore for simple things like fishing."

Murphy noticed his wistful tone, and she wondered if he was also talking about himself. When she was young, she remembered many a lazy Saturday when she'd spend the entire day at her grandmother's place, fishing until suppertime. It was a memory she held dear. Probably fishing with her father was a good memory for Kayla too.

"Turn up here, to the left," he said.

"I don't remember this drive at all," she said. "Of course, we usually only went to the pond when we came out here." When the cabin came into view, Kayla's eyes widened. "Oh, my God."

"Yeah, it's a far cry from that old hunting shack."

"It looks like a real cabin."

"He put those half logs on for siding And added on some rooms in the back."

"Don't see a vehicle," Murphy said from the backseat.

"Drive on around to the side," her father directed with a wave of his hand. "If he's here hiding, then he's got his truck parked around back in the woods."

They didn't make it around to the back though. A man came out onto the porch with a shotgun in his hands. A man who she assumed was Ned Dixon.

"That damn fool," her father mumbled. "Stop the car."

She and Kayla got out too, but Kayla stopped her with a touch on her arm. "Let him go first. Uncle Ned looks a bit… well, a bit scary."

His face had several days of stubble on it and a baseball cap was hiding his hair, which still stuck out around the edges. His clothes were wrinkled and scruffy. He looked as disheveled as a homeless man. She assumed this wasn't his normal look.

"Put the damn shotgun down, Ned."

"What do you want?"

"What the hell's wrong with you?"

"I'm fearing for my life, that's what the hell is wrong." He motioned with his gun. "Who's that with Kayla?"

"Put the damn shotgun down," her father said again. "That there's my new officer, Murphy. You'll scare her half to death waving that thing around."

"Is it just me or do you also feel like there should be banjo music playing?" she whispered, causing Kayla to laugh quietly.

"He's not a crazy mountain man," Kayla said. "At least he used to not be." She nudged her elbow. "Come on."

They went inside the cabin, into a kitchen. It looked like a rustic home, comfortable enough to live in. Nothing about the inside indicated it was an old hunting shack. She glanced around quickly, her eyes lighting on the nearly empty bottle of whiskey on the table. Ned sat down and poured a shot. Judging by the smell around him, he'd been drinking for a while.

"Kinda early for whiskey, ain't it?"

"I guess it depends on your state of mind, now don't it?" he held the bottle up to Earl. "Want a shot?"

"Don't believe I do, Ned." Earl leaned his arms on the chair next to Ned. "You gonna tell me what you're mixed up in?"

"Ain't got nothing to say to you, Earl."

"No? Well, you already said you were fearing for your life. I got Guy Woodard shot dead. Now Lance Foster shot dead. Hell, half the town thinks we got a serial killer on the loose." He stood up, walking around behind Ned. "And we come up here and find you hiding out, clutching a damn shotgun in your hands...fearing for your life." He put an arm around his shoulder. "So don't you tell me you ain't got nothing to say to me."

"What are you doing here anyway? With them, no less."

Earl looked over at her and Kayla. "'Them', as you say, are my two best officers. Murphy...tell Ned here what you found."

Murphy walked around the table so that she could face Ned Dixon. His eyes were slightly bloodshot, and she wasn't sure if it was from the whiskey or lack of sleep.

"Mr. Dixon, I'm Officer Murphy. Kayla and I discovered a link between Guy Woodard and Lance Foster. It seems that Mr. Foster videoed his meetings in his office. He kept the memory cards locked up."

"Videoed?"

"Yes, sir. With a hidden camera. His secretary was aware of the memory cards. Besides Guy Woodard, your name was mentioned, as well as the mayor, Floyd Niemeyer."

"Billy N," Earl interjected. "Now what the hell were you doing meeting with Lance Foster?"

"You say you got video recordings?"

"No, we're saying they existed. They've been taken, apparently."

Kayla sat down at the table beside him. "What's going on, Uncle Ned?"

"You just get back in town?"

"Last week." Kayla smiled at him. "And this is my first week on the job. It's been rather busy, to say the least." Murphy watched as Kayla put a hand on her uncle's arm. "What's going on?" she asked again. "To hear Dad tell it, you and Lance Foster couldn't stand each other."

"Yeah, well, that didn't change." He poured another shot of whiskey. "Lance Foster got us into a bit of trouble. Now, it seems like we all got prices on our heads."

Earl walked around the table. "For what, Ned? Prices for what?"

"Lance got me involved in something—something bad." He tossed back his whiskey. "Drugs, Earl. He got me involved in the drug business."

"Drugs! What do you mean, the drug business?"

"I mean we were moving them from Houston to other cities."

"Cocaine? Marijuana? Something else?" she asked.

"Cocaine, mostly," he said.

Earl slammed his fist on the table. "Cocaine? I'm the goddamn chief of police and you're dealing cocaine? Are you out of your mind?"

"Look, I didn't want to do it. But Lance and Guy came out to the plant one day last year. Said they had someone in Houston who needed to move the drugs. They had this plan. We'd hide it in the concrete statues and ship it out."

"Ship it out where?" she asked.

"There's this company that I sell my stuff to. It's like a distribution center. They then sell it to Lowes and Home Depot and places like that."

"So where the hell does it end up?" Earl asked.

"I don't know. My part of the deal is to put the cocaine in the statues and ship them out. That's all I know. What happens after that, I have no idea."

"How do you get the drugs in the first place?" she asked.

"That was Billy N's part of the deal. All I know is, once a week I'm stuffing drugs into my molds as the concrete hardens."

"I'm sorry, Uncle Ned, but this makes absolutely no sense. Why would a drug dealer involve outsiders like you and Lance Foster in his drug business? I mean, you're only moving it a few hundred miles, aren't you?"

Ned shrugged. "Look, I told you, Guy and Lance came to me with this scheme. And the distribution center services not only Texas, but Oklahoma, Arkansas and Louisiana too."

"Why would you go along with it, for God's sake?" her father demanded.

"Because they offered me a lot of money, that's why."

"How was Guy Woodard involved?" Kayla asked.

"He washed all the money through the bank."

"How much money are we talking?" Kayla asked.

Ned shrugged. "I don't know. My cut was ten grand a week."

"Jesus Christ, Ned. That was *your* cut? Exactly how much of this crap were you sending out?"

"A lot—forty or fifty statues a week."

"One kilo per statue?" she asked.

He nodded.

She whistled. "Street value is what? Eighteen, twenty thousand per kilo?"

"We've seen it go for twenty-five in the Dallas area," Kayla said.

"So you're telling me you package close to a million dollars of cocaine a *week*?" Earl said. "Are you out of your *mind*?"

"If your cut was ten grand, what do you think Guy Woodard and Lance Foster were getting?" she asked.

"More than me, that's all I know."

"So something went wrong, obviously, if they're dead," she said.

"Yeah, something went wrong. Lance started skimming off the top, that's what. Each kilo wasn't a kilo anymore. It was ten or fifteen grams short."

"He was selling it on the side?" Earl shook his head. "Jesus Christ. In *my* town?"

"No, Earl. He claimed he had somebody in Dallas."

"Who is Mr. X?" Kayla asked.

"That's…that's the dude in Houston. I don't know his name. That's what Lance and Guy called him."

"How is goddamn Billy N involved in this?"

"He's got that trucking company. Best I can tell, that's how they get the drugs from Houston to Sawmill Springs."

"So you—Ned Dixon—got involved with the likes of Guy Woodard, Lance Foster and goddamn Billy N? None of the three would give you the time of day out in public, you know that, right? Hell, you and Billy N used to get into fights in high school nearly every damn day! Yet you go into business with him? The goddamn drug business?" Earl again slammed his fist on the table. "Now what the hell am I supposed to do?"

"You've got to protect me, Earl. First Guy, then Lance. Me and Billy N are next, I just know it. You've got to protect me."

"Protect you? Hell, I should throw your ass in jail, that's what I should do," he said loudly.

Murphy rubbed her eyes, then glanced over at Kayla. They both knew Earl would do no such thing.

"Does this Mr. X know who all was involved? Does he know about you?" Kayla asked.

"Sure he does. He knows we use the statues."

"Have you met him?"

Ned shook his head. "No. Like I said, I have no idea who he is. Some dude from Houston, that's all I know."

"Judging by Lance Foster's appointment book, he met with the guy at least once a month," she said. "If Niemeyer's trucks brought the cocaine up here, then why would this Mr. X need to be that involved? I mean, here in Sawmill Springs. Why would he even come to the area?"

"Maybe he's not the boss. Maybe he's just checking on their investment," Kayla suggested.

"Does Charlotte know about this, Ned?"

"No. She thinks the concrete business is doing exceptional this year," he said as he rubbed the stubble on his chin.

"What excuse did you give her for you hiding out here at the cabin? She wouldn't tell me where you were."

"I told her I had some repairs to do on the deer blinds and that I was going to take a few days off. And I told her not to tell anyone. Told her I didn't want company."

"Then I suggest you keep yourself here," Earl said. "Let us try to figure out what the hell we're going to do."

"Oh, and you're going to need a new chain for your gate," Kayla told him.

Ned looked up at Earl. "What'd you do?"

"I cut the son of a bitch, that's what. You changed locks on me."

"Oh, yeah, forgot to give you the new one. Well, I've got some chain out in the shed. I'll take the four-wheeler down there and replace it."

"And answer your damn cell phone," Earl said.

"I know you're mad at me, Earl."

"Mad don't even begin to touch what I feel right now, Ned. Now you just hang tight until we figure out what's going on."

Murphy would have handcuffed him and brought him in. His confession of drug trafficking needed to be addressed, and he would be safer locked up in jail than anywhere else. She knew Earl wouldn't go for that though. A small town like this? The news would spread like wildfire.

It was a silent ride back into Sawmill Springs with her and Kayla exchanging glances several times in the mirror. They both had questions, no doubt, but neither of them voiced them.

When they got into town, Earl said tersely, "Drop me off at the station. I've got some calls to make."

"Shouldn't we discuss this? Come up with a plan of action?" Kayla asked.

"Yeah, as soon as I have one, I'll let you know what it is."

"Dad…"

"You two get over to Billy N's trucking company. It's on the other side of the interstate. Bring his ass in and we'll question him."

"Okay."

"And don't take a patrol car. Either you or Murphy drive. Don't want to call attention to anything."

"We're wearing uniforms," Kayla reminded him.

"Then change into street clothes. I don't want anything getting around town just yet, until I figure out what in the goddamn hell I'm going to do." Kayla had barely pulled to a stop before he opened his door and got out. "Bring him in around back. Make sure Lori doesn't see you. Use the back door to my office."

"Wouldn't it be simpler if we said we were bringing him in as the mayor, just to discuss the current situation with the murders?" Murphy suggested.

"Yeah, it might be," he snapped. "But I don't have time to think about it, so do as I say." He slammed the door and hurried into the station.

Kayla turned around in the seat to face her. "I like your suggestion. It makes it all simpler."

"Yeah, but I guess I wouldn't mind getting out of this uniform," she said.

"Oh, I don't know." Kayla smiled at her, her blue eyes twinkling. "You look awfully cute in it."

Murphy's eyebrows shot up. Did Kayla really just say that? God, she hated it when straight women flirted with her. But when they were as cute as Kayla was…well, she supposed she could make an exception.

CHAPTER SEVENTEEN

Kayla stood in Murphy's kitchen, eaten up with envy at how large it was. There was at least four times more counter space in it as in her duplex.

"Planning a meal?"

She turned, finding Murphy in jeans and a polo shirt. Her own change of clothes was into pressed khakis and a light blue blouse. She'd have much rather slipped into her jeans instead.

"I was coveting your counter space," she said, answering Murphy's question.

"Well, feel free to plan a meal. I make an excellent taste-tester."

"Really? Then how about tonight?"

"Sure. But, you know, food-wise, it's pretty bare."

"So we'll go by the grocery store," she said, mentally going over her menus, trying to find one that wasn't too complicated.

"Deal. I'll buy, you cook." Murphy smiled broadly. "I get leftovers, of course."

"Of course." They went out the front and she waited while Murphy locked the door. "Your truck or my car?"

"I'll drive," Murphy offered.

"It still smells new," she said when she got inside the white truck.

"Yeah. I got it right before I moved here. Wanted something that would blend in better than the sports car I had."

Kayla nodded. "I can see you in a sports car, I guess, although I think this fits you." As usual when Murphy drove, the air conditioner was on and the driver's window was opened.

"Do you mind the window?"

"Not at all," she said as she tucked her hair behind her ears to prevent it from blowing.

"So…this Floyd Niemeyer, do you know him?"

"I'd recognize him, yes, but I wouldn't say I know him. He's older than my father, so his kids were older than me in school. I don't recall there ever being any interaction between our families."

"You haven't really said anything about your uncle."

"I think I'm still in shock," she said honestly. "I know my dad is." She turned to look at her. "You would have cuffed him and brought him in, right?"

Murphy nodded. "He confessed to trafficking drugs…yeah, I'd have arrested him on the spot. But again, I'm used to the city where there are checks and balances and things are done by the book."

"I know. Me too. I've had to tell myself to step back and look at it from a different angle. Small towns like this—small counties—it's still a good old boy network. Judge Peters has a lot of power, but he's also good friends with most, if not all, of the big names in town. Not to mention a lot of these men and their businesses are linked in one way or another. My uncle, on the other hand, isn't a big name in town even though he's got a successful business," she said. "All of these men were born and raised here, and they all went through school together. A lot of the pecking order was established way back then."

"So you're saying that even if it wasn't your uncle—say it was Floyd Niemeyer who had confessed all of that—we still wouldn't have cuffed him and brought him in."

"That's right. And that's the reason my dad wants this to remain secret. He wants us to bring Floyd in to find out what's going on. He's not looking to arrest him—at least not right now."

Murphy's phone rang, and she picked it up from the console, her expression changing as she looked at it.

"Excuse me," she said and Kayla nodded. "Hey…what's up?"

Kayla glanced out the window, trying to give Murphy some privacy and not just blatantly listen to her conversation. Judging by her casual manner, it was a friend.

"Yeah, I know. Been super busy with it all." A pause. "No, nothing much to tell."

So maybe not a friend. Someone looking for information.

"Dinner? Tonight?"

Kayla brought her head around, finding Murphy looking at her. "Can't tonight. Already have plans."

Okay…so not just a friend…someone asking for a dinner date.

"I'll have to let you know, Gloria. With everything that's going on, it's hard to say what my weekend will be like." A quick nod. "Okay. I'll call you. Bye."

Kayla had to bite her lip to stop herself from asking the most obvious question. Fortunately, Murphy volunteered the information.

"Gloria Mendez," she said. "She's a sheriff's deputy."

"Oh. So you're passing on a dinner date?"

Murphy smiled. "Well, yeah. I thought you were cooking. You know, I get leftovers that way."

"Well, if you want to ditch me for someone else, I'll understand. Are you…dating?"

"Gloria? No. I mean, we've gone out a few times. She had me over for dinner one night."

Had her over, meaning they didn't go out to eat. Was it an intimate dinner? she wondered. Even if they weren't technically dating, that didn't mean they weren't sleeping together. That, of course, was absolutely none of her business. Her curiosity, however, got the better of her, and she feigned ignorance as to who Gloria Mendez was.

"Is she new there? I don't recall her name. Not that I know everyone at the sheriff's department, but in this town, women on the force are rare."

"She's fairly new, yeah. She's young. Twenty-four, I think."

"So not dating but there's a possibility?"

Murphy raised an eyebrow. "Are you fishing for gossip to share with Lori?"

Kayla nearly blushed. Yeah, she was fishing for gossip, but she was only being nosy for herself. She shrugged as nonchalantly as she could. "No, just being curious, that's all."

They crossed over the interstate, getting caught at the light on the other side. Murphy stopped behind an eighteen-wheeler, then pushed the button to roll her window up.

"No breeze and the smell of diesel," she explained. "Reminds me too much of the city." She said nothing else, so apparently she didn't feel the need to answer the dating question. Kayla didn't blame her really. It wasn't any of her business who—or if—Murphy was dating.

When the light changed to green, they drove past several of the newer travel stops that combined gas and diesel with a convenience store and fast-food places. Taco Bell, Burger King, Whataburger, Sonic, Pizza Hut, Subway, Arby's...you name it, it was here. When she was growing up, their only option besides the local Dairy Mart had been when McDonald's had come to town. She still remembered the grand opening...their high school band had performed. Looking at all of it now, she thought she much preferred the old days. Now, it was just a conglomeration here along the interstate, seemingly no rhyme or reason to any of it.

"Do you know how far down it is?"

"Dad said it was on the right, just past all of this mess."

Murphy laughed. "I see you're not fond of chain restaurants either."

"It just clutters up everything, doesn't it? Although, I'm sure most of the locals like having all these choices now."

"Yeah, and I'll admit, I've popped into the Subway a couple of times. And I've had a pizza delivered."

"There's the sign," she said, pointing to Niemeyer Trucking.

"What is it that he does?"

"I have no clue."

There were two cars parked outside the office building. Three large trucks—tractors—were parked against the fence, but there were no trailers in sight.

They heard laughter coming from inside the office. Murphy pushed the door opened, and the laughter ceased almost immediately. Two young women, early twenties, were sitting behind two desks.

"May I help you?" one asked.

"Looking for Mr. Niemeyer," Murphy said.

The girl shook her head. "Oh, sorry. He didn't come in today."

"Are you looking to rent a truck?" the other asked. "'Cause we can help with that."

"No, actually we're just wanting to speak with Mr. Niemeyer," Murphy said.

"Would we be able to find him at his home perhaps?" Kayla asked.

"There was an email from him this morning that said he wouldn't be in, that he had to go out of town," the first girl said. "So I don't guess he's there. Are y'all friends of his?"

She and Murphy exchanged glances. The last thing they needed was to tell these two young girls that the cops were out looking for their boss. They'd be on the phone before the door closed behind them. Apparently Murphy thought the same thing.

"Yes," she said. "He'd told us to drop by sometime. I guess we should have called first."

The girl smiled and nodded. "He's usually always here. Unless he's got some business to do. You know, he's the mayor and all."

"Yes. Say…you don't happen to have his cell phone number, do you?"

At that, the girl hesitated. "Well, I do, but in the past, he's asked us not to give it out to anyone."

"I understand," Murphy said. "Well, we'll stop by another time then."

They walked back to the truck in silence. Only when they'd both gotten inside and Murphy had started it up did they speak.

"Well, what do you think?"

"We could go by his house, but if he's truly out of town and his wife is there, it'll raise some questions," she said.

"So we'll make up something," Murphy said as she pulled away. "We need his blessing as mayor for some charity event we want to start."

"Okay, I'm game. Only I don't know where he lives."

"Well, thanks to Tim, he's taken me around town enough that I think I can find it. There's a really nice subdivision out past the high school. Guy Woodard's house is out that way too."

Murphy pulled into the driveway of the house she was "ninety percent certain" was the Niemeyer's place. Just to be sure, Kayla did a quick Google search on her phone to verify.

"Yes, this is it."

At the front door, Murphy rang the doorbell. It was a rather loud, obnoxious chime that could be heard easily from the front porch. However, they neither saw nor heard any movement from inside. She rang it again, then knocked. Still nothing.

"I'll go peek in the garage," Kayla said.

The garage doors were solid without windows so she walked around to the side, hoping the neighbors weren't watching her. She glanced through the side window, finding the two-car garage empty. She turned, surprised to find Murphy standing behind her.

"Empty," she said, answering Murphy's silent question. "No one's home."

"I guess you better call the chief and find out what he wants us to do."

CHAPTER EIGHTEEN

It seemed a little strange to be at the grocery store, picking up things to cook dinner—albeit for a very attractive woman—in the middle of a murder investigation. However, her father had told her to "just lay low," whatever that meant, until morning. He was going to try to find the mayor himself. He had connections, he said. Again…whatever that meant. He was being extremely secretive, and no amount of questioning on her part had gotten anything out of him. He told her not to worry and that if she wanted to—as long as there was no police business discussed—she could come over for dinner. She declined.

So here she was with a list of ingredients needed to make two different dishes. Something simple that wouldn't take too long—a skillet casserole. That was her first choice, although she had no idea how stocked Murphy's kitchen was. Did she even have a skillet? Her second choice was chicken parmesan, but then that meant doing some side dishes. The skillet casserole had broccoli in it. No need for an added veggie dish.

"What if she doesn't like broccoli?"

"Excuse me?"

She smiled at the lady standing next to her. "Sorry. Talking to myself." She sighed, then pulled her phone out of her pocket. Murphy answered on the first ring. "Do you have a cast-iron skillet and do you like broccoli?"

Murphy laughed. "Are you at the grocery store already?"

"Yes."

"I told you not to go to any trouble," Murphy reminded her. "But yes, I like broccoli."

"And the skillet?"

"Let me look. All this kitchen stuff was already here." She heard cabinets opening and closing and finally an "ah ha."

"Does that mean yes?"

"It's like a cast iron convention. There's at least ten different ones here. Who needs that many?"

"People who cook. See you in a bit."

She was smiling and she wasn't entirely sure why. Was it just the prospect of having dinner with an attractive woman after nearly eight long months of celibacy? Not just celibacy. But she hadn't even been on a date since she'd ended things with Jennifer. Not that this was a date. Neither of them had even suggested anything of the sort. But yeah, she liked Murphy. They got along well as work partners and they seemed to be in tune with each other. Professionally was completely different than personally, though. She knew that firsthand. Still, she thought Murphy might be interested in getting to know her better as well, even if it was only as friends. At least they would each have someone to hang out with. Of course, there was Gloria Mendez. Maybe Murphy already had someone to hang out with.

That thought made her smile fade somewhat as she selected an onion from the bin. So they'd have dinner, hang out, watch TV or something, that's all. It wasn't a date.

* * *

The kitchen was already clean and tidy, but Murphy wiped down the countertop again anyway. She didn't know why she was feeling nervous. Maybe because she hadn't entertained another woman at her place in a very long time. One of the benefits of not cooking was never having people over. She would go to their place instead. That way, she could end the evening whenever she wanted, depending on how the date was going.

Of course, this wasn't a date. Kayla Dixon was straight. Gorgeous and straight…a damn shame. At least Kayla was open to being friends though. She hadn't known her long, but she already knew that she clicked better with Kayla than she did with Gloria. Again, it could just be the age difference with Gloria, but there really wasn't any attraction there. Kayla? Yeah, those blue eyes seemed to draw her in, and she had a hell of a time getting back out again—which was why she had to constantly remind herself that Kayla was straight.

Maybe being friends with her wasn't such a great idea after all. Gloria would definitely be the safer option. She stared off into space, trying to picture Gloria's face. She was having a hard time recalling any features. An image of Kayla popped into her mind easily, though…the blue eyes that seemed to be filled with light, the tiny laugh line that showed when she smiled, the barest hint of a dimple in one cheek. She sighed.

"She's straight. Remember that."

Later, however, she was having a hard time clinging to her self-warning. She'd volunteered to cut up the broccoli, volunteered to help *cook*, of all things. Even though it was a very large kitchen, it was much too small, as they seemed to be bumping into each other at every turn. When Kayla's hip nudged hers, scooting her out of the way, she very nearly dropped the knife.

"It is such a joy to have a big kitchen again," Kayla said. "You lucked into this house."

"Yeah, I know. When we get this into the oven, I'll show you around. The backyard and porch are wonderful." She wiped her hands on a towel, eyeing the wine bottles on the counter. She had brought out two—both red. Kayla had brought along a bottle of chardonnay which she'd slipped into the fridge when she got there. "You want a glass of wine?"

"Sure. You can choose," she said. "I'm not at all picky when it comes to wine."

"I'm not an expert on food pairings, but I assume one of the reds would go better with dinner. How about I open the chardonnay?"

"That's fine. I'm about ready to assemble this thing, then it's forty minutes in the oven."

Murphy leaned against the counter, watching as Kayla mixed in the ground beef with the pasta.

"So Earl said to lay low, huh. What do you think he's up to?"

"I wish I knew. And Uncle Ned? I still can't believe he's mixed up in this. No matter how Dad tries to spin it, Uncle Ned is looking at some serious charges."

"Unless Earl plans to ignore it."

"Ignore it? Ned confessed to three cops. How can he ignore it? How can we ignore it?"

"Oh, come on, Kayla. You worked for the FBI. I've been around long enough to know that this sort of thing happens all the time. Things get swept under the rug depending on the circumstances." She shrugged. "It's common knowledge."

Kayla turned around to face her. "Yes, sure, I admit I've heard of things like that. But I've never been a part of it. This is different, though. Dad won't have the clout of the FBI to back him. If it got out—and it will—that he covered this up to protect his brother, not only would his career be over, but he'd be looking at obstruction charges." She shook her head as she turned back to her casserole. "It's his brother, I know, and that makes it personal, but I still can't see him ignoring what we know. If it was just me…maybe he'd try. But you were there too."

"Well, it wouldn't be the first time I've had to follow an order I didn't agree with," she said.

"If it was only Uncle Ned, then maybe. But there are too many other players involved. And as it stands, it's because of the drugs that Guy Woodard and Lance Foster are dead. It's all going to come out, one way or another."

Murphy leaned over and opened the oven door, getting a smile from Kayla in return as she put the casserole inside.

"Now, how about a tour of that back porch? I've had enough police talk."

"Sure, come on." She pointed to a small door off the kitchen. "That goes out to the porch too, but we'll be formal and use the doors in the living room."

Kayla picked up her wineglass and followed her. "So all of this furniture was here? This is a beautiful hutch," she said, running her hand along the wood.

"Yeah. When I landed this house, I sold all of my stuff but my bed. I figured it would be easier to buy new things when I needed it rather than go through the hassle of moving everything." She shrugged. "Besides, I didn't have anything that special."

Kayla nodded. "I think if I'd scored a place like this, I'd have sold my furniture too."

The double glass doors that opened out onto the covered back porch were one of her favorite features of the house. She opened them wide, then stepped aside to let Kayla go out.

"Oh, my God. This is fantastic," Kayla said. "It's big enough to make an outdoor living room out here." She turned to her, her eyes wide with a smile on her face. "What a *great* place to watch football games!"

"Is that a hint?"

"Yes! I'll even bring the food. We could have a tailgate party right out here."

Her enthusiasm was infectious, and Murphy had an easy time imagining them enjoying a game together.

"Great yard too," Kayla continued. "Do you have to keep it up?"

"No. She already had someone coming once a week, so I kept them on. I'd be lost. I haven't mowed a lawn since I was ten."

"Ten? Isn't that when you said your family moved to Houston?"

Murphy nodded. "Yeah, I was devastated at first. I thought my world was ending. Didn't want to leave my friends, my cousins, my grandmother," she said, smiling. "I still miss my grandmother."

"She's still alive?"

"Oh, yeah. Still lives in Eagle Lake. When my parents retired, they built a house on her property so they're right there, but she still gets around. She still has a garden. She's eighty-three and shows no signs of slowing down."

"Do you visit much?"

"Not enough, no. Of course, I was a lot closer when I lived in Houston, but there never seemed to be enough time. I'd get back for a day here and there. Two days if I was lucky."

"What's that area like? Eagle Lake."

"Oh, the town itself is a lot like Sawmill Springs, like most small towns, really." She leaned against one of the banisters. "Coastal prairie, farmland, rice farms. Got wooded areas but not like here. Live oaks, mostly, some yaupon thickets, cedars. Not the rolling hills and big tall trees like we've got here, but still pretty."

"So when you left Houston, why here? Why Sawmill Springs?"

"There were openings in other towns, some smaller than this, some larger, but when I visited here, I felt like it was the right size. Plus, it wasn't too far from the city if I wanted to go back and it's not that terribly far from home, less than four hours." As their eyes met, she knew what the next question was going to be.

"Why did you leave Houston?"

She swirled the little bit of wine that was left in her glass before drinking it. She sighed, meeting Kayla's eyes again. "I killed someone."

The blue eyes that stared back at her were filled with nothing but compassion. "You want to tell me about it?" she asked softly.

Another sigh. Did she want to tell Kayla about Leon? About the drug bust the FBI had all arranged...the one that went horribly bad? She hadn't told her family; hadn't told her grandmother. In fact, she hadn't told anyone. The guys in her squad knew what happened, her lieutenant, her captain. And the FBI knew, of course.

She walked back inside, the smell of the casserole in the oven reminding her of how hungry she was. She opened the fridge and took out the wine bottle, filling her glass nearly to the top. She turned, finding Kayla beside her. She added to her glass as well before corking the bottle again.

"His name was Leon," she said. "He was my informant. He was my friend." She swallowed a sip of wine. "And I shot him."

Kayla pulled out a chair and sat down at the table, waiting for her to continue. She took a deep breath, blowing it out quickly. She sat down across from her, her fingers twisting the stem of the wineglass aimlessly as scenes from that night danced through her mind. Darkness, then bright lights, then darkness again. Shouts. Screams. Gunfire. People running. The fire. Sirens. And more screams.

She ran a hand through her hair, brushing it away from her eyes. "I was approached by the FBI—two pricks who are lucky I didn't shoot them," she said bitterly. "Leon had been secretly working for them. Leon's cousin was in deep with a gang and they were running drugs. That wasn't the real reason the FBI wanted them though. They'd killed someone from a rival gang, someone who was set to testify in some big drug case. This was more about revenge on their part."

"If Leon kept it a secret from you, then they must have had something on him," Kayla said.

"When Leon refused to help them, they planted drugs in his apartment, then did a fake bust."

"So if they had him, why did they come to you?"

"I was working a homicide. Leon's cousin told him who'd shot this kid during a drive-by at a bus stop. My investigation was getting in their way, apparently." She put her wineglass down. "Anyway, long story short, we were doing a joint bust. I'd get my guy and they'd get theirs. Leon wasn't supposed to be there. I'd told him to stay away." She met Kayla's gaze across the table. "They'd told him he *had* to be there. They needed him to ID their guy."

Kayla reached over and covered her hand with her own. "Leon got caught in the crossfire?"

Murphy nodded. "It was pretty much chaos from the beginning. Shots were coming from all directions. This guy was running and I went after him. I yelled for him to stop. When he turned around, he had a gun. That's all I saw." She swallowed. "Four people died that night. And I shot Leon."

"I'm so sorry," Kayla whispered.

Murphy looked away from Kayla, afraid that the tears she'd kept hidden would surface. "He was…well, over the years, we'd become friends." She slowly turned back to her, meeting her eyes again. "Not friends in the sense that we hung out or anything, but we had a mutual respect for each other that had evolved. I knew about his family, his life. He knew about mine. We talked. It wasn't always just business." She cleared her throat before continuing. "That's the main reason I left Houston. I couldn't do the job anymore. I felt like I was killing myself by being there. Once I made the decision to leave, well, I didn't know what I was going to do. I only knew I wanted to slow down, I wanted things to be sane. I was tired of working homicides." She smiled slightly. "So I wanted to go somewhere where they hadn't had a murder in seven long years."

Kayla smiled too. "Yes. And here we are." Then her smile faded. "Do you still blame yourself?"

"As opposed to blaming the FBI? I'm the one who pulled the trigger, not them." She picked up her wineglass again. "I've accepted it. I've made peace with myself, I guess. He had a gun in his hand. I shot. I didn't know it was Leon. Leon wasn't supposed to be there. So I've made peace with myself. Am I over it?" She shook her head. "No. I think it'll probably stay with me for a very long time."

"Did you come here right away?"

"It happened in March. I started here in mid-July," she said.

"So it's still very recent. I'm sure your emotions are still raw over it." She smiled gently. "I won't bring it up again. If you feel the need to talk about it, though, I'm a good listener."

Murphy nodded. "Thanks."

Kayla stood up. "Let me check on dinner. I don't know about you, but I'm starving."

They decided to pass on opening the red wine, both choosing a bottled water instead. Kayla put a heaping pile of the casserole on a plate and handed it to her. She stabbed a fork into it even before sitting down.

"Oh, yeah. This is delicious," she said as she swallowed her first bite. "I'll share the leftovers with you."

"Thanks. I was going to try to sneak out with some anyway," Kayla said as she joined her at the table.

"I don't like to cook, but it's more about the fact that I don't know *how* to cook," she said. "My mother wasn't a good cook, even by her own admission. My grandmother, that was a different story, but she was old school. I remember staying with her and she'd have this old crock by the stove, full of lard." She shook her head. "Disgusting to think about now, but she'd get a spoon and scoop some out and plop it in the pan, then fry whatever she was having that day. I was a kid and all I knew was that it was delicious. No way I'd eat that today."

"Does she still cook that way?"

"No. That was back when my granddad was still alive. They had a farm, and they butchered a pig a couple of times a year. That's where the lard came from." She shook her head. "I'm sure that contributed to his early death. Now, instead of bacon and eggs every morning, she does the oatmeal thing."

"I hate oatmeal."

"Yeah, me too. Kinda slimy."

Murphy took a big swallow of her water, wondering a bit about Kayla's personal life. So far, she'd offered very little. She thought asking about her ex-husband—who still lived in town—would be a safe subject.

"So…you're really friends with your ex-husband's wife?"

Kayla smiled, laughing lightly. "Friends with *both* of them, yes. Kevin and I were best friends in high school, only we didn't call each other that. At the time, it seemed like a natural progression to start dating. It wasn't until after we were married that we realized—well, me particularly—that being together as lovers was a huge mistake."

"You were young?"

"Eighteen and right out of high school. To his credit, he was very understanding, even though at first, it was a little strained around the apartment. We talked though. Honestly, sincerely, no beating around the bush. I mean, we were kids still, but we always had this more grownup relationship between us."

"So he came back to Sawmill Springs and you stayed."

"Yes. And we kept in touch, despite how awkward it was at first." She smiled. "I did refrain from going to his wedding though."

"Is she from town?"

"No. He commuted to college at Sam Houston and he met her there. She's really nice and I get along fine with her. There's no reason not to. I have no designs on Kevin in the least and I'm certainly not a threat to her."

"I think it's great that you remained close."

"What about you? Any ex's that you're still close with?"

"Well, first, there would have to be an ex to begin with."

"Oh, no. Don't tell me you were one of those cops who was married to the job?"

"Afraid so." She shrugged. "I mean, I dated here and there, but certainly nothing that would be considered a long-term relationship. I don't think I was very good at it."

"Dating?"

"Yeah, I had a hard time leaving work behind. I rarely gave my full attention to my date. I can remember times when we'd be having dinner and I'd be pretending to listen to a particular story all the while I was going over evidence in my head and inventing suspects where there were none."

"Yes, that does make for a bad date." Kayla smiled and wiggled her eyebrows teasingly. "I don't get the impression that you're distracted tonight, though, so thank you for that. You've been very attentive."

Murphy had a difficult time swallowing the bite she'd just taken. What did Kayla mean by that? Was it an innocent statement or was she flirting again? Well, if Kayla wanted to play that game, Murphy was willing, even if she thought it was a very—*very*—bad idea to be flirting with a straight woman.

"Of course I'm attentive. You're a beautiful woman. What else is going to hold my attention?" She was surprised by the slight blush on Kayla's face. "As a bonus, you're a very good cook."

"Thank you." Their eyes held. "For both compliments."

Yes…very bad idea, she thought as she struggled to find her way out of Kayla's blue eyes.

After taking a second helping of the casserole—much smaller portions than the first—they shared kitchen duty. The old house didn't have a dishwasher so Murphy washed while Kayla dried. The leftover casserole had been evenly divided, and she put hers in the fridge. Kayla's was on the counter.

"I had a good time," Kayla said as she was getting ready to leave. "It was fun to cook and I enjoyed spending time with you. Glad we had a chance to talk."

Murphy nodded. "Me too. It was nice to have company. We'll have to do it again."

"Football season starts in two weeks. I'll start planning my first spread," she said with a smile. "Spicy wings, maybe."

"Oh, yeah. Let's start with that."

They stood at the front door, a little twilight still left in the sky negating the need for the porch light. Murphy shoved her hands in her pockets and Kayla shifted her leftovers from one hand to the other. With the briefest of nods, she turned to go. Then she stopped and turned back around. Murphy wondered at Kayla's indecision, but she didn't have to wonder long. Kayla stepped closer, hugging her quickly.

"Thank you," she murmured as she pulled away. "See you tomorrow."

Murphy stood there, speechless, as Kayla walked down the sidewalk and to her car. She stood there long after the taillights of Kayla's car disappeared down the street.

"God…I wish she wasn't straight."

CHAPTER NINETEEN

The next morning, as Kayla was putting on her uniform, her mind drifted back to last night. A hug? Really? What had she been thinking?

Well, she hadn't been thinking sanely, obviously. It was just that Murphy had looked so vulnerable, standing there in the shadows with her hands tucked into her pockets. She looked like she *needed* a hug and Kayla had been unable to resist. Yes, she found her attractive. Yes, she enjoyed spending the evening with her. Yes, she hoped they became friends. And the hug? Was it inappropriate? Perhaps. They certainly didn't know each other well enough for hugs. At least Murphy wasn't shying away from her subtle flirting.

"Flirting…right," she said with a roll of her eyes. She was so out of practice in that game she was surprised Murphy had even noticed her attempt at it, however slight.

Today was a new day, though, and it was back to their so-called murder investigation. She hoped her father had come to some sort of a decision. They should be scouring financial records, phone records and credit card receipts of the four men involved. That's what they should be doing in their attempt to locate the common denominator, which she assumed would be the mysterious Mr. X. Maybe Murphy had some contacts in Houston she could call in for a favor. First things first…they needed warrants, and the only person to go to Judge Peters for that would be her father. So without his blessing, they were doing little more than treading water.

She hated treading water…waiting for the next victim to surface. Because this time, that victim could be her uncle. Doing prison time for drug trafficking was a whole lot better than being dead, regardless of what her father might think.

She pulled into the back of the station, not sure whether to praise or curse her luck—Murphy was just getting out of her truck. And damn, but did she look good in a uniform or what? She pulled in beside her and Murphy waited, leaning against the side of her truck while she parked.

"Good morning," she said with a smile as she got out. "Perfect timing."

Murphy nodded. "I'm used to starting my shift at six so getting here after seven feels like I'm slacking."

"I see you went back to the uniform too," she said, trying not to be too obvious as she looked her over. "I haven't spoken to my dad yet. I don't know what's on the agenda today."

"Remember when this thing first started and he put the two of us on the case?"

She nodded. "Right. You were supposed to be the lead investigator."

"Uh-huh. So how receptive do you think he'd be to requesting a warrant? We've got to start digging into their activities."

"I know. I was thinking the very same thing. Financials, phone records, credit cards. We should already be deep into it by now."

"So?"

"Let's talk to him. We need to get back on point with this."

"Good. I'm glad we're in agreement."

She stopped walking. "I know this whole thing is unorthodox. My uncle being involved complicates matters. At the end of the day, though, I'm certain that my dad—the chief—will do the right thing." God...she hoped so anyway.

Her phone rang just as they reached the back door. "Speak of the devil," she murmured. "Hey...what's up?"

He didn't bother with pleasantries on this early morning. "Where are you?"

"Walking inside the station. Where are you?"

"On my way to a crime scene."

"What's going on?" she asked, glancing at Murphy, who was listening.

"Goddamn, Kayla, this thing's unraveling faster than I can get a grip on it," he said, and she recognized the distress in his voice.

"What now?"

"Got two bodies out off Mason Road—down by the swimming hole."

"Two?"

"Male and female. Call went in to the sheriff's department. Sheriff Ramsey just called me. Nothing positive yet on the ID, but the guy who found them, he said it's Floyd Niemeyer and his wife."

"Oh, my God."

"Where's Murphy?"

"She's here."

"Okay, then you two get out here. You remember where it is?"

"Where Mason Road crosses Mill Creek? Yeah, I went there enough times as a teenager, I should remember."

"Meet me there."

She grabbed Murphy's arm as she was going inside, stopping her. "Two bodies: the mayor and his wife, most likely," she said as she pulled Murphy back outside.

"Jesus...not at their house, I hope. Because we—"

"No, no. Out at Mill Creek. I don't know anything else. He said we should meet him there."

"Outside of the city limits?"

"Yes. Sheriff's department got the call."

"So we're not the only ones involved anymore. Harder to keep a lid on it all."

"My dad and Sheriff Ramsey are tight. I'm certain they'll agree on whatever course of action we take. They've got a good working relationship. And knowing my dad, what we learned from Uncle Ned won't be shared with Ramsey just yet."

"I hope Earl knows what he's doing. This could all end up biting him in the ass."

"I know," she said with a nod of her head. "I doubt he's worried about that right now." She stood between her car and Murphy's truck. "I'll drive. I know the way."

"We're in uniform," Murphy said. "We should be in a patrol car."

Kayla nodded. "Yeah, okay." There were only two still in the lot. It would be quicker to take her car, but Murphy was right. They were in uniform, not plainclothes.

"Be right back," Murphy said as she jogged into the station, presumably to get the keys and a radio for each of them. She followed her progress until she disappeared inside the station, then she turned away with a sigh. Now was *so* not the time for her libido to be kicking in. After her affair with Jennifer ended, she never even looked twice at another woman. She was simply happy to be single again, happy to lose the constraints that the relationship had put on her. She had no desire to date, had no need for intimacy. She was happy and free. But damn if Murphy—looking so sexy in her uniform—didn't stir something within her. She sighed again. Now was *so* not the time.

When Murphy came back, she tossed the keys at her with a smile. "You can still drive, hotshot."

Kayla caught them in one hand, returning her smile. "Thank you. I'm quite familiar with the old swimming hole." She got inside. "Or did Tim take you out that way?"

"No. I have no idea what you're talking about."

"It's Mill Creek. It runs, oh, I don't know, six or seven miles outside of town. The creek bottom is where it flows under Mason

Road. Upstream is a nice swimming hole. It used to be private property, but as kids, we all went there," she said, remembering many a trip with Kevin when she was in high school."

"So you were a trespassing little deviant when you were young, huh?"

Kayla laughed. "On both sides of the bridge, there were turnouts," she said. "It was just a creek on the downstream side, but upstream, the Pattersons owned it. Kids used to crawl through the fence there, but by the time I started going, the fence was gone and a make-do road went right along the creek. It was definitely a local hangout, even for families trying to escape the summer heat. But the Pattersons feared that someone would drown and they'd get sued, so they sold that strip of land to the county, making it public. That happened the summer after I left town," she said, remembering how much fun it had been to *sneak* onto the property. She wondered if, now that it was legal, it had lost some of its appeal.

"So it's like a park?"

"It's like a park that no one keeps up. There are no amenities, if that's what you mean. I think they put a trash barrel back there, that's about it."

She was actually surprised she remembered the route. A couple of small twisting and turning roads took her to Mason Road, a narrow dirt road that crossed the creek and eventually hit the paved county road to the north, which would take you up on Braden's Hill. God, that brought back memories; she and Kevin parking, pretending to watch the moon as they kissed and fumbled around like the teenagers that they were.

"I hope you know how to get out of here because I'm completely lost," Murphy said.

"If we stay on this road, there's a great spot to go parking up on Braden's Hill," she said, giving Murphy a wink. That comment was met with a shocked stare, and she silently scolded herself. She really, *really* needed to stop flirting with Murphy.

When they approached the creek bottom, flashing lights from no less than four sheriff's deputies' cars greeted them. Other than her father's patrol car, the only other vehicle there was an old Chevy truck with an assortment of fishing gear on the back. It must belong to the guy who found the bodies. She was surprised they hadn't sent him on his way already. Unless, of course, he was buddies with—or even a relative of—one of the deputies, which was a very good possibility.

She parked behind her father's car on the shoulder of the road. There was a sheriff's deputy to direct traffic, in case a car or truck came through. Chances of that were slim as Mason Road wasn't exactly a thoroughfare. More likely, word had gotten out and some curious onlookers might swing by.

"You must be Kayla Dixon," the deputy said with a smile. "I remember you from school."

Kayla smiled back, not recognizing the young man at all. Even his last name—Capers—didn't sound familiar. "Yes, I'm Kayla. I'm sorry, I don't remember you."

"Don't imagine so. Todd Capers. I was a freshman when you were a senior." He looked over at Murphy and nodded. "Officer Murphy, right? I've heard Gloria talk about you."

Murphy's expression remained blank as she motioned with her head. "Where are the bodies?"

"Way back along the lane, down by the swimming hole."

So maybe this Gloria and Murphy were closer than Murphy let on, if Deputy Capers knew about their…what? Relationship? Affair? Dating habits? Well, it wasn't any of her business, she told herself. Besides, if she was that curious about it, she should just come right out and ask Murphy what was going on. Again… it wasn't any of her business. It was probably better left alone anyway. They worked together. They were becoming friends. That should be enough. Surely she'd learned her lesson with Jennifer.

"I can't believe you used to swim in this," Murphy said.

She glanced at the creek, the brownish water not looking inviting in the least. "I don't remember it being that color when I was a kid," she said with a laugh. "A swimming hole was a swimming hole. But now? There's no way in hell I'd get in the water."

They saw the group standing near the edge of the woods and lane, her father's white Stetson making him easy to spot. Most turned to look as they approached and she wasn't really shocked to see a female among them. This must be Gloria Mendez. She didn't need to see her name on the uniform to know. The look, the smile she gave Murphy was enough to clue her in. And yes, that look said that they were more than friends.

Damn.

Murphy, however, remained professional in her demeanor, getting right to work. "How were they killed?" she asked of no one in particular.

"Each shot in the head," one of the deputies said.

The bodies were lying face down, their hands tied behind their back.

"Execution style," she murmured.

"The male, Mr. Niemeyer, also has what appears to be a knife wound on his side here."

"If you've already taken your photos, I'd like to turn them over," Murphy said. "With permission, of course."

The man standing next to her father—Sheriff Ramsey—nodded. "Yeah, I know you were a homicide detective back in Houston. Any help, we'll take." He looked the same as the last time Kayla had seen him…a lit cigarette dangling from his fingers, the ash growing long as if he'd forgotten it was there.

"I done told the sheriff here that we need to have a joint investigation. We've got two killings within the city limits, now this. All of them prominent people in town. No sense in us all going off in different directions."

She was surprised her father had offered, but knowing him, the joint investigation would involve them working the case and only sharing what they deemed necessary—or as little as possible—with Sheriff Ramsey.

She squatted down beside Murphy as she turned the mayor over onto his back. His shirt was bloody from multiple stab wounds.

"Wounds meant to inflict pain but not kill," Murphy said quietly with a quick glance at her.

"Torture?" Yes, maybe their killer wanted information. Like the names of who all had double-crossed him. Like her Uncle Ned. She glanced up at her father, but his stare was solely on the body.

"There was nothing here at the scene," a female voice said. A very pleasant female voice, she noted. "No shell casings. They weren't dragged. They were made to walk."

"Where was the killer's vehicle parked?" Murphy asked.

"Hard to say. Bubba Howard drove right up here," Sheriff Ramsey said. "And of course, he trampled around here too before calling us."

"With all the leaves and pine needles down, it's hard to make out tracks," another deputy said.

"Any blood splatter?" she asked. "Was he stabbed here then shot or was he stabbed somewhere else?"

They all turned in circles, looking at the ground around them. She walked back toward the lane, trying to imagine where a car or truck would have been parked. As he'd said, there was too much ground cover to make out tracks. She found no blood. Neither did anyone else. She walked back to the circle in time to see Murphy turn Mrs. Niemeyer over. Unlike her husband, she had no other visible wounds other than the kill shot to the head.

"Look where they would have been standing," Murphy said as she took a step back. "The area here around the female is mostly undisturbed. Whereas here, next to him, it's trampled, the leaves scattered about, blood." Murphy looked over at her again. "I think the killer shot the wife first. Then he toys with the mayor, stabbing him several times before killing him."

She nodded. "If he stabs him while she's still alive, she's going to fight him, or try to, to save her husband. The ground would be disturbed."

"Sounds great in theory, but that doesn't really help us, does it?" Sheriff Ramsey said. "Like the other killings in town, this was likely done by a professional. Someone who knows what he's doing. To find out who the hell he is, we need to find out why he was targeting these people."

She looked at her father, meeting his gaze, but he remained silent. She and Murphy did as well.

"You've got the president of the bank, the mayor and his wife, and Lance Foster, probably the richest man in town," the sheriff continued.

"They all had money," one of the deputies said.

"If he's targeting rich men, makes me happy for my measly cop's salary," her father said, drawing laughs from the others. "I suppose Brett Newberry's been called?"

The sheriff nodded. "The news will be all over town soon. And we got Guy's funeral tomorrow. Lance will be laid to rest on Monday." He looked at her father. "Not sure how much more of this people can take, Earl. You don't have *any* suspects?"

"Our crime scenes looked like this one. Nothing but a goddamn body. Not any evidence left behind. Hell, Guy was shot from a distance. There wasn't even a scene to speak of."

"Well, they're obviously linked somehow."

"We're working on that angle," her father said. "Haven't got anything concrete yet."

"Well, they apparently all pissed off the same guy."

"Makes you wonder if there are any others in town with a target on their back," Gloria Mendez said, getting nods from her colleagues. She, Murphy and her father all remained expressionless.

Her father cleared his throat then, taking a step back. "Well, I guess we're out of here. You'll let me know when you get the coroner's report, right?"

"Will do." Then the sheriff shook his head. "We're sure keeping those boys down at Montgomery busy. *Damn*. Now Billy N." He shook his head again. "Earl, we better catch this bastard and soon or we'll both be looking for a new line of work."

"Well, if you look at it that way, Sheriff, we're pretty safe. The three most powerful men in town are dead. Who's going to run us out of office?"

"Except for Judge Peters, and he's the one with the real power."

"True. But both you and I know that he normally didn't act without one of these fellas being in his ear. He might likely be lost now."

She looked at Murphy, trying to read her expression. She hoped it was only nervousness that had them talking this way. There were too many people listening—unless the deputies were loyal to Sheriff Ramsey and wouldn't dare dream of repeating any of this. She knew for a fact that if Tim Beckman was here, loyal to her father or not, this conversation would have been spread to his uncle as soon as they left the scene. Then Ray would have communicated it to whoever was playing dominoes at his store. Based on this line of thinking, Judge Peters might be the next one on the list.

She drew her brows together. If Judge Peters was such good buddies with these three men, did it stand to reason then that he was somehow involved in this drug business? Uncle Ned hadn't mentioned his name, but...

"Well, we'll get out of your hair," her father said. "Keep me in the loop."

"If you find a link, you'll let me know, right?"

"You'll be the first one I call."

Kayla struggled not to roll her eyes at her father's blatant lie. She and Murphy fell in line with him as they walked back down the lane to Mason Road. When they were out of earshot, her father glanced at her.

"What's running through that pretty head of yours?"

She looked past him to Murphy. "And what's running through yours?"

Murphy met her gaze. "Judge Peters."

She smiled. "Yes."

"What about him?"

"Hey...Murphy, wait up," Gloria Mendez called from behind them.

"Be right back," Murphy said to them, pausing to meet Kayla's gaze for a second. "I'll catch up."

Kayla had to prevent herself from turning around and watching them. Their conversation was too muted for her to hear. She sighed and continued walking.

"So are they an item or what?" her father asked.

She shrugged. "I don't know."

"You've been riding with her for several days now...you don't talk?"

"They've gone out to dinner, I think," she conceded. "Why? What do you know?"

"Hell, I don't know anything. I got enough to worry about without keeping tabs on who's dating who," he said. "Now, back to Peters. What are you thinking?"

"Maybe he's involved too. I know Uncle Ned didn't mention him, but maybe—"

"I'll ask Ned. But doing drug business with your buddies is one thing...getting a goddamn county judge involved is a completely different animal all together."

"I suppose," she said. She glanced behind them, seeing Murphy heading in their direction. "It's something to consider, though. He may need protection."

"Yeah...I'm glad you brought that up." He paused as Murphy joined them. "You through jibber jabbering with that gal?"

"Yes. Sorry," she said.

"I got a job for the two of you." He held his hand up. "And I don't want any feedback or smart comments," he said, looking at her. "I've made this decision and it's the best one."

She sighed. *Now what?*

He looked around them, seeing some of the deputies coming back. "We'll talk in my office. Let's go."

He headed to his car without another word, and she looked at Murphy, both of them shrugging at the same time.

"He's your father. What do you think's on his mind?"

"At this point, I'm afraid to even guess." She got behind the wheel. "He doesn't seem convinced that Judge Peters is involved, but he said he'd ask Uncle Ned."

"It would be quite risky for a judge," Murphy said. "There's corruption then there's corruption. With the amount of drugs they've been moving through here, that's dealing with the big boys, not some small-time amateur drug dealers. I can't see *them* allowing a county judge to get involved."

"You're probably right." She glanced over at her. "What do you think about calling in help?"

"Help?" Murphy's eyebrows rose. "You mean FBI?" She shook her head. "There's no way your father would go for that."

"Would you?"

"You know how I feel about the FBI."

"I know. And I don't mean have them come in and take over the case. But they have resources. If Niemeyer Trucking was used to bring the drugs to Sawmill Springs, they could retrace the route."

"We can do that too. All we need is a warrant for his records."

She sighed. "You're right. It goes back to resources though. We need someone who can compile the records, sort them, throw them in a database or something and spit out the information."

"Not used to doing legwork, huh?"

She shook her head. "I'm used to calling Kabir. He was my go-to computer geek. He could hack into anything."

Murphy pretended to be shocked. "Now don't tell me the FBI did some illegal hacking."

She smiled. "Of course not. I have no idea what you're even talking about."

It wasn't until they got back into town that she mentioned Gloria Mendez. It wasn't any of her business, no, but she couldn't hold back the questions any longer.

"So…that was Gloria, huh? She's cute."

Murphy nodded but said nothing else.

"So…got a date or something? I mean, she sought you out. Or was it about the case?"

Murphy laughed lightly. "No, it wasn't about the case. She wanted to know my schedule, when my off-days were."

"Oh. So…got a date?" she asked again.

"She's got some friends from college coming to visit. She wanted me to join them for dinner."

"Sounds like fun," she lied.

Murphy laughed. "No, it doesn't."

"Okay, no, it doesn't. She's young. I remember when I still wanted to hang out with my college friends."

When they pulled into the station, Murphy turned to her, her dark eyes looking into her own. "So to answer your not-so-subtle questions, no, I don't have plans with her."

Kayla hoped she wasn't blushing. "I guess with this case and all…"

"Right."

CHAPTER TWENTY

Murphy stood next to Kayla, watching as Earl locked his office door behind them. When he said that he wanted to keep things between the three of them, he wasn't kidding. He also got right to the point.

"You two are going to be on protection detail. And as I said out there in the woods, I don't need any comments."

Kayla was the one to speak first. "Okay," she said a bit hesitantly. "So what's the detail?"

He stared at them for a moment. "Something ain't right about this whole thing. I don't think we're looking for your mysterious Mr. X. I think it's a local who's been doing the killing."

She and Kayla looked at each other. He'd been insistent since the beginning that there was no way in hell that a local could be involved. Why now? But Kayla seemed to be on the same page as her father.

"Because only a local would know about the place on Mill Creek," she said, causing her father to nod.

"Even if you're driving around, looking for a secluded place to do your killing, you're not going to find that old swimming hole without directions," he said. "A local would have known Guy Woodard's habit of stopping for gas on Mondays. A local would have known Lance Foster rarely left his office before six *and* would have known that Lou Ann left at five sharp every day."

"So you're suggesting there's another player in this game besides the four of them? Your brother didn't mention any other names. If Lance and Guy were skimming off the top, you've got an angry drug dealer," she said.

"I'm not saying this drug dealer is not involved. He's probably the one giving the order to kill, but my gut says he's not the one doing it."

"So protection detail?" Kayla prompted.

"Ned. Out at the cabin."

Kayla shook her head. "You can't be serious."

"Look, Chief—"

He held his hand up. "It's not really up for discussion, but if it makes you feel better, Ned's not exactly thrilled about it either. I told him we could either do it my way or bring him in here and guard him at the station."

"I think the station would probably be safer and definitely more appropriate," Kayla said.

"I'm not hauling my brother in like he's some common criminal."

"Well, not to state the obvious," Murphy said, "but he did confess to drug trafficking."

Earl turned and stared at her, his eyes narrowing.

"Just sayin'…"

"Might just be for a few days," he said, ignoring her comment.

"Dad…Murphy and I are the lead on this. There are so many things we should be doing. Pulling phone records…"

"Financials," she added.

"Credit card details," Kayla said. "We need to get a warrant for Niemeyer Trucking so we can look at their records and try to trace the drug path. And you want us to be stuck out in the woods on protection detail?"

"Couldn't Tim and someone else do it?" Murphy asked.

"I said this wasn't up for discussion," he said loudly. "You'll do as I say, goddamn it. I'm the chief, the boss." He pointed at them. "You two are officers. Hell, I could say you're both still on probation, so I certainly don't need any kind of pushback from you." He tapped his chest. "I'm in charge. And when we catch this son of a bitch, then and only then will I deal with this drug mess that my brother is mixed up in. Because right now, all I'm trying to do is keep his ass alive."

Murphy remained silent and Kayla finally nodded. "Okay. You're the boss. You want us guarding him instead of digging for evidence, that's what we'll do."

"Look, I know what all we need to do. I know we need a warrant to pull records. Kimbro is our computer guy. He's good. I'll have him look into what you want. Phone records and such."

"Financials," Kayla said. "Starting at the bank."

"Yes, okay. He can do all that. But I want you two out at the cabin. I don't trust anyone else to keep my brother safe. Right now, that's all I'm concerned with."

* * *

"This is so wrong," she said for the second time as she followed Kayla down an aisle in the grocery store.

"If we're going to be stuck there for a few days, I refuse to live off chips and bean dip," Kayla said with a glance at Murphy's contribution to their basket.

"Kayla...the case. Not your plan to cook."

Kayla smiled. "Of course I knew what you meant. And of course I agree with you, but what can we do?"

"Take your laptop. We can still do some research."

"I can take my laptop and I can use my phone as a hotspot, but that won't really help. I can't access the databases from my laptop."

She nearly growled in frustration. "I hate this. I really, really hate this. I feel like we're handcuffed."

"That's because we are."

"So he's thinking it's a local? There are no leads, no evidence. How the hell does he think he's going to find the killer?" she asked, trying to keep her voice low. "We should be doing something, not shopping for groceries and babysitting. Two of the guys could have done this."

"Again, I agree," Kayla said as she grabbed a bag of potatoes. "You like potatoes, right? Everybody likes potatoes."

"I especially like mashed potatoes and gravy."

"My gravy sucks. You'll have to make do with baked." She turned to look at her. "My father is stubborn and set in his ways. When he makes his mind up about something, there's no changing it. I learned that at an early age."

"Meaning we do this detail and hope he stumbles upon the killer?"

"Meaning we do this detail, and maybe the killer stumbles upon us. My dad may be right. If the killer is a local and he's eliminating everyone in this little operation, then my uncle is surely next on the list—most likely *last* on the list. This might be our only opportunity."

"So we babysit?"

"I'd rather think of it as witness protection. I had that detail a few times in my career." Kayla stood staring into the meat cooler. "I'm thinking I can bake a whole chicken tonight. Tomorrow—"

"We've got that casserole," she reminded her. "Although I had some for breakfast so I don't know if it's enough for three."

"Breakfast? Liked it that much, did you?"

"I loved it. Couldn't you tell?"

Again, Kayla turned to look at her, but it was a different kind of look. The blue eyes seemed to be searching hers, and Murphy wondered what she was looking for. As their stare continued, Murphy felt her pulse increase, the steady slow pace speeding up as she sunk deeper into those blue depths. A straight woman should not have this effect on her.

Kayla finally blinked, breaking their stare. She cleared her throat slightly before speaking. "I had some for breakfast too.

How about you decide on tomorrow's meal. Is there a favorite that you like?"

"Italian."

"Italian? That's a rather wide range."

Murphy shrugged. "I like stuff with pasta. My choice would be lasagna, but I think that's rather involved, isn't it."

Kayla nodded. "If you don't mind store-bought Alfredo sauce over your pasta, I could do something with shrimp and veggies. How's that?"

Murphy smiled. "When this is over with, can we arrange for a once-a-week dinner date and you cook for me?"

Kayla's eyes captured hers again. "A once-a-week dinner date could easily lead to two." Her eyebrows rose teasingly. "Or even three."

Murphy knew they were getting into dangerous territory, but she couldn't resist. She took a step closer, still clinging to Kayla's eyes. "Three nights a week? People will think we're dating."

Kayla took a step closer as well, her blue eyes twinkling. "Or having *really* good sex."

Murphy's heart lodged in her throat, nearly choking her as Kayla's hand lightly touched her arm as she moved past her. She took a breath, wondering what the hell kind of game they were playing.

CHAPTER TWENTY-ONE

It was late afternoon before they got out to the cabin, and as before, Uncle Ned met them on the porch with a shotgun in his hand. The stubble on his face was thicker, and he appeared to be in the same clothes.

"I told that stubborn father of yours that I didn't need a damn babysitter," he said.

"Yes, well, as you said…stubborn," she said. "We brought provisions. Weren't sure what the food situation was like here."

"How long you plan on camping out here?"

Kayla shrugged. "He said two days."

"Thinks he's going to catch him a killer, does he?"

Murphy walked up beside her carrying the bags from the grocery store. "He seemed pretty confident that he would, Mr. Dixon."

He stared at her for a moment, one hand absently scratching his beard, the other still holding the shotgun. "Officer Murphy is it? You can call me Ned. What should I call you?"

"Murphy is fine."

The three of them stood on the porch, looking at each other silently for a moment, then he finally opened the door and motioned them inside.

"Come on in. It's still damn hot out here, isn't it? I'm about ready for summer to be over with."

The inside of the cabin was cool from the air conditioner, and Kayla had to agree that she was ready for fall as well. Especially since fall meant football weather and she hoped to have a standing football date with Murphy each Sunday, if their shifts allowed it. Whether that involved really hot sex or not was another matter. That thought made her look over at Murphy, and she couldn't contain her smile as she remembered their conversation in the grocery store. Murphy had been rendered speechless by her statement. Who knew flirting would be so much fun?

"There ain't much in the kitchen except for some canned stuff. I wouldn't mind a decent meal, I guess. You cook?" he asked, his question directed at Murphy.

She laughed. "No, sir, not a bit."

His glance slid to her. "Kayla? I hope you're not relying on me to cook."

"I can handle the meals, Uncle Ned." She looked at his shotgun pointedly. "I think you can put that thing up now."

"You lock the gate?"

"Yes. I'll keep the key, if you don't mind."

He nodded. "Give it back to Earl after this is over with."

She found Murphy in the kitchen, putting away their things in the fridge. She looked over her shoulder, seeing it nearly empty inside. There was a jar of mayo and a jar of pickles. A stick of butter that was half used was on the top shelf and two beer bottles lay on their sides next to it.

"Never thought I'd see a fridge that looked worse than my own," Murphy murmured quietly as her uncle stood watching them.

"Well, if you pay attention, you might learn a few cooking tips," she said, touching her back lightly as she moved behind her. "Then you can stock your fridge."

"If I learned to cook…then what would you do?"

Kayla paused, turning around to look at her. Murphy seemed embarrassed by her statement.

"I mean…during football games and such."

Kayla held her gaze a moment longer, and then smiled. "I'm sure we could find *something* for me to do." She wiggled her eyebrows, which caused Murphy to blush and look away. She bit her lower lip. God, she *really* needed to stop flirting with her. In front of her uncle, no less. She turned to him then.

"Got TV out here? Or better yet…Internet?"

He snorted. "That Internet crap? Are you kidding me?"

"TV?" Murphy asked hopefully.

"No, this is a getaway cabin. If I brought TV and Internet up here, hell, might as well stay at home." He scratched his stubble. "Would probably have more company too and they'd stay longer."

Kayla laughed. "If you're talking about us, we'll get out of your hair as soon as we can. Besides, I'm sure you're ready to get back home to Aunt Charlotte." She met his gaze. "What have you told her?"

"She doesn't know what's going on, and I'd like to keep it that way. I told Earl that he's not to say a word to her."

"You don't think she'll get suspicious with you hanging out up here?" Murphy asked.

"Suspicious? Like I'm having an affair with someone?" He laughed. "Since I fixed this place up, I come up here a lot. She thinks I'm redoing the deer blinds."

"Can't believe she let you come up here without food," Kayla said. She looked at him pointedly. "What *have* you been eating?"

"Grilled me a steak the first night. Had a can of chili last night."

"Steak sounds good. Canned chili…not so much." She motioned to both of them. "Let me start on dinner. You two… out." Her uncle left, but Murphy lingered.

"I can help," Murphy offered.

Kayla simply couldn't resist. Or maybe she could, but the words came out anyway. "You'll only distract me if you're in here."

Murphy held her gaze, but her eyes were questioning. Kayla took a step toward her, her head tilting slightly.

"What?" she asked quietly. She saw Murphy take a breath.

"This could be a dangerous game, Kayla," Murphy nearly whispered.

"Game? What makes you think it's a game?"

Their eyes were locked together, but again, questions filled Murphy's. Questions and something else. Was Murphy afraid of her? Maybe she was coming on too strong, flirting too much. God, she was so out of practice at this. She found Murphy attractive...she liked her. She wanted to spend time with her, get to know her. She was attracted to her. Yes, sure she was. But was *now* the time to initiate something between them? No, of course not. They were working. Her uncle was here. No wonder Murphy looked uncomfortable.

She finally sighed and took a step back. "Go on," she said. "I need to get the chicken in the oven."

CHAPTER TWENTY-TWO

Murphy couldn't concentrate on the cards in her hand, and Ned beat her easily in their first two rounds of gin.

"You *have* played before, right?"

"Yeah, sorry," she murmured as she picked up the cards he'd dealt her. She looked at them without seeing them, her mind still on Kayla. *You'll only distract me.* She should just tell her that while she was very flattered, she did not—ever—mess with straight women. No, not even when they were as attractive as Kayla Dixon was…a blond beauty with deep blue eyes that she wanted to dive into. Oh, and that smile. That smile could melt her on the spot. She needed to tell Kayla to stop smiling at her. She needed to tell Kayla to stop touching her. And she really needed to tell Kayla to stop flirting with her. Her eyes widened a bit. Maybe Tim was right. Maybe she *was* a siren or something.

Ned cleared his throat, and she looked up sheepishly. "Sorry." She picked up Ned's discard, surprised that she had two other nines in her hand.

Out of the corner of her eye, she watched as Kayla took her laptop to the sofa and kicked off her shoes. She was going to check email, no doubt. Kimbro had promised to keep them updated with every little detail that turned up, no matter how minute. She turned back to the cards, but Ned's attention was now on Kayla.

"You ever going to tell me what that brother of mine is up to?"

"He doesn't think the killer is your drug dealer. He believes it might be a local."

"A local? What the hell's Earl thinking? I done told him about Lance skimming off the top."

"Only a local would know about the swimming hole," Kayla said.

"So he thinks one of the fine citizens of Sawmill Springs is doing the killing? That's crazy." He looked over at her. "What do you think?"

"I think I'm still on the side of the drug dealer," she said honestly, hidden swimming hole or not. "Makes more sense."

"Yeah…that's what I'm saying," Ned said. "Not some local. Good God, Earl must have a screw lose." He shook his head. "And he thinks I need babysitting in case some damn local fool comes calling?" He laughed. "My brother, the police chief. I always was a better shot than him, anyway. I think I can take care of myself."

"No offense, Uncle Ned, but hunting and taking a deer is quite different than shooting a person, more so if it's someone you know."

Murphy looked overhead to her right, eyeing the twelve-point buck that was mounted there. Other antlers were hanging on the wall but none as nice as that monster.

"Got him in 2012," Ned said, following her gaze.

"Out here?"

"Yep. He wasn't interested in coming to my feeder. He was chasing him up a doe. I saw him through a clearing and I about shit my pants," he said with a laugh.

"Tough shot?"

"Oh, yeah. Well over two hundred and fifty yards. Damn lucky shot, I will admit, but I dropped him in his tracks."

"What caliber rifle do you use?"

"I used a Winchester 30-06. I've got a Remington 243, but I prefer the Winchester. It sights in better for long shots."

"Uncle Ned, when did they first approach you?" Kayla asked. "I want to give Kimbro a date range so he doesn't have to go through too much data," she explained.

"Guy and Lance?" He rubbed his chin thoughtfully. "Let's see, it was back...late last year, I think." He nodded. "Still hunting season. Before Thanksgiving, I think."

"Okay, good. I'll get him to check from November to present," Kayla said.

"What's he searching for?"

"He's going to start with phone records."

Murphy got up from the table and walked over to her, eyeing Lance Foster's appointment book. "Why not search around the dates of when this Mr. X was in town? Maybe he'll hit on a phone number."

Kayla smiled at her, and Murphy's heart fluttered...like a damn teenager's. She was about to go back to the table when she felt Kayla's hand on her arm. She turned back to her, her skin burning where Kayla's fingers rested.

"This is going to be useless if our killer used a burner phone. Maybe we should have him start with financials."

"Lance had a phone like that," Ned said. "A burner, like they say."

Kayla sighed. "Great. Financials it is," she murmured.

"I think Guy did too," he continued. "They were a little paranoid."

"Do you have their numbers?" she asked.

"No. They rarely called me. Most of our...our *business* was done face-to-face."

"How about Niemeyer Trucking?" she suggested. "Log of routes or something. He could start there."

"That won't get you nothing," Ned said as he scooted his chair away from the table. "Bogus manifests and routes. On top of that, Billy N even deleted the fake records too. Ghost trucks, he called it."

"Well, you're just full of good news," Kayla said.

"They weren't no dummies, Kayla." He picked up his shotgun and headed for the door.

"You need to stay inside, Uncle Ned."

"Gonna sit on the porch and smoke a cigarette. I think I'll be safe."

"Stubborn like my dad," Kayla murmured.

"I'll go out with him."

Kayla nodded. "I'll email Kimbro back; tell him to forget phone records. I think we should target financials. If Guy Woodard was using the bank to run the cash through, he had to have left a trail." She paused. "I hope this isn't over Kimbro's head."

"And if it is?" she asked.

"I've got some contacts at the FBI. I can always try to sweet-talk somebody into helping us."

"I'm sure you could sweet-talk the devil himself," she said without thinking.

Kayla slowly turned her head toward her, her lips twitching in a smile as their eyes met. "Is that what you think? Even the devil?"

"I think so," she said quietly. "He wouldn't stand a chance."

"How about you? Would you stand a chance?"

She needed to pull away. She needed to break the spell. She needed to…to get closer…she needed to drown in those eyes. She needed…

"I need to…I think…I should…I should…check on Ned," she managed as she got up and hurried toward the door.

"Murphy?"

She stopped and took a deep breath before turning back around.

"Do I make you nervous, Murphy?"

Murphy's heart was pounding as if she were about to be interrogated. She swallowed, then nodded. "Yeah, you do."

Kayla got up and walked toward her. "Why?"

"I don't…well, I don't do this," she said.

"Do...*this*?"

"I'm...I'm uncomfortable when...when straight women, you know..."

Kayla's eyes widened. "*Straight* women?"

"Yeah. I mean, you're very attractive and yes, I admit I'm attracted to you," she said. "And if I were...you know, if I were younger, I might have been inclined to—"

"Oh, my God! You think I'm *straight*?" Kayla put her hands on her hips. "Why would you think I'm straight?"

"Well...well, you were married, for one."

"Yeah, I was eighteen!"

"Well, then you said you had that affair with that guy, that agent."

"That guy's name was Jennifer," Kayla said. "They do have female agents, you know." She took a step back and held up her hands. "Oh, my God. That's why you said I was playing a dangerous game. You thought I was straight, and I was coming on to you. God, I can't believe you thought I was straight." Kayla rubbed her forehead with her fingers. "How embarrassing," she murmured. "Look. Forget it. Just forget it."

"Forget it? Forget what?"

"Yeah, forget it. Forget that I ever found you attractive. Let's just do this stupid babysitting thing and...and forget all about it."

Murphy stared at her...still in shock. Kayla *wasn't* straight? The meaning of that finally hit home. She was gay and she was flirting with her. Kayla found her attractive. Oh, God. Now what? She met her eyes again.

"I...I..."

"Forget it, Murphy. I'm an idiot."

"No, no, no...*I'm* the idiot," Murphy said.

Kayla smiled slightly. "Yeah, okay...I'll give you that. You *are* an idiot."

"Okay. Yeah. Well...then..."

Kayla pointed at the door. "Check on Uncle Ned. We won't *ever* talk about this again."

Murphy drew her brows together. "Ever?"

CHAPTER TWENTY-THREE

"An idiot," she murmured to herself. No wonder Murphy wasn't responding to her overtures. She thought she was *straight*, for God's sake. It was just as well. They had no business mixing work and pleasure. For one, her father would kill her. And two… yes, she *had* learned her lesson with Jennifer. Work and play did not mix. Friends? Sure. But anything else? No. It was out of the question. It was best to forget it and move on.

"The chicken was delicious."

She didn't turn around at the sound of Murphy's voice. "Thank you," she said as she continued to put the leftovers away.

"I'll wash dishes," Murphy volunteered.

"I'll let you. Give me a few minutes and you can have the kitchen to yourself."

She heard Murphy sigh and felt her move closer.

"Kayla…lct's—"

"Forget it," she finished for her. She finally turned around, facing her. "Where's Uncle Ned?"

"He's got the cards out. I assume he's looking for another victim."

"I guess it's my turn to be the victim," she said. "I need to check my email first. It's Friday evening. I doubt Kabir has had a chance to delve into anything yet, but you never know."

"I thought you were going to sweet-talk him?"

"Yes, well, I tried to temper that a bit. Don't want him to think that I'm straight or anything."

Murphy laughed. "Yeah, don't confuse him." Her smile faded a little. "I—"

Kayla held her hand up, stopping her. "No. Let's don't talk about it. I'm embarrassed enough."

"It never occurred to me that you were gay," Murphy said. "The married thing...and Tim calling you a...a siren and how he got all tongue-tied around you and—"

"A *siren*?" She rolled her eyes. "God...*men*." She met her gaze. "You really thought I was a straight woman coming on to you?"

Murphy nodded. "I did. And if it helps, I was really, really wishing you weren't straight."

"Well, imagine that. Your wish came true." She cleared her throat. "But we should forget about it. We're working. And I'm obviously very out of practice."

"We are working, yes, but I wouldn't say you're out of practice."

She took a deep breath. What did that mean? Were they going to forget about it or not? "I'll...I'll get out of your way. Thanks for doing dishes."

"Sure. Thanks for cooking."

They stepped around each other as she left the kitchen, and Murphy claimed the sink. Her uncle was sitting at the table, playing solitaire, a bottle of whiskey and a glass sitting next to him. Behind him, the living room was dark except for a lone lamp in one corner. There were no curtains or blinds on the windows, and if someone were outside, they would be easy targets.

"Do you mind if I put the porch light on?"

He glanced up at her. "What for? You going out?"

"Something to offset the light in here."

"Worried about a sniper being outside, are you?"

"We *are* supposed to be protecting you," she reminded him.

He put his cards down. "I've never had anybody from town out here before. Always kinda liked having it to myself. My boys come out to fish occasionally, that's about it," he said, referring to his sons. "We use it for family barbeques and such."

"According to my dad, you missed Memorial Day this year."

He nodded. "Yeah…well, I was…busy," he said rather sheepishly. "What I'm trying to say is, if you're worried about somebody finding us out here, don't be."

"If you have a price on your head, they'll find you." She walked over to the door and flipped on the porch light. "It's not hard to track cell phones."

"You think someone can track this old flip phone of mine?"

She smiled. "You still have that thing?"

"I just need a phone. Don't need a damn computer in my hand."

"You sound like Dad," she said as she picked up her laptop and joined him at the table.

"You gonna play?"

"I need to check email first." However, her phone rang before she logged in. It was her father and she hoped he had some news. "Hey," she answered.

"Y'all okay out there?"

"We're fine. Just had dinner and now Uncle Ned is about to beat me in gin rummy," she said, smiling at her uncle. "Any news on your end?"

"Got a break. But not sure how it'll help us. Kirby found the bullet that killed Guy Woodard—embedded in the outside wall. Must have hit Guy and kept right on going. Damn lucky it didn't fly right through the store and take out Kirby too."

"Caliber?"

"A 30.06. Common enough. Gonna send it off for testing though. Also got the preliminary report on Lance Foster. They were able to retrieve the bullet. A nine mil," he said.

"That's good news. Maybe a break…finally."

"You got anything going?"

"I've been in email contact with Kimbro. He hasn't found anything. I also emailed a friend at the FBI," she said. "If Kimbro gets stuck, I'm sure he'll help us."

"Kimbro said you told him Niemeyer Trucking was a dead end."

"Yes. According to Uncle Ned, they used what he referred to as ghost trucks."

"Yeah, and Lance and Guy used burner phones. I guess they learned that from watching too many spy movies," he said. "Got Guy's funeral tomorrow at ten. It'll be a huge event. The Lutheran Church will be overflowing."

"You haven't said…are you taking much heat?"

"Nothing I can't handle." His voice lowered a bit. "How's Ned treating you?"

"Fine," she said, glancing over at him.

"I guess he's right there, huh?"

"Yes. Murphy's doing dishes."

"Well, unless we get a hit on something, I guess I won't talk to you again until after the funeral. I'll let you know how it goes."

"Okay. If we have any excitement out here, I'll call you."

She put her phone down, surprised to find Murphy leaning against the kitchen doorway, watching her.

"Dad," she said unnecessarily.

"Any news?"

"Yeah, actually. They found the slug that killed Guy Woodard. Kirby found it in the wall of his station. A 30.06. And it was a nine millimeter that killed Lance Foster."

"Well, that's something, at least." Murphy came closer. "We looked all over for that slug."

"I know."

"A 30.06, huh?" her uncle said. "That's a pretty common rifle. So's the nine mil."

"Yes," Murphy said. "But if we find the gun, we can use ballistics to match the bullet."

"So…if you had a suspect, you could get a warrant to confiscate his weapons?"

"Yes," she said as she sat down at the table beside her.

"And match the bullet to the gun? Just like on TV?"

"Well, things take a little longer in real life, but yeah, just like on TV."

He shoved the bottle of whiskey across the table toward Murphy. "You want a drink?"

"It looks inviting, but I'm working. I'll have to pass."

"Kayla?"

"No, thanks."

He filled his own glass. "You never were much of a drinker that I recall."

"I left here when I was eighteen, hardly drinking age."

He took a sip of the whiskey. "Got married and left town," he said. "Kevin Lade returned alone. Heartbroken, the way I hear it."

"That was a long time ago, Uncle Ned. Kevin is married with kids. Hardly heartbroken." She looked over at Murphy. "Nothing new on email."

"I guess you didn't sweet-talk enough to your FBI friend," Murphy said with a smile.

"I guess not." She closed her laptop and shoved it aside, then glanced at her uncle. "Ready to beat me in gin?"

He shuffled the deck of cards one more time before dealing them out. Murphy picked up Lance Foster's appointment book and flipped through it idly, her glance going to their card game occasionally.

"No, not that one," Murphy said. "Pick up the three he discarded."

"You're a fine one to offer advice," she said. "Did you even win a hand?"

"I came close."

"What's your version of close?" her uncle asked as he drew a card.

"I had four of a kind once," Murphy said as she leaned back in her chair, taking the appointment book with her.

Kayla watched her for a second, wondering what she was looking for. They'd both been over the book several times already. Her uncle tapped the table impatiently.

"Sorry." As soon as she discarded a seven, he scooped it up, then laid his cards out.

"Gin."

"Damn. That was fast."

"Told you to take the three," Murphy murmured without looking up.

"Yes, I'll take your expert advice next time," she said as she shuffled the cards.

Murphy was flipping back and forth between pages, her brows drawn together in a frown. Then she closed the book and held it to her chest, a thoughtful expression on her face. Kayla was about to ask what she'd found when Murphy got up and went into the kitchen. She shrugged, then dealt out the cards.

Her uncle's gaze was on Murphy as she stood at the kitchen counter, her back to them, hands shoved into the pockets of her jeans.

"She doesn't talk much," he stated.

"That's what Lori says too, although she's not quite as quiet as I first thought." She looked at the cards in her hand, then glanced again at Murphy. Murphy had turned and as their eyes met, Kayla knew something was up. Murphy motioned her into the kitchen. She nodded, then laid her cards down. "Be right back."

Murphy moved deeper into the kitchen, out of her uncle's line of sight. Kayla moved up beside, her brows drawn together.

"What's wrong?" she asked quietly.

"Look at this," Murphy said, pointing to the last entry in the appointment book.

Kayla nodded. "Yes. Mr. X."

"The handwriting. It's different than all the others." Murphy flipped to another entry for Mr. X then another. "The X has a curl on each of them. See?"

"Yes. Go back to the last day." There was no curl. She stared at her. "What are you thinking? That the killer made the entry to make it look like this Mr. X was there?"

"Yes."

"Then…"

"There are only four people who knew Mr. X existed. Three of them are dead."

"We were going with the assumption that Mr. X was the killer," she reminded her. "If he was the killer, he wouldn't have made the entry. Unless he didn't know they called him Mr. X."

"I think the chief is right. It's a local." Her gaze went out into the living room. "Your uncle….he's a good shot. He took that deer with a Winchester 30.06."

Her eyes widened. "You're not suggesting that Uncle Ned is the killer, are you?" she asked in a shocked whisper.

"Four men were involved in this drug scheme. Three are dead. He's not exactly acting like there's a killer out looking for him."

"When we came here with Dad, he was hiding. He was scared. He was—"

"Acting," Murphy finished for her.

Kayla ran a hand through her hair nervously. Was Murphy serious? Did she really think Uncle Ned was the killer? *Her* Uncle Ned? He was an accomplished hunter, yes. The deer antlers on the wall were a testament to that. A 30.06 was a popular hunting rifle though. Her uncle wasn't the only person in Sawmill Springs to own one. It was all circumstantial, at best. The forged appointment with Mr. X, however, pointed at her uncle. As Murphy had said, four men knew of Mr. X's existence and three of them were dead.

She looked at Murphy, their eyes locking together. "I can't believe this," she whispered. She shook her head. "What if you're wrong?"

"What if I'm right?"

She nodded. "Okay. Yes. It's something we should consider." She glanced behind her. "I should get back out there. He's probably suspicious of us being in here."

"Just act normal. Go back to playing cards."

"What are you going to do?"

She held her phone up. "I'm going to call your father."

Kayla grasped her arm and squeezed. "He'll never believe you."

"I know." Murphy motioned with her head. "Go on. I'll be right there."

She took a deep breath before walking back out, but her uncle was no longer sitting at the table. She nearly panicked and her heart was beating wildly in her chest, but then she saw movement and turned. He was standing at the window with a glass of whiskey in his hand. No, he certainly wasn't acting like he was a target. He would be in plain sight of anyone outside. She pushed that thought away and pointed to the table.

"Sorry. Want to finish?" Her voice sounded nervous, odd, to her own ears. She wondered if he recognized the change in her.

"What were you two in there whispering about?" he asked before bringing the glass to his lips.

"Just...work. I...I need to email Kimbro. Murphy...there was a date in the appointment book that Murphy wants Kimbro to...to concentrate on," she said lamely. She glanced toward the kitchen, hearing Murphy's strained voice. She imagined Murphy was finding it hard to argue with her father while trying to whisper.

She went back to the table and sat down, but her uncle made no move to join her. She picked up the cards, then remembered her lie. She was supposed to email Kimbro, so she pulled the laptop in front of her and opened it up. Her uncle moved to the kitchen door, and she wondered if he could hear Murphy on the phone.

"Should I deal again?" she asked nervously. "Or did you have a good hand?"

He pointed his glass at her. "Yeah, why don't you shuffle again." His glance slid to her laptop. "After you do your email, of course. I'm in no hurry."

"Sure." She opened up her mail, wondering what she could email to Kimbro that would make sense. What if her uncle stood over her shoulder and read it? *Christ!* She tapped her fingers nervously, then began typing, deciding to go with the lie in case Uncle Ned did indeed read it. However, he was still standing by the door, not paying her any attention. Should she email her father instead and tell him to come out there? No. He never checked his email from home. Maybe she should alert Kimbro and ask him to send her father out. She was about to type a quick message when her uncle turned and looked at her. Afraid he would come investigate what she was writing, she simply clicked out of the email, pretending to send it, then closed the laptop with a tentative smile.

"All set," she said as she picked up the cards. He made no move to join her and she shuffled the cards with shaking hands. She couldn't help but glance up at the deer mounted on the wall. A beautiful buck. Well, beautiful once, when he was still wild and free, running the woods. What did her uncle say? Over two hundred and fifty yards away? They'd estimated the shot that took out Guy Woodard was close to three hundred. Could her uncle have made that shot?

Murphy came out of the kitchen, and as Kayla glanced over at her, her uncle grabbed her around the neck and brought a handgun from behind his back, pressing it to Murphy's head. The cards spilled across the floor as Kayla jumped up, knocking the chair over in the process. She drew her weapon, pointing it at her uncle.

"Uncle Ned, what the hell are you doing? Put the gun down," she said as evenly as she could manage.

Uncle Ned walked Murphy closer to her, the barrel of the gun pressed directly against her temple. Kayla took a step back, holding her gun in front of her.

"Put your gun on the table, Kayla. You're not going to shoot."

"Uncle Ned—"

He shook his head. "You know, I always thought there was something funny about you, Kayla."

"Funny? What are you…what are you talking about?" She gripped her weapon tighter, wondering if she dared to take a shot. He was all but hidden behind Murphy. She met Murphy's eyes, but they weren't steeped in fear like she thought her own must be. They looked back at her calmly and she relaxed a little.

"The way you and Kevin divorced…so quick," he continued. "You living there in Austin, Earl never saying a word about it, keeping it all a big secret."

"Me being gay was never a big secret," she said. "Didn't think anybody cared."

"No…I don't care," he said. "But I've been watching you two. Seen the way you been acting." He pulled Murphy up tighter against him. "I think you like Murphy here, that's what I think."

Kayla laughed nervously. "Well, yeah…we're kinda partners, so yeah, I guess I like her."

"Yeah…I don't think you want me to shoot her. But shoot her, I will, if you don't put your goddamn gun down," he said, his voice louder now.

"Uncle Ned…please…she's a cop. You can't do this."

"This late in the game…don't matter much to me if I kill another one, cop or not. Put your gun down, Kayla. You're not going to shoot through her to get to me."

It was basic training 101…*never* willingly give up your weapon. But her uncle's finger was on the trigger of his gun, and the barrel was pressed against Murphy's head. There was no way she could attempt to disable him.

"Kayla…don't do it," Murphy said.

He grinned…an evil grin that transformed his face into something other than her uncle's once familiar smile. "Oh, I think she likes you too, Kayla," he mocked. "How sweet." The smile on his face faded completely. "Now…drop your gun. I'm not afraid to shoot her." He stared into her eyes. "I'll do it. You know I will."

Yes, she had no doubt that he would. She, then, would shoot him a second later. That scenario flashed through her mind… Murphy lying in a pool of blood, her head split open from the gunshot. Her uncle lying beside Murphy, two—maybe three— shots to the chest, blood seeping from his wounds. Both dead.

She lowered her weapon.

"Kayla…no! He won't shoot me."

Kayla put her gun on the table as he'd instructed. "Yes, he will."

CHAPTER TWENTY-FOUR

Murphy strained her wrists against the rope, to no avail. He had the knot tight and secure. She looked over at Kayla, who was tied, like her, to a chair next to the table. She, too, was trying to loosen the rope that held her.

"Won't do you no good to struggle," he said as he walked in from the bedroom carrying a duffel bag.

"And it won't do you any good to run," Kayla shot back. "Uncle Ned, think about what you're doing."

"Oh, I've been thinking about it for the past several months," he said as he put his bag on the table and collected their guns and phones. He took the time to pour a glass of whiskey and knocked it back quickly. "My plan didn't include killing Billy N's wife, but I had no choice," he said, almost to himself. He looked at them. "Of course my plan also didn't include my meddling brother thinking I needed police protection." He laughed. "Kind of ironic, ain't it?"

"Why kill them?" Murphy asked.

"Why? Because I was doing all the goddamn work, I was the one taking all the chances. Them? All they were doing was getting rich. I found out their take was twice what mine was." He zipped up his bag, then shoved his gun into the waistband of his jeans. "When I called them on it, Lance said he'd make good. Said he had a stash of money from what he was selling on the side. Guy didn't even know about it." He smirked. "But I think I know where he hid it. I'll find it."

"Floyd Niemeyer wouldn't give up the location then?" she asked, remembering the knife wounds he'd suffered.

"Billy N was squealing like a pig when I shot his wife. But no, he apparently didn't know where Lance had hidden it."

"Who is Mr. X?" Kayla asked.

He laughed. "Lance was a paranoid son of a bitch. That's what he called the guy from Houston who brought the money."

"And the camera? The tapes?"

"Lance was an idiot. Yeah, I got all that and it's been destroyed. He was trying to be secretive about this little business we had going, yet he tapes our conversations? Goddamn idiot."

He paused beside Kayla's chair and patted her cheek. Kayla jerked away from his touch. "You always were my favorite, Kayla Ann," he said. "Aunt Charlotte's too. It probably would have broke her heart if I'd had to kill you."

"Aunt Charlotte knows?"

"Of course she knows. How do you think I got into Bernice's shop?"

"Jesus," Kayla murmured.

"No, I'm afraid he can't help you now." He stared at her for a moment longer, then took a step away. "I would have shot her, you know. I would have shot you too if I had to."

"Yes, I don't doubt that."

"Yeah, well, remember that." He took another step away. "You two sit tight." Then he laughed at his play on words. "Tight. Get it? I'll be back before daybreak. Then we'll decide how the rest of this is going to play out."

They watched him leave, and he paused at the door, looking back at them. He turned the lights out, plunging the cabin into darkness, then locked the door behind him.

"Great," Kayla murmured.

"You okay?"

She heard Kayla sigh. "Oh, yeah. Just peachy. Although when I envisioned having you tied up, this wasn't exactly what I had in mind."

Despite their situation, Murphy pictured that very thing. "Had me tied up, did you? Was I naked at the time?"

"Yes, you were very naked. So was I." She heard Kayla struggling with her rope. "So...do you miss Houston yet?"

Murphy moved her wrists up and down, feeling the rope cutting into her skin. "Oh, yeah...kinda getting there. You miss the FBI?"

"Well, I'm thinking I wouldn't be in this predicament if I was still an agent." She let out a frustrated breath. "My rope isn't loosening a bit."

"Mine either." She stopped struggling with the rope, trying to relax. "So...when I was in the academy, we had this session on what to do in a standoff, and I'm pretty sure handing your weapon to the perp wasn't part of the deal."

There was silence for a moment. Then Kayla cleared her throat. "He would have shot you," she said quietly.

"Then you would have shot him."

"Yeah...but he still would have shot *you*." Another pause. "And...well, I kinda like having you alive. I mean, we haven't even kissed yet and I'm already picturing you naked, in my bed."

Murphy smiled at that, wishing she could see Kayla through the darkness. "So you're saying when we get out of this mess, we're going to kiss?"

There was no response for the longest time. Then she heard Kayla shift in her chair. "I haven't been with anyone since Jennifer. I haven't even gone out on a date in eight months. The first time I laid eyes on you, though..."

"I felt like a nerdy teenage boy with a crush on the head cheerleader," she admitted. She twisted her wrist slightly to the side, feeling the rope give. "And, of course, in my mind, you were straight."

"I can't believe you thought I was straight. I was blatantly flirting with you."

"Yes, I know." She could now move both wrists, and she curled her fingers, trying to reach the knot.

"You flirted with me too."

"I couldn't help it." She felt the rough edges of the knot, and she moved the rope back and forth, trying to loosen it.

"Have you slept with her?"

Her head jerked up. "Who?"

"Gloria Mendez."

"No."

"Kiss?"

Murphy lifted a corner of her mouth in a smile. "Well…"

"She wanted to sleep with you?"

"Oh, yeah. She didn't keep that a secret."

"Kinda like I'm not keeping it a secret?"

Murphy's hands stilled. "Do you want to sleep with me?"

"I do. Which is a little odd for me. I normally go much slower."

"So you're not a first-date-hop-into-bed kinda gal?"

"Not even second date. Well, there was the one time in Miami…" Kayla said, her voice trailing off. "I blame it on the rum."

She felt the knot give, and she tugged on the rope. "So no third date?"

"No. The sex was okay, but I wasn't really that interested in her."

It was a double knot. The second knot was always looser than the first one. The triumph she felt as the knot came loose subsided when the remaining knot refused to budge.

"What about you? Were you serious the other day when you said you didn't leave an ex behind in Houston? No broken hearts?"

"Why would you think there'd be broken hearts?"

"Because you don't look like the settling-down type. I can imagine some poor girl falling in love with you and you leaving her with her heart broken."

Murphy's fingers were cramping, and she flexed her fist several times. "No broken hearts. I never really took the time for romance," she admitted. "Woke up one day—alone—and I'm over thirty and I wondered where the time had gone."

"You gave it all to the job? A lot of cops are like that."

"Yeah." She tried the knot again, surprised to find it loosening. "And most live to regret it."

"You?"

"I do. Because I *am* the settling-down type." She paused in her attempt to untie the knot. "I just never met anyone I wanted to settle with, I guess."

"Yes. Dating is hard work…weeding through all of the castoffs to find that perfect mate." She sighed, and Murphy heard Kayla's chair shift. "I can't fucking believe this is happening. What did my dad say?"

"You want verbatim or should I just paraphrase?"

"I know he didn't believe you, but what did he say?"

"'You're out of your goddamn mind, Murphy,'" she said, trying to mimic Earl. "'And don't go brainwashing my daughter with that crap either. Ned ain't no goddamn killer!'"

Kayla laughed. "Oh, Murphy…that was good. I think even Dad would appreciate your impersonation of him."

The sound of Kayla's laughter in the darkness made her smile.

"So where do you think the money's hidden?" Kayla asked.

"I don't know. Maybe Lance Foster had some property somewhere. Maybe he had something like this, back in the woods."

"If he did and it was kept secret, I'm not sure how Uncle Ned would find it."

Murphy's hands stilled, shocked that the knot was starting to pull free. "Just a little more," she murmured.

"I hope that means you're making progress on your rope. I was about to fling myself to the floor, hoping the chair would break apart. You know, that works in the movies," Kayla said.

"Don't go to all that trouble," she said as the rope fell away from her wrists. She flexed her arms. Her hands then made quick work of the rope tied around her thighs. She stood, pausing to rub her sore wrists.

"You got it?" Kayla asked excitedly. "Come untie me!"

Murphy held on to the table, sliding around it. Ned had left them on opposite sides and she banged into one of the other chairs, wincing at the pain in her shin.

"Damn…I can't see a thing."

"Turn to your left. The light switch for the hallway is right there."

Murphy held her hands out, feeling for the wall. She found it, then slid her hands up and down, finally finding the switch. She flipped it up, but nothing happened.

"What the hell?"

"Jesus…you think he turned the power off outside?"

"Considering how hot it's gotten in here, I'd say yes."

"I thought it was getting hot for another reason," Kayla murmured.

Murphy walked toward the sound of her voice. She nearly fell in her lap as she collided with her chair, her hands reaching out to steady herself. She gasped as her hand settled on something soft and round.

"Jesus, Murphy…we don't have time for you to feel me up," Kayla said with a quick laugh.

"I'm so sorry," she said as she jerked her hand away from Kayla's breast. "I can't see a thing." She kept her hands on Kayla's shoulder, moving behind her, sliding them slowly down her arms until she reached the knot.

"I know this is so not the right time, but I'm incredibly aroused," Kayla said lightly.

Murphy's hands shook as she tried to untie her. Aroused? Yes, there was something about it being completely dark in the room, something about having to use her hands instead of her eyes. It would be like making love blindfolded. And Kayla tied to the bed. Her hands stilled as she pictured just that.

"Murphy?"

She shook her head to chase the image away, her fingers tugging at the rope again. It finally loosened, and she pulled it away, releasing Kayla's hands.

They both moved at once, bumping into each other with quiet laughter.

"I'm heading to the door," Murphy said. "Where are you going?"

"Yeah, do you know where the door is?"

"How can it be so freakin' dark in here?"

"We're out in the middle of the woods and I'm guessing we have no moon," Kayla said as she took her hand. "Let's stay together."

"Ouch!"

"Okay, that'd be the sofa," Kayla said.

Kayla moved them around it while Murphy held out her other hand, trying to ward off any objects that might be in their path. They came to the wall, then felt along it for the door. She heard Kayla fiddling with the lock. Then she opened it, letting in more darkness.

They stumbled out onto the porch then down the three steps to the ground. Looking overhead at the clouds drifting by, proved Kayla right. The sliver of a half-moon above barely shed any light on their surroundings. There wasn't even one sparkle of a star in the sky.

"Great night to have cloud cover," Kayla stated dryly.

They stood still for a few seconds, letting their eyesight adjust to what little light there was. Kayla's car was parked where they'd left it, and they headed in that direction.

"He took my keys, but I have a handgun in the glovebox," she said. "And a flashlight. Can't guarantee the batteries are still good." When she opened the door, the interior light was a welcome sight. She turned on the headlights too, then leaned across the seat and pulled out a gun and small flashlight.

Murphy took the light and turned it on. It had a surprisingly sharp beam.

"Do you know how to hotwire a car?"

"Give me an older model car and sure, I'd be all over it. These new cars? I wouldn't know where to start." She flashed the light around them, landing on the tires. "Doesn't matter much," she said. "He must have knifed your tires."

"That son of a bitch. Tires cost a fortune."

"So? We walk?"

Kayla blew out her breath as she turned the headlights off and closed the door. "Yeah, I guess we walk." She took the flashlight from her. "Be right back. Water bottles," she explained as she headed back into the house.

Alone in the darkness, Murphy heard rustling in the brush. She turned, looking toward the woods. She felt her heartbeat increase, felt her senses on full alert as she listened. She didn't imagine it would be Ned or any other person. She hoped it was nothing more than a raccoon or armadillo. Still…it seemed like an eternity before Kayla returned.

"Found a flashlight in the closet."

Murphy took it and cast the beam of light in the direction of the noise. Sure enough, a harmless armadillo scurried away.

Kayla laughed quietly. "Thought it was a mountain lion or something?"

Murphy let out a nervous breath. "Or something."

Kayla handed her a water bottle, and they started walking along the road. It was relatively quiet, the sounds of crickets and cicadas breaking the silence occasionally. Far off in the distance, they heard coyotes and the faint hooting of an owl.

"I missed the night sounds," Kayla said after a while. "Living in the city—traffic, horns, people talking, music playing, dogs barking—you don't realize what the *real* night sounds like."

"When I was a kid and I'd stay with my grandmother, we'd sit on the porch after dark—her in her rocking chair—and we'd listen to the frogs down at the pond."

"You had a fishing spot too?"

"Yeah, nothing big, but I could spend a whole Saturday out there drowning worms," she said, remembering those carefree days. "Once we moved and I got involved with new friends in the city, I kinda forgot how much I liked it there."

"You didn't go back much?"

"At first, we went back a couple of times a month, but as time went on, our visits got fewer and fewer. Special occasions, holidays, we still went for that. By the time I was in high school,

I had new interests and new friends, so I didn't miss it." She shrugged. "Or at least I convinced myself I didn't."

"I quit trying to pretend that I didn't miss it. I sometimes wish I had come back sooner than I did, but I wasn't ready, I guess."

They were quiet again as they continued walking, both with their flashlights on, illuminating the road ahead of them. It was only then that she thought to look at her watch.

"I didn't realize how late it was," she said. "Nearly eleven."

"I would imagine that by the time we make it to the county road, our chances of hitching a ride are going to be slim."

"I just hope we make it to the county road. I'm completely lost out here."

"Once we get through the gate, we go left. That's Zimmerman Road. We'll take another road to the right which will take us to the county road." Kayla sighed. "And I'm tired just thinking about how far it is. I'd guess it's at least six miles to reach the county road."

"Maybe we'll get lucky and someone will come along."

"Yeah, the way our luck's running that someone will be Uncle Ned." Kayla turned to her. "I still can't believe it's him. I would have never thought him capable of doing something like this."

"Money makes people do crazy things," she said. "We've seen that plenty of times in our line of work."

"True. But does he really think he can simply take the money and disappear? Does he plan to head to Mexico or something?"

It was her turn to sigh. "We had him, you know."

"No. He had us," Kayla corrected her. "Your instinct was right, and when I went back out, I should have been better prepared."

"If he wasn't your uncle, I think you would have been. What were you going to do? Come out of the kitchen with your weapon drawn?"

"He was suspicious the moment I came out. I could see that. So yes, I should have drawn on him."

"And he obviously had a nine mil tucked in his pants. Would you have been able to shoot him if he'd drawn on you?"

"Yes." She pictured that scenario, then shrugged. "That's easy to say now, of course."

"Yet you gave up your weapon."

"He would have shot you, Murphy."

"You gave up your weapon. He could have shot me anyway, just for the fun of it. He could have shot both of us."

"Look, I know all of that. I know what I should have done. I've been through countless hours of training, and no, I should not have surrendered my weapon. I was clinging to the hope that he was still my Uncle Ned and he wasn't going to shoot us." Kayla leaned closer and nudged her arm. "In case you didn't know, I'm very attracted to you, and I let that cloud my judgment."

She laughed. "Well, I guess I'm really happy about that, because yes, I think he would have shot me."

Kayla stopped walking and so did she.

"After this is over with, do you think we can...I don't know, maybe—"

"Have a date or something?"

Kayla smiled. "Well, I was thinking more like, get naked and have a date...you know, like in bed." Then she laughed. "God, I'm not normally *ever* this forward. Maybe a near-death experience has made me lose all my inhibitions."

"So you want to...skip the date and just—"

"I want to sleep with you," Kayla said bluntly. She tilted her head. "Do you want to sleep with me?"

The tone of her voice was teasing, playful, but Murphy wondered if Kayla doubted her interest. If they weren't on foot, in the middle of the woods, and on the run from a murderer, she'd take the time to show her just how interested she was. However, she didn't want their first kiss to be out here. She smiled and started walking again. Kayla fell into step beside her.

"So...is that a yes or a no?"

Murphy laughed. "Can I use my handcuffs?"

Kayla laughed too. "Not the first time. I want my hands free to touch you." Her voice lowered. "All over."

Murphy nearly stumbled and Kayla grabbed her arm to steady her.

"We should probably change the subject," she said. "You're dangerous."

Kayla's laughter rang out again, and Murphy walked beside her, a smile on her face as she imagined them in bed together. Most likely, it would be an experience she would never forget.

CHAPTER TWENTY-FIVE

Kayla saw the headlights seconds before Murphy did. "Kill your light," she said and moved them to the side of the road.

"I thought we wanted to flag someone down?"

"It's a truck. It could be Uncle Ned on his way back to the cabin."

He'd locked the gate behind him, but she still had the keys in her pocket. Once on Zimmerman Road, they'd headed north, walking mostly in silence. They'd reached the first road, taking it to the right. She thought they were making good time. It had only taken them twenty minutes to reach the gate and another fifteen on Zimmerman before they turned. Her hope of flagging down a vehicle was vanishing with each step and each tick of the clock. Even though it was a Friday night, there weren't many residences out this way. It would be pure luck for someone to be out. She thought they would have a better chance once they reached the county road, even though it would be after midnight before they got that far.

Now, as headlights approached, she feared they were sitting ducks. They went into the ditch and up against the fence, taking cover behind a small cedar tree. As the truck approached, it seemed to slow, and she gripped Murphy's arm tighter. When it passed by, she relaxed. It was a light-colored truck. Her uncle's truck was black. Even so, she didn't put her flashlight on to try to get their attention. She let them drive on. For some reason, she had gotten a bad vibe.

"What is it?"

She stared in the direction of where the truck had gone. "I'm not sure." She took a deep breath, wondering at her nervousness.

"Well, come on. Let's hit it."

She nodded, following Murphy back out onto the road. They walked on in silence, their footsteps barely making a sound on the pavement. A few times, the clouds parted, revealing the half-moon, but it was soon swallowed up again. Their flashlights cast a gentle glow that bounced around them as they walked. The night, while humid, wasn't overly warm and she felt comfortable with the slight breeze that blew through the trees. Still, she looked forward to a cool shower and sleeping in air-conditioned comfort. She glanced over at Murphy. When they got back to town, dare she suggest they share a bed? She mentally shook her head. No. Now wasn't the time. Who knew if they would even get to bed? Her uncle was out there somewhere…looking for hidden money. Finding him was at the top of the list. Sleeping with Murphy would have to wait.

"I hear a car."

Kayla heard it too, but there were no headlights to be seen. The woods were thick and the road curved. She looked behind them, but all was dark. Up ahead through the trees, they saw a flash of light. As before, they got to the side of the road, but it wasn't a truck that was heading their way.

"Let's flag them down," Murphy said, stepping out onto the road. She waved her flashlight around as Kayla stood beside her, waving her arms over her head. The car slowed and Murphy moved to the middle of the road.

"Be careful."

"Yeah…they're stopping."

It was a newer model Honda, and when the window buzzed down, a teenaged boy stared back at them. Kayla stepped forward, giving him a smile.

"We're having a little car trouble," she said. "We could really use a lift into town."

He looked at her suspiciously. "Where's your car?"

She pointed behind them. "Several miles down on Zimmerman."

"I could maybe take a look at it for you. I'm pretty handy with that sort of thing."

Murphy leaned down, looking into the window. "We just need a ride into town."

"I'm Kayla Dixon," she said. "Chief Dixon's daughter," she clarified. "If you could take us to the police station, that would be great."

He nodded. "Okay…yeah, sure." She heard the doors unlock and she opened the back. "Those beer cans back there…those aren't mine," he said nervously.

Murphy got in the front beside him, and Kayla slipped into the back. Her feet rattled the beer cans around. There were at least six.

"Had a little party, did you?"

"No, no. Like I said, those aren't mine. My dad must have—"

"Right."

"You have a rather youthful appearance for being over twenty-one," Murphy said, her lips twitching as she tried to hide a smile.

"Yeah…well…I'm…you know…"

"I was a teenager once too," Murphy said. "No worries. Just be careful."

He made a wide turn and headed back toward the county road. He was driving at least ten miles per hour slower than the speed limit, which suited her fine. When they got into town, he slowed even more, and they were nearly crawling as they approached the station. When he finally came to a stop, he sat upright, both hands clutched on the wheel, his eyes staring straight ahead. She leaned forward and touched his shoulder.

"Thanks for the lift."

Murphy turned to him, waiting until he looked at her. "We're both police officers, by the way," she said. "Don't let us ever catch you driving around this town after you've been drinking."

"Yes, ma'am."

"Look, if you're going to sneak beer, you sure as hell don't drive around with the empty cans in your car."

"No, ma'am. We…we had a six-pack. I just had one beer, I swear."

"Okay, kid." Murphy got out, then stuck her head back inside. "You be careful going home."

"I will. Yes, ma'am."

He pulled away slowly, and they stood there watching him. Kayla finally laughed.

"He probably won't sleep tonight."

"Good. He looked like he was barely sixteen."

"Well, as you said, we were all teenagers once."

"You were a cop's daughter. Don't tell me you did that too?"

They headed into the station and she nodded. "Kevin and I would each sneak a beer from our parents' fridge and go out to Braden's Hill. By the time we got there, the beer was warm, but we didn't really care."

Yolanda, the night dispatcher, was the only one at the station. Kayla thought they should let her know that they were there, but Murphy was already going into the squad room so she followed. It was after midnight, but her father answered his phone on the second ring.

"It's me," she said.

"Where the hell are you? I've been calling you for the last two hours," he said. "Ned's not answering his phone either. I was about to head out there and check on you."

"Yeah, well, you would have found us tied to chairs," she said. "Everything Murphy told you is true. Ned—"

"Ain't a goddamn killer!"

"He is a goddamn killer," she yelled back. "You've got to listen to me, Dad. He took our phones and our weapons. He knifed the tires on my car. He took off. He left us tied up. He—"

"He's my brother. He wouldn't do that," he said stubbornly.

"But he *did* do it."

"There has to be some mistake. He's scared. There has to be—"

"It's not a mistake."

Murphy took the phone from her. "Goddamn it, Earl, quit burying your head in the sand. Ned Dixon killed four people. Ned Dixon held a gun to my head. Ned Dixon threatened to kill your daughter, for God's sake! Now what in the hell are we going to do to find him?"

Kayla met Murphy's gaze, watching as Murphy nodded. "Fine." She handed the phone back, and Kayla took it.

"Aunt Charlotte knows, Dad. She knows what he's done. Apparently Lance Foster hid some cash and he's looking for it. Then, I don't know, he said he'd be back."

"Goddamn," her father muttered. "Okay. Jesus. Okay, I'll go by their house. I'll bring her in."

"We'll meet you there."

"I don't need any goddamn help!"

"Tough. And bring Mom's cell phone. I'll need to borrow it." She hung up the phone and looked at Murphy. "What did he say to you?"

"He said I better be right about this or I'd be looking for another job."

"He's so stubborn," she said. "Come on. We're meeting him at their house."

"They're not going to be there."

"I know."

CHAPTER TWENTY-SIX

Ned and Charlotte Dixon lived on the south side of town in an old neighborhood with large homes and yards, much like the one she was renting. She slowed as they approached, finding Earl's patrol car parked in the driveway. He was standing beside it, pacing.

"Nobody's here," he said when they walked up to him.

"Cars?"

"Nothing. Her car is gone too."

"He said that Lance Foster had hidden money somewhere," Kayla said. "Do you know if he owned some property other than his house?"

"Something like Ned owned, back in the woods," she added.

Earl took off his white Stetson and scratched his head. "Not that I know of. But hell, he was the real estate guy. He could own several places, for all I know." He put his hat back on. "Are you *sure* Ned's mixed up in this?" His question was directed at Kayla, not her.

Kayla nodded. "I'm sorry, Dad, but yes. He…he grabbed Murphy, held a gun to her head, threatened to kill her too. He said he found out that they were taking a bigger cut of the money than he was. Lance was supposed to have had some cash from the drugs they were selling on the side. That's what he was after."

Earl shook his head slowly. "My own goddamn brother."

"Maybe they decided to leave without the money," she said. "Or maybe he found it already."

"Could be headed to Mexico by now, I guess," Kayla said. "But I don't think he'd leave without the money. That was the whole point of this, wasn't it?"

"Maybe the point was revenge. He was pissed at all of them."

"Pissed?" Earl said. "You don't go kill four people because you're *pissed*."

She shrugged. "Pissed. Angry. Furious." She shrugged again. "I'm just saying, maybe it wasn't only about the money. You said yourself that they wouldn't have given him the time of day out on the street. In his eyes, he's doing all the work; he's taking all the chances moving the drugs. They're the ones raking in the cash though, not him."

Kayla nodded. "I agree with Murphy. I think most of this was driven by anger. He felt slighted. I imagine he felt like he was being taken advantage of."

Earl pounded the side of his truck. "This makes no goddamn sense. When we went out there, Ned was scared. Hell, you both saw him. There's got to be some explanation for this. Maybe this Mr. X is making him do it. Maybe—"

"There is no Mr. X," Kayla said. "That was just something Lance Foster came up with. Ned said he was the guy who brought the money." Kayla wrapped her fingers around his arm. "Dad, I know this is a shock to you. It is to me too. But we've got to do something. Put a BOLO out on their vehicles, something. You need to let Sheriff Ramsey know. You need—"

"No. Not yet."

"Dad—"

"No! As far as Ned knows, you two are still tied up. I'm going out there, wait on him."

"Earl—"

"Goddamn it! I'm in charge here, not you two."

"He may not go back there," Murphy said. "Once he finds the money, what reason would he have to go back?"

"He said he'd be back by daybreak," Kayla reminded her. "As far as he knows, Dad doesn't know anything. He thinks we're still out there. Guy's funeral is tomorrow. Well, today now, I guess, but really, the whole town will be there. He's got to feel like he's got time."

"But why go back out there?" she asked again. "What's there that he would need?"

"He's got cash somewhere," Kayla said. "Maybe he has his own hiding spot out in the woods. He finds Lance's stash, then comes back, packs up and heads out to...I don't know...maybe Mexico. The funeral is at ten. I'm sure he thinks he has until eleven or so before Dad is free and tries to contact us."

"I don't know. That seems kinda reckless. You find Lance Foster's money, then you get the hell out of town." She pointed at the house. "Your aunt is gone. He's obviously contacted her. I think we should be looking for them around town." She turned to Earl. "Kayla is right. We should put a BOLO out."

"I don't give a goddamn what you think, Murphy. He's going back to the cabin because you two are supposed to be at the cabin. Unfinished business."

Kayla's eyes widened. "You think he's going to return to the cabin to kill us?"

"As much as it pains me to say it, yes."

"Then why not kill us up front?" she asked.

"I don't know. Maybe he wanted you for leverage, in case something went wrong. Leverage against me," Earl clarified. He reached in his pocket and brought out a phone. He handed it to Kayla. "Here. It's your mom's. She said to bring it back in one piece."

"What do you want us to do?"

"Get some sleep."

"We should go out there with you," Kayla said.

"I can handle Ned," he said.

"Dad—"

"If he doesn't show, then we'll get the ball rolling first thing in the morning. I'll call Ramsey, we'll put the alert out, everything. But if I can bring him in quietly, without getting the whole goddamn town involved, then that's what I want to do."

Murphy glanced at her watch. It was nearly two. "He said he'd be back by daybreak."

"I'll give it until six thirty or so," Earl said. "Now, go get some sleep. We'll meet in the morning."

He got in his car and slammed the door, ending the discussion. They stepped away as he backed out of the driveway.

"I don't like the plan either," Kayla said before Murphy could speak. "I just hope Kabir has something for me in the morning. The warrant we got didn't include Uncle Ned, but I'll see if he can include him in the loop too."

"You think financials will help us at this point?"

"I don't know. We still have the drugs to consider."

"And that'll get pushed down to Houston and it'll go nowhere," she said. "If they were using Niemeyer's so-called ghost trucks and some dude named X was bringing the cash, it's a dead-end. Especially without the recordings that Lance Foster made."

"How do you think Uncle Ned knew about the camera?"

She shrugged. "How do you think he got Lance Foster to pull the memory cards out of his secret hiding place?"

"He probably admitted to killing Guy Woodard and maybe threatened Lance's wife or something," Kayla said. "Lance was scared enough to hand them over."

"If that was the case, why didn't he also give up the hiding place of his cash?"

"I don't know. Lance Foster was all about making money. Maybe the cash meant more to him than the recordings did. Maybe he knew he was going to be killed one way or the other, so why give Ned what he wanted?"

"I guess," she said with sigh. "Come on. I'll take you home."

They walked toward her truck, but before either of them opened their doors, Kayla stopped and looked at her across the hood.

"If you take me home, then you'll just have to come pick me up in the morning."

The streetlight cast just enough light for her to make out Kayla's eyes. She smiled back at her.

"Well, I guess you could stay with me. There's like four bedrooms in the place."

"Right. I guess I'll have my pick then."

They swung by Kayla's duplex so she could get a change of clothes, but by the time they were heading to Murphy's house, they were both yawning profusely. Wherever Kayla decided to sleep, sleep was just what they'd do.

"I haven't used this bathroom, but I think there are some towels in there," she said as she pointed out the spare room to Kayla.

"Go take your own shower. I'll find everything I need."

Murphy went into the kitchen and got a bottle of water from the fridge, drinking nearly the whole thing. As she made her way to the back bedroom, she heard the water running in the shower. She tried not to picture Kayla—naked—standing under the warm spray. She shook the image away and stripped off her clothes, relishing her own shower. It had been a very long, very stressful day, and she felt some of the tension slip away as the water bounced off her shoulders.

When she went back into her bedroom, she wasn't really surprised to find Kayla in her bed. She was, however, a little disappointed to find that she was fast asleep. She covered her mouth to hide a yawn, her body telling her that it was going on three a.m. and she needed some sleep. So she quietly pulled the covers back and slipped in beside Kayla. Kayla's only response was to reach out a sluggish hand and wrap her fingers around her arm. Murphy sighed contentedly and closed her eyes.

CHAPTER TWENTY-SEVEN

Kayla rolled her head slightly, shocked to find herself pressed against a warm body, her arm draped across a slim waist. She opened her eyes, seeing the barest hint of daylight breaking the darkness outside. She was tired and her eyelids were heavy. All she wanted to do was close her eyes and snuggle closer to the woman next to her.

Murphy hadn't exactly offered her bed last night, and Kayla had made a half-hearted attempt to find another one to sleep in. The first bedroom she'd gone into did indeed have furniture, but the bed was covered in only an old quilt. There were no sheets and she was too tired to look for some. So while Murphy showered, Kayla had gone into her bedroom and simply crawled under the covers, the scent of Murphy lingering on the pillow she used. Her intention was to stay awake, of course. But the sound of the shower was lulling her to sleep and even though she pictured Murphy naked and dripping wet, it wasn't enough to keep her eyes from closing.

She smiled now as that image came back to her. Would Murphy be as lean and toned as she imagined? Would she still be soft to the touch? She couldn't stop her hand from moving… slowly, surely as it snaked under Murphy's T-shirt. Warm skin under her fingertips sent her heart racing. Was it six? Six thirty? Should they be up and on their way to the station? The murder investigation faded from her mind as quickly as it had come. She didn't care what time it was. She was too tired to care.

Her hand settled just under the swell of Murphy's breast. She sighed contentedly and closed her eyes. They hadn't even kissed yet. No need to rush things.

* * *

Even though Murphy knew exactly who she'd fallen asleep with, it was still a shock to wake and find a warm hand mere inches from her breast. She moved her own hand, touching Kayla's fingers. Her eyes slipped closed again as she moved Kayla's hand up to cover her breast. Kayla's fingers closed around it and she let out a quiet moan.

"We don't have time for this," Kayla murmured.

"I know." Murphy rolled her head toward Kayla. "It's just been so long since someone's touched me."

Kayla shifted, her eyes fluttering open, meeting her gaze. "When's the last time you made love with someone?" she whispered.

Murphy looked into those eyes, trying to see past them, trying to recall the last woman who'd touched her. No name or face would come to her.

"I don't know. It's been a really long time, I guess."

Kayla's eyes gentled and she leaned forward, brushing her lips against her own. "When this is over with, I want to spend hours making love with you."

Murphy was suddenly afraid this would never be over with. She rolled them over, holding Kayla beneath her as her hips pressed down. She found Kayla's mouth, their moans mingling as they kissed. Kayla's thighs spread, inviting Murphy closer.

But T-shirts and underwear got in the way, hindering her desire to touch. No, they didn't have time for this. She should stop. Kayla, however, pulled her closer, her tongue dancing around Murphy's, her hips pressing upward.

Before she knew what was happening, Kayla had pulled her T-shirt off, her hands going to her breasts, thumbs raking across her nipples. God, were they really going to do this? Murphy had no more time for thought as one of Kayla's hands cupped her from behind, then slid inside her underwear, caressing her hip.

"Take these off," Kayla whispered.

"We don't have time," she protested weakly, even as she was helping Kayla push them down.

"We're going to make time," Kayla countered.

Murphy found herself on her back, completely naked. Kayla knelt over her, pausing to remove her own T-shirt. When Murphy's hands lifted to touch her, Kayla captured them and held them behind Murphy's head, her mouth silencing any protest she might have.

"Pretend you're handcuffed," Kayla whispered into her mouth, she then moved lower, her lips and tongue swirling around her nipples, one…then the other.

Murphy tried to remember the last time she'd been this aroused, but no memory would come to her. It was just Kayla— here and now. She longed to touch her, but she kept her hands over her head, letting Kayla have her way. A hot mouth was locked on her breast and a hand slid across her belly, then lower. She moaned in anticipation, imagining Kayla inside her. She was wet, she could feel it against her thighs, and she opened them wider, silently urging Kayla to touch her.

Kayla paused, her fingers brushing lightly, teasingly against her. Murphy groaned in frustration. Then her hips jerked as Kayla's fingertip found her clit.

"You're very wet," Kayla murmured. "I like that." Her fingers slid into her opening, then back out, back to tease her clit once more.

"Please…" she whispered. It was all she could do to keep her hands off Kayla. If she didn't end this torture soon, she'd—

The phone's ringtone was sharp, loud, and it pierced the quiet sounds of their lovemaking.

"Oh…God…*no*," she groaned as Kayla's hand stilled.

"Don't move," Kayla whispered as she reached across Murphy to grab the phone. She took a deep breath, then answered. "Hello."

Murphy turned her head, burying her face in the pillow. It would be Earl. Time to go to work.

"Okay." A pause. "Yes, I'll let Murphy know." Kayla lay back down beside her. "You were right. We didn't have time for this."

Murphy only sighed.

Then Kayla rolled toward her, her mouth teasing her own. "We could shower together."

Murphy smiled. "You enjoy torturing me, don't you?"

Kayla's tongue ran across her lower lip. "I want to hear you scream." She sat up and pulled Murphy with her. "Come on. Let's hurry."

CHAPTER TWENTY-EIGHT

Murphy sat at the desk, her eyes moving across the words on the screen without seeing them. No, all she saw was Kayla's mouth at her breast, Kayla's hand between her legs. It was probably the quickest shower she'd ever taken…yet it was one she would most likely never forget. She looked up, finding Kayla watching her. They smiled at each other…the slow, gentle smile that new lovers shared.

Oh, yeah, she was ready for this case to be over with. She was ready for *normal* again—something she'd hoped to find when she'd first moved to Sawmill Springs. What she hadn't thought she'd find was a lover though. And she was definitely ready for *that* too.

First things first, however. Earl had spent a fruitless night—morning, really—waiting for Ned to show back up at the cabin. At seven, when there was no sign of him, he'd come back into town. Ned's house was still empty too. So, according to Kayla, Earl was planning to meet with Sheriff Ramsey this morning. Her gut told her Ned and Charlotte were long gone, but Kayla didn't think so. She didn't think he'd leave without the money.

So then where was the money?

She turned her attention to the notes once again, absently reading through them—notes she'd made and had already gone over countless times before. She went back to the beginning, to Guy Woodard's murder, reading through what little facts they had. The notes on Lance Foster weren't much more detailed. They had more questions than answers. She stopped when she came to the list of foreclosed properties they'd pulled. The only one that was linked to Guy Woodard and the bank had proven to be a dead end—a dilapidated mobile home sitting on a long-forgotten lot. She tilted her head as she stared at the description of the property. Why was it forgotten?

"What is it?"

"Why do you think this property," she said, pointing at the screen. "This foreclosed property we looked at that day…why do you think it's still sitting?" She looked at Kayla. "I mean, we saw it, yeah, it's junk. But it's got a water well, it's got septic, there's electricity there. Haul off the trailer house and you've got a nice piece of property with utilities."

"Are you looking to buy? It'll probably be cheap."

"Right. So why hasn't it sold?"

"What are you thinking?"

"The bank owned the property. We couldn't find where it had ever been put up for auction or for sale. But what if it had?" She leaned forward. "What if it was a transaction done, you know, under the table or something? What if Lance Foster bought it?"

Kayla nodded. "Okay, yeah. I think maybe we're reaching here, but if you're right and Lance did buy it, then it would be a perfect place to hide…whatever it was he needed to hide." She picked up the phone on the next desk. "I'll call Kabir. He can hack into anything. I'll see if he can find the title or deed or whatever."

"It's Saturday morning," she reminded her.

Kayla smiled. "So I'll sweet-talk him."

She laughed quietly. "Yeah, I hear you're pretty good at that."

* * *

Kayla had no luck finding Kabir, however. All of her contact information for him was on her phone, which Uncle Ned had snatched. She finally tracked down someone who had his cell number, but she was told he was in London on assignment. No wonder he hadn't answered any of her emails.

Murphy came back in carrying two cups of coffee. She let her eyes roam over her—the jeans loose enough to be comfortable, tight enough to show her curves. They weren't enough, however, to keep Kayla from picturing Murphy as she'd been that morning…naked, wet, wanting. Oh, the quickie in the shower wasn't nearly enough to assuage her appetite. No, quite the opposite, in fact. All it did was fan the flame. She could have spent hours making love. She *wanted* to spend hours in bed with Murphy. And as soon as this was over with, she hoped to do just that.

"What?"

Kayla smiled, forgetting that she'd been staring. "Just… remembering our shower," she said quietly.

Murphy met her gaze, holding it. "I'd really like for you to stay with me again tonight." She smiled quickly. "You know, maybe go to bed about eight or so."

Kayla laughed. "I was thinking seven sounded good."

"Seven sounds great." Murphy wiggled her eyebrows teasingly. "Don't forget your handcuffs."

"Oh, honey, don't you worry." Her voice lowered to a near whisper. "I'll have you begging."

Murphy's expression turned serious. "You don't need handcuffs to make me beg."

The look in Murphy's eyes made Kayla want to forget where they were. That look made her want to get up and go to her. Go to her and kiss her, touch her. It made her want to unbutton her jeans and slip her hand inside. She stood up, afraid she might do just that when the outer door opened.

They both turned, finding her father standing there. He looked…well, he looked awful. Lines of worry etched his face. His normally clear, sharp eyes were cloudy, tired.

"Anything?" he asked gruffly.

She shook her head. "You?"

"Hell, got Ramsey's guys all on alert. He put the BOLO out." He took his hat off and ran his fingers through his hair. "On both vehicles. Charlotte's too."

"Have you been in touch with Boyd and Wayne?" She turned to Murphy. "That's their sons," she explained.

"I drove by both of their houses on the off chance that Ned's truck was there, but no, I didn't stop in. Hell, what would I tell them?"

"Dad, you can't keep this from them. You can't keep it a secret any longer."

"It won't be a secret for long. As soon as Timmy hears the BOLO he'll be on the phone to his Uncle Ray. Won't take long for it to spread all over the goddamn town."

"What about Kabir?" Murphy asked.

Kayla shook her head. "No. He's out of the country."

"Who's that?" he asked.

"I worked with him. A computer whiz. A hacker."

He raised his eyebrows. "For what? I thought Kimbro was handling all that for us."

"Kimbro is working off a warrant," she said. "Kabir wouldn't have those restrictions."

"Damn FBI thinks they can hack into anything," he muttered. "No wonder nobody trusts them."

"Murphy had an idea. I wanted Kabir to check it out."

He looked at Murphy. "What?"

"There's a piece of property that the bank owned—foreclosed on. We went out and looked at it after Lance Foster's murder."

He nodded. "I remember. The old Schneider place. What about it?"

"Well, there's no record that it was put up for auction. No record that it was ever sold."

"Yeah. So?"

"Maybe Lance Foster bought it," Kayla said.

He frowned. "Are you trying to say that you think this might be the secret place where he's got money hidden? Out at that old dump?"

"It's a dump, yeah. But you take off the house and you've got a nice wooded lot, five acres. You've got septic and a water well."

"What the hell are you talking about, Murphy? You going into the real estate business?"

"I'm saying, there's no reason that it wouldn't have sold. Which makes me think that it *did* sell."

"And you think Ned knows this?"

"He seemed pretty sure that he knew where the money was hidden," Kayla said. "If that's the case, he may have already found it."

"It won't hurt to go take a look, Earl."

He looked between the two of them, finally nodding. "I guess it beats sitting around here waiting on Ramsey to call. My stupid, goddamn brother," he mumbled with a shake of his head. "I still can't wrap my head around all of this. Are you *sure* he—"

"We're sure, Dad."

CHAPTER TWENTY-NINE

Even though her father had wanted to go in Murphy's truck—less conspicuous, he'd said—they took his patrol car. She'd convinced him they needed as many resources as they could get. She let Murphy ride in the front with him despite Murphy's offer to sit in the back. Sitting behind them gave her the opportunity to observe Murphy freely. And observe, she did. Murphy was all business and looked very much like the detective she used to be. When she'd shoved the Glock into the leather holster at her waist, she positively oozed with confidence. Murphy's walk had just enough swagger to make her look like… well, dare she say a badass? Oh, she loved looking at Murphy in her uniform, but this…this was something else entirely.

"You know this is probably a waste of our time," her father said for the second time.

"We got no other leads," she said.

"You call this a lead?" he scoffed.

She didn't reply. No, it wasn't a lead. It was a hunch. It was a long shot. At least it would eliminate the one possibility that they had. Kimbro was doing a title search, which he said could take days. Her suggestion was to call Lance's wife to see if she knew of any property he owned, but her father didn't want to involve her. "She ain't even buried him yet. No sense in getting her involved in this mess."

She was going to have to be involved very soon anyway, but Kayla let him have his way. This mess, as he called it, was going to turn into one giant scandal once everyone in town learned that Lance Foster, Guy Woodard and Floyd Niemeyer were mixed up in dealing drugs. Mixed up deep enough that it got them killed. She sighed. Killed by the police chief's brother, no less. How in the world was her father going to survive this? Would he resign? Would he be run out of town like he'd first feared? He'd been the chief for a decade and a half. Whenever a new mayor was elected, they'd not deemed it necessary to appoint someone else, leaving her father to run things as he always had. What now? Would a new mayor want him out? Would he appoint Pete Wilson to replace him? If that was the case, what would she do? Would she want to stay in Sawmill Springs and work for someone other than her father?

Her glance slid to Murphy. What about her? Would she stay on? Their romance was in the early stages, just budding. Could it survive a move of one or both of them? She put a halt to her thoughts. She was getting way ahead of herself. Speculating on the future would do no good.

"Ain't seen a single car since we left town," her father said. "Whole damn county is probably there for Guy's funeral."

"I guess a lot of people are more curious about what's going on than they are grieving," she said. "Won't you be missed there?"

"I should be there, yes," he said. "But I imagine that by the time the funeral rolls around, it'll be spreading like wildfire that Ned is our only suspect. I think I'd just as soon *not* be there for that."

"Might be good to be there," Murphy said. "Show everyone that you're still in charge."

He looked at Murphy sideways and laughed. "In charge? Not with the way you two have been trying to boss me around."

"Sometimes you're too close, Dad. You let it get personal."

"Hell, yeah, it's personal. That's my goddamn brother! My *only* brother. Your first instinct is to protect, you know." He shook his head. "I tried to protect him, all right. Had him under goddamn police protection. Wait until *that* gets out. I'll be the laughing stock."

"I was under the impression that we were keeping a close eye on him, not protecting him," Murphy said. "Apparently your instincts were right. He *needed* to be watched."

"You trying to put some kind of a fancy spin on it, are you?"

"Well, there's only been the three of us involved in this. Don't know how much of a spin it'll take. As far as anyone needs to know, we were keeping Ned under police surveillance."

Kayla would have hugged her if she could have. Her father needed to hear that. Her father needed to know that they had his back. For all his bravado, she could tell he was worried, not only about Ned, but about himself too. If he lost his job, there's no way he could continue to live in Sawmill Springs. What would he do?

Her father slowed as he approached the property. She saw immediately that someone had been there. Murphy did, too.

"Weeds are mashed down on the driveway," Murphy said quietly.

"That don't mean that Ned's here. Could be from anybody."

Frankly, Kayla was surprised that there were tracks there at all. Murphy's hunch that maybe Lance Foster owned this property had been simply that…a hunch, a gut feeling on her part. At the time, she'd thought they were grasping at straws, trying to find some kind of lead, *any* lead. The chances that they'd stumble upon Ned had been slim, at best. Now, as her adrenaline kicked in, she had a feeling that's exactly what had happened.

"We've got to check it out," Murphy said as her father continued past the house.

"Don't see any cars. No truck. If somebody was here, they're long gone," he said.

"Could have stashed the truck back in the woods. That's what he did at his cabin," Kayla said.

"You think he's back there hiding? He's bound to know we're looking for him by now."

"How so? He thinks we're still tied up. He thinks you're on your way to a funeral, along with the rest of the town."

"That may be, but a part of him has to think that you could have escaped by now," he said. He glanced over at Murphy. "How did you get untied, anyway?"

"Flexible fingers," she said, holding her hands up and wiggling her fingers.

Kayla nearly snorted with laughter. "You don't say?"

Her father looked back at her but said nothing as he turned his car around. "Guess it won't hurt to drive in and see if we can follow the tracks."

The five-acre lot was open in the front where the mobile home was, only a few trees remaining, including the huge dead one that hovered directly over the house. Beyond the house, however, the woods were thick and overgrown. If Lance Foster did indeed own this and he was using it to hide cash, why not stash it in the house somewhere? But the tracks didn't stop at the house. They continued on into the woods, the old lane now overgrown with weeds and small saplings.

She was as shocked as anyone to see a black truck squeezed into the woods, the driver's door standing open. Her father came to a sudden stop, jarring them all in their seats.

"That stupid son of a bitch," he muttered.

Like Murphy, she was scanning the area around them, but she saw no movement. The tailgate on the truck was down and two shovels were tossed on the back.

"Okay, if you're Lance Foster, are you really going to bring cash out here in the woods and dig a hole and bury it?" Murphy asked. "I only saw him a couple of times, but he was always dressed impeccably…suit, tie, the works. I don't see it."

"I was thinking the same thing," she said. "Why not put it in the house?"

"Lance Foster didn't bury any goddamn money. And if he did, how in the hell would Ned know where to dig?"

They all got out, and while her father's attention was solely on the truck, she and Murphy were looking around them, into the woods. They weren't so thick that you couldn't see, but the trees were plenty big enough for someone to hide behind.

"No keys inside, but he did leave this behind," he said as he carried a duffel bag around to the back of the truck. He unzipped it and held up two cell phones. "These possibly yours?"

Kayla snatched hers out of his hand and held it lovingly to her chest. "Yes, thank you very much." She raised her eyebrows. "I don't suppose our weapons are in there, huh?"

"Nope. I guess he thought he might need those." He tossed the other phone to Murphy. "Nothing much in here. Change of clothes, some socks. No money, in other words." He looked down the road from which they'd come, his gaze on the old house. "My guess is, they did what Kayla suggested…stashed his truck back here in the woods, took off in Charlotte's car." He left the duffel bag on back of the truck and headed back to the patrol car. "We'll check inside the house, and then report to Ramsey that we found his truck. I'm afraid to say it, but you may be right. They could be heading to Mexico with a bag full of cash."

Kayla paused at the car, her brows drawn together in a frown. Something didn't feel right. It was almost too easy. If he was really trying to hide his truck, why park it there? Sure, it couldn't be seen from the county road, but still, it was hardly hidden. She tried to picture Uncle Ned and Aunt Charlotte out here, searching for cash, frantically trying to get away before the police or sheriff's deputies found them. Uncle Ned? Yes, he seemed crazy enough to do it. But Aunt Charlotte? She couldn't see it. She couldn't even fathom that she'd been a part of the murders—that she'd helped him. But she recalled that conversation with Miss Bernice when she'd casually mentioned that Charlotte had been into her shop. Aunt Charlotte didn't sew. Was it a coincidence that she'd picked the very day that Guy Woodard was killed to browse for fabric?

"What are you thinking?"

She glanced at Murphy. "I don't know. Something doesn't feel right. It's like…like it's staged or something."

"Hidden but in plain sight?"

"Yeah."

"What are you two going on about now?"

"The truck," she said. "It wasn't really hidden."

"Sure it was. We couldn't see it until we drove right up to it."

"But it wasn't hidden. It was parked between two trees. If he was trying to hide it, he would have driven farther back, parking behind some yaupon thicket or something."

"You're overthinking this," he said as they got inside the patrol car. "I doubt Ned's smart enough to try to stage something. What for?" He backed up, and then turned the car around. "Come out, get the money, leave. I think he pulled his truck back here so it couldn't be seen from the road and they took off in Charlotte's car," he said, repeating his earlier assumption.

Maybe she *was* overthinking it. Perhaps Ned did just drive back here far enough to hide the truck from the road. They would be in a hurry, no doubt.

When they got close to the house, there was evidence that a vehicle had driven around to the back. Was this where Aunt Charlotte's car had been?

"These tracks look big, like from a truck," Murphy said. "What kind of car does Charlotte drive?"

"One of those little Ford things, a Focus or something," her father said. "But yeah, these tracks look too big for that."

He stopped in the back of the house, on the same tracks. They all got out. Everything seemed quiet. The house appeared to be empty. As her father walked to the back door, she and Murphy exchanged glances. Something wasn't right. Did Murphy feel it too?

"Door's unlocked," he said. "Let's take a quick look. Murphy, go around to the front. Check that door."

Murphy nodded and took off in a slow jog to the front, leaving Kayla standing alone. She looked around the back, seeing the twisted metal of an old lawn chair sticking up in the weeds. A couple of terra-cotta pots, dirt still in them, stood up against the skirt of the trailer, weeds growing inside where flowers had perhaps once been. A couple of crows landed in the dead oak beside the house, their calls echoing over and over again, as if scolding them for being there. She slid her gaze from them to the old, rusted-out car that was mostly obscured by weeds. She frowned. The weeds appeared stomped down in places. Had someone been snooping around the car?

Instead of following her father into the house, she walked over toward the car. Yes, the weeds had been trampled on. She squatted down. Were those drag marks? She went closer to the car, her eyes widening as she saw a shape inside, in the backseat. Someone was slumped against the door, away from her. She reached for her weapon but before she could pull it from its holster, her arm was twisted from behind. She gasped and spun around, swinging her other hand up, only to find herself grasped around the neck, the cold metal of a gun barrel pressed against her temple.

"I'll surely pull this trigger, Kayla Ann. You know I will."

She stopped struggling, even as his arm tightened around her neck. "Uncle Ned…please," she said. "You can't do this."

"Too late for that." He pulled her up close against him as he leaned next to the car. "Got your Aunt Charlotte in there. It pained me to tie her up. Once I'm out of here, if you could see that she's properly taken care of, I'd appreciate that." He jerked her up hard, then walked toward the patrol car. "Earl! You need to come on out here now," he yelled. "Earl!"

Her father burst through the back door, his weapon in his hands, his eyes wide. "What in the goddamn hell are you doing, Ned?"

"What does it look like? Kayla here is my shield…so you don't shoot me." He backed them up some as Murphy came running from around the side. Her weapon was drawn as she took aim, her arms stiff, following their movement. "Now you just stop right there, Officer Murphy. We all know how this is going to play out."

"Goddamn it, Ned. You've lost your ever-loving mind."

"You don't know the half of it, Earl."

"Put the goddamn gun down, Ned."

Ned shook his head. "Always got to get in the way, don't you Earl? Couldn't leave well enough alone, could you?"

"Well enough alone? Christ, Ned, you not only got mixed up in goddamn drugs, but you killed four people!"

"They had it coming."

"Billy N's wife? What the hell did she do?"

"Well, that was unfortunate, yes." He jerked Kayla around as Murphy took a step to the side.

"No, no, no. See…Earl's not going to shoot because this here's his daughter. And you're not going to shoot because this here's your lover. So just back up!"

"What? Her goddamn what? *Lover*?"

He stared at her and Kayla shook her head. "Oh, Dad…not now, please," she whispered.

"Ned…I'm warning you, you stop this right now. You let her go," her father demanded.

Ned laughed. "Or you'll do what, Earl?"

"Yeah? Well, what do you think you're going to do? You think I'm going to let you walk out of here with her?"

"Gonna take your car, Earl. That's what I'm going to do."

She stared at Murphy, realizing that she'd yet to say even one word. Their eyes locked together and she saw it with such clarity, she could have been reading Murphy's mind. She panicked for a moment.

Oh, my God…she's going to take a shot!

Ned and her father's voices faded into the background as she stared into Murphy's eyes. Everything seemed to stop and she felt like she was moving in slow motion—each breath she took, each beat of her heart, each thought that ran through her head. She heard nothing, no voices, no sound. All she saw when she looked into Murphy's eyes was a quiet confidence, a quiet calm. She didn't know how Murphy planned to pull this off, but she trusted her. As her uncle and father traded barbs and threats, as the barrel of her uncle's gun pressed harder against her temple, she relaxed, ignoring the tight squeeze of his arm around her neck. One more look into Murphy's eyes, then she counted silently to three before slowly moving her head toward her uncle's shoulder.

The shot was loud in her ears, and she fell to the ground with her uncle's arm still around her neck. She was stunned. Was she shot? Could she feel her legs? Was she breathing? Time again stood still. How many seconds did she lay there? Minutes? Whose hands were touching her? Whose voice was she hearing?

"You're okay. Look at me."

She turned her head to the sound of the voice, finding Murphy leaning over her. She finally dared to breathe…to blink her eyes.

"Have you lost your goddamn *mind*?" her father bellowed.

Murphy helped her into a sitting position, away from her uncle. Kayla turned to look at him. Murphy's shot had hit him square between the eyes. She squeezed Murphy's hand, meeting her gaze.

"Thanks."

Murphy pulled her to her feet, then into her arms. Kayla clung to her and buried her face against Murphy's neck.

"That was so damn close, Murphy," she murmured.

"I guess I forgot to tell you that I was a sharpshooter, huh?"

Kayla gave a nervous laugh as she pulled out of her arms. "Oh, yeah. *That* would have been nice to know." She turned to her father. "I'm okay."

But her father's stare was directed at Murphy. "What in the hell were you thinking?"

"I was thinking that your daughter was in danger."

"You could have shot her!"

"I wouldn't dare shoot her."

"Dad…stop. I'm okay."

"Goddamn it," he muttered. He slid his glance to Ned, slowly shaking his head. "Goddamn," he said again. He squatted down beside him, one hand moving over to touch Ned's shoulder.

Kayla was going to reach out to him, to offer some comfort, but Murphy stopped her.

"Let's give him a minute."

Kayla nodded, then took a step away. She pointed to the car. "Aunt Charlotte's in there."

Murphy opened the door, the rusted hinges screaming in protest. Kayla watched as she reached inside, then she gasped as Aunt Charlotte's limp body rolled to the seat.

"Oh, my God. He said he…he tied her up. But—"

"She's dead," Murphy said. "Gunshot to the chest."

"Oh…Jesus," she whispered. She turned toward her father. "Dad…"

CHAPTER THIRTY

Murphy wet a path between Kayla's breasts, relishing the quiet moan she heard. She tried to recall the last time she'd felt a connection with someone like this and nothing would come to her. It had been so long—far too long.

Soft hands rubbed across her back, pulling her subtly closer. Her mouth closed over Kayla's nipple, sucking it into her mouth as Kayla's hips pressed up against her. She felt nearly intoxicated as the scent of Kayla—the taste of her skin—seemed to flood all of her senses at once. She slipped a thigh between Kayla's legs, feeling her wetness as it coated her own skin. That wetness is what she wanted to feel, what she wanted to taste.

She moved lower, her lips nibbling lightly below Kayla's breast, her stomach. She was already spreading Kayla's thighs with her hands, pushing them apart as she moved lower still, pausing at the curve of Kayla's hip, kissing her way down. The soft hair between Kayla's thighs was damp with her arousal and Murphy simply wanted to bury her face there. Kayla's hips were rolling, as if searching for her mouth and Murphy waited no longer.

She cupped Kayla from behind, holding her still as her tongue snaked its way past her soft curls and into the wetness she sought. She moaned with pleasure at her first taste, feeling Kayla's response as she reacted with a slight jerk of her hips and an answering moan of her own. Her tongue teased her swollen clit, then slid lower, finding her hot and wet. Kayla clutched at her shoulders, holding her close and Murphy's tongue flicked in and out before going back to her clit. Her lips closed around it, sucking it hard into her mouth, causing Kayla to push up against her, her hips rocking now against her face.

Murphy could hear Kayla panting, could feel her trembling beneath her. Her orgasm was close so she pulled her mouth away.

"Oh, God...*no*," Kayla hissed.

Murphy sat up, her fingers finding Kayla wet and ready. She plunged deep inside of her.

"Oh, God...*yes*."

Murphy leaned forward, capturing Kayla's mouth in a fiery kiss. Their tongues battled, their moans mingling as they kissed. Murphy's fingers were dripping wet as she pushed in and out of Kayla, faster, deeper, letting Kayla set the pace that she needed. Hands clutched at her, gripping her tightly, almost painfully so. She lowered her mouth to Kayla's breast, sucking a nipple inside. Kayla held her close, her breath coming in quick bursts, her hips undulating wildly against her hand. Then Kayla arched, one last thrust before screaming out, her thighs squeezing tightly against Murphy's hand, holding her there as her body quaked from her orgasm.

She finally relaxed and Murphy pulled her fingers out of her, feeling Kayla jerk slightly as she brushed her sensitive clit.

"God, Murphy...that was better than the last time."

Murphy smiled as she leaned down and kissed her. "That's what you said last time."

Kayla drew her into her arms. "I'll probably say it next time too. Making love with you is fantastic."

Murphy smiled contentedly as she lay down next to Kayla. Yes, it was fantastic. Kayla had said she wanted to spend hours in bed. They'd done just that.

"Is this your way of trying to keep my mind off everything that's happened?" Kayla asked as she kissed her.

"Has it helped?"

Kayla sighed. "Yes, it has. I needed to…to lose myself for a while." She rolled over, staring at the ceiling. "My mom is making dinner tonight. I want you to go with me."

She groaned. "I'm not sure I'm ready to face Earl."

"We have to face him eventually."

"He could shoot me, you know."

Kayla laughed. "Yes, he could. Despite everything's that happened in town, I'm sure he's still wondering if we're really lovers or not. I can't believe Uncle Ned said that." Her smile faded. "Jesus…I can't believe he shot Aunt Charlotte." Kayla rolled over and faced Murphy. "What do you think happened?"

"I don't know. Maybe she wasn't really in on it at all. He said she knew, but maybe she didn't."

"But why kill her?"

"We'll never know what really happened, I guess."

"They still haven't found her car," Kayla said. "None of it makes sense. Uncle Ned was always just a…a normal guy, you know. For him to do all of this…the drugs, the killing, I…I can't wrap my mind around it all. And…and he threatened to kill me. He had a gun held to my head. He had a gun held to *your* head. This could have so easily ended differently."

Murphy reached over and brushed the blond hair away from Kayla's eyes. The blue orbs that looked back at her were misted with tears.

"It could have, but it didn't. We're both okay."

"I don't want to *ever* go through something like this again. I want Sawmill Springs to return to the sleepy little town that it's always been. I want to write traffic tickets and do crowd control at Friday night football games. I want to go up to Braden's Hill and catch some teenagers drinking beer that they stole from their parents' fridge."

Murphy smiled. "That could be fun. The kid who gave us a ride…I've got the license number. We could harass him."

Kayla smiled too and wiped at a tear that had escaped. "That was kinda funny, all those empty beer cans in the back."

"We should have called his parents."

"I know. But we were kinda busy."

They were quiet for a moment, saying nothing, just lying beside each other, touching. Murphy rolled her head to the side, looking at Kayla. Kayla turned too.

"You know, I'm supposed to have a dinner date tonight."

Kayla's eyes widened. "Oh?"

"Gloria. You remember…college friends in town."

Kayla shook her head. "No. No, no, no. You'll have to call and cancel."

"I will?"

"Yes. Sorry, but I've got you tonight." Kayla leaned closer, kissing her softly. "I kinda think I might want you every night." She smiled against her lips. "You can tell Gloria that you're going to be busy for a while. Quite a while."

CHAPTER THIRTY-ONE

Kayla stood patiently as her mother hugged her tightly, her hands patting her face, then her shoulders, as if making sure she was okay. She surprised Kayla by turning to Murphy and hugging her as well.

"I'm just so thankful you're both in one piece."

Kayla could tell she was fighting back tears. "We're fine, Mom. Part of the job."

"Well, you'll probably tell me that these last few days have been mild compared to your FBI stint, but I don't believe it for a minute."

Kayla smiled at that. "That's because I never told you about my undercover work in New Orleans. I knew you wouldn't be able to sleep at night if you knew what I was doing."

Her mother held her hand up. "Well, please don't tell me now."

"How's Dad?" she asked quietly.

"Keeping everything to himself, as usual." She motioned with her head toward the den. "He was on the phone with Judge

Peters. I'm sure we'll have to beat it out of him to get the scoop on that conversation." She then linked arms with both Kayla and Murphy. "To change the subject to something much more pleasant…how are you two doing?"

"Doing?"

"You're glowing, honey. Sex used to do that to me too."

Kayla blushed. "Oh, my God! You did not just say that!"

"I knew this would happen," her mother continued. "I could tell."

"She thought I was straight," Kayla said, pointing at Murphy. "Tell her."

It was Murphy's turn to blush. "No. I'd rather not talk about it."

Kayla laughed. "I was flirting with her and she was trying her best not to flirt back because she thought I was straight."

"Why did you think she was straight? I thought you had… what's it called…'Gaydar?'"

Kayla laughed again, finally taking pity on Murphy. "Because I was once married and because she thought Jennifer was a guy."

"In my defense, you never said her name," Murphy said.

"True." She smiled at her mother. "To answer your question, we're doing fine."

"Good. Because you look happy. You both do." She tugged them along into the kitchen. "Come help me with dinner. Your father said he didn't have much of an appetite so I made his favorite, hoping to tempt him."

Kayla turned to Murphy. "You'll never guess what his favorite thing is. You'd think a big roast or something, but no."

"Swedish meatballs over buttery egg noodles," her mother supplied. "I will admit, I make pretty good meatballs, but I think it's the gravy that gets him."

"I don't know that I've ever had homemade Swedish meatballs," Murphy said.

"Then you're in for a treat."

* * *

Murphy felt a little awkward sitting at the table across from Earl. She didn't know if it was her imagination or not, but he appeared to be glaring at her. She avoided his eyes as much as possible.

"I don't suppose anyone at this table is going to fill me in on what really happened, are you?" Bobbie Dixon asked.

Murphy glanced at Kayla. Kayla shrugged.

"It's probably best left unsaid, Mom."

"I see. Gonna make me read it in the paper then. I heard from Donna Everett that it had something to do with drugs."

"No sense hashing it over," Earl said gruffly. "There'll be enough of that in the next few days, I'm sure."

"I went by Wayne's house," Bobbie said. "Dropped off a casserole. They're just heartbroken." She shook her head. "I don't think it's set in with me yet either."

"The whole situation…it's…well, it's awful," Kayla said.

"Awful don't begin to cover it," Earl said. "Now I've got to explain my goddamn brother's actions, as if I had something to do with it."

"Is that what Judge Peters thinks?" Bobbie asked.

"He's in shock like the rest of us. Sheriff Ramsey and I are meeting with Gavin Craft in the morning. I imagine Judge Peters will be there too."

"Gavin Craft?" she asked.

"District attorney."

"Do you need us to go along?" Kayla asked.

"I think I can handle it." He raised his eyebrows. "Are you thinking I won't be able to put the right spin on it?"

"What spin are you talking about?" Bobbie asked.

Murphy, Kayla and Earl all exchanged glances. It was only then that Murphy realized that Bobbie had no idea what had really happened. She'd heard a rumor about drugs, so Earl hadn't said anything to her, apparently. She obviously hadn't been told that Ned had a gun held to her daughter's head…and she most likely didn't know that it was Murphy who'd shot him. Murphy stared at Earl, wondering why he'd kept her in the dark.

Earl put his fork down. "Yeah, there were drugs involved. All of them…Guy, Lance, Billy N and Ned."

"So that was true? My goodness, I never would have believed it."

"Uncle Ned was hiding cocaine in his concrete statues and birdbaths, then shipping them out," Kayla said. "Their business arrangement hit a rocky road."

Bobbie shook her head. "I can't believe he'd kill over it. And poor Charlotte…"

"It's over with now," Earl said abruptly. He looked at her, then at Kayla. "Gavin will want to interview both of you too. Especially Murphy. Might not be a bad idea for you two to come along tomorrow. Maybe we can get it all over with at once."

Kayla nodded. "Sure."

Earl picked his fork up again and bit into a meatball. He glanced again at Kayla. "Got your car towed in to Kirby's. He's gonna get some tires for you."

"Good. Thank you."

"Drove by your duplex this afternoon. Was gonna let you know about the car."

Murphy shoved a forkful of food into her mouth, watching as Kayla's expression changed from serious to amused.

"Did you now? I wasn't home."

"I gathered that when you didn't answer the door." He turned his attention to her, and Murphy nervously picked up her glass of tea.

Earl tapped the table with an index finger, over and over. Murphy finally looked at him, meeting his gaze.

"What Ned said…was that true?"

Murphy didn't need him to clarify what he meant by that. Before she could answer, Kayla reached over and squeezed her arm, letting her fingers linger.

"Dad…quit trying to intimidate her."

"I'm asking a question, that's all."

"You already know the answer. Yes, Dad…we're lovers."

Murphy nearly spit out her tea.

CHAPTER THIRTY-TWO

Kayla stood beside Murphy at the dresser, looking at their reflections in the mirror. Murphy was a little taller, not much. Her dark hair hung below her eyebrows and Kayla had to stop herself from brushing it away. Murphy saw where her gaze was as she impatiently moved the hair to the side.

"I need a trim."

"I like it. It's sexy." She turned to her. "Speaking of sexy, you in this uniform…I could just…eat you up."

Murphy's lips twitched in a smile. "Yes, I think you already did that."

Kayla laughed. "Sex with you is so much fun. I never thought I'd like handcuffs."

"Don't you *ever* tell your father that."

"God, no." She leaned closer, kissing Murphy lightly on the mouth. "And despite how he acts, he really does like you."

"You think so?"

"Yes. How else do you think we got the same shift?"

"I can't believe they're still making you ride with Tim for another four weeks though."

"I think it's good," she said. "I have experience in a lot of things, but I've never been on patrol before."

"Tim's got a crush on you, you know."

"So you say." They stopped in the kitchen on their way out, each pouring a cup of coffee for the road. "Speaking of that…I think I've got a huge crush on you, Detective Murphy."

"Oh, yeah?" Murphy gave her a lopsided grin. "I kinda have a huge crush on you, too, Agent Dixon."

Their eyes held for a long moment. "Come to my place tonight," she offered as she leaned against the counter.

"Okay. You gonna cook for me?"

"Not a chance," she said with a smile.

"Want me to pick something up on my way over?"

"Sure." She shoved off the counter, smiling as her lips met Murphy's. "Get something we can eat in bed."

* * *

Murphy was whistling as she drove down the street to Kayla's duplex. She stopped up short however when she saw Earl's patrol car parked along the curb. Now what? Did something happen? She glanced to the seat where the large pizza sat…a loaded pizza. She was starving. But Earl was there. Should she drive on by? Should she stop? She slowed as she passed by, not sure what to do. She could always text Kayla, ask her if it was safe to come in.

She blew out her breath. She was being childish. Of course it was safe to go in. It was only Earl…her boss and Kayla's father.

Yeah…right.

So she drove on past.

Her escape was short-lived, however, as her phone rang.

"I saw you sneaking away," Kayla said. "Come in. He's got some news."

"Good or bad?"

"He won't say."

"Okay. Be right there."

She turned around, wondering what news Earl could have. Was he resigning? God, she hoped not. He was ornery and cantankerous, but she was used to him now. If he resigned, then Sergeant Wilson would most likely be appointed, if only temporary. She liked Pete okay, but he wasn't police chief material. That made her smile. Was Earl?

She took the pizza with her, finding the door opening before she could knock. She and Kayla stood there smiling at each other, their eyes meeting. She hadn't seen her since six that morning.

"Hey."

"Hey, yourself," she said. She looked past her, seeing Earl watching them. "Are we in trouble or something?" she asked quietly.

"I don't think so." She stepped aside. "Come in."

Murphy walked in, nodding at Earl. "Chief," she greeted.

"Pizza?"

"Yeah, you want a piece?"

"No, better not. Bobbie will have dinner waiting."

Kayla took the pizza from her and put it in the oven to keep warm. They all stood in the living room, no one making a move to sit. She looked at Earl expectantly, wondering what was on his mind. He was twisting his Stetson in his hands.

"Pete Wilson resigned this morning."

"You're kidding," Kayla said. "Why?"

"Said he felt like it was time. I didn't try to stop him."

"You two have worked together for years."

"Yeah, we have. He'll turn sixty in a couple of months. Says he's gonna work with his son for a few years." He motioned for them to sit. "He's got that portable building place over on the interstate."

She and Kayla sat next to each other on the sofa. Earl continued to stand. The room was small and he stepped around the end table, pacing in the space between the living room and the kitchen. He tossed his hat on the bar that separated the two rooms.

"Gonna shuffle things around a bit." He stopped and looked at them. "Don't mind saying that the thought of me resigning has crossed my mind a time or two." He rubbed the hair of his mustache with an index finger and thumb. "I wouldn't have been shocked, either, if I'd been relieved of my duties. Doesn't look like that's going to happen."

"I thought the meeting went well," Kayla said. "In fact, they were impressed, I think."

"Thanks to you two," he said. "If it'd been left up to me and Ramsey, I imagine Ned might just have gotten away with it. And that would have mostly been my fault. You two are the ones who followed up with Lou Ann, found out about the tapes, found the link. Hell, I'd—"

"Dad..."

He held his hand up. "I know what you're going to say, but the fact of the matter is, I let my personal feelings get in the way of the job. Lesson learned the hard way." He started pacing again. "I'm gonna move Timmy up to sergeant. He's been here long enough to warrant the promotion. Y'all got a problem with that?"

"No," she said.

"Not at all," Kayla said.

"Good. I haven't told him yet." He looked at her, meeting her gaze. "I'm creating a new position. Captain." His gaze went between the two of them. "Captain Murphy. It's got a ring to it, don't you think."

Her eyes widened. "Me?"

"Yeah, you. You got a problem with it?"

"I don't know the first thing about being a captain, Earl," she said.

"Well, I imagine being a captain in Sawmill Springs will be a whole lot different than being one in Houston," he said with a laugh. "For one thing, you'll still be on patrol."

"Why are you doing this?"

"You deserve it. You have enough experience. You ran this case." His mustache lifted up at the corner of his mouth as he smiled. "Besides, it wouldn't look too good if I gave that position to my daughter."

Kayla leaned against her. "I think it's a wonderful plan, Dad."

Earl pointed his finger at them. "And no playing favorites when it comes to assignments."

"No, sir."

Kayla got up and went over to him, hugging him tightly. "Thank you."

"Well, we'll see how the guys handle it." He looked over at her. "Don't expect much of a pay raise."

"Of course not." She got up too, walking over to shake his hand. "Thank you. I guess."

"You're a good cop, Murphy. And what happened this week in Sawmill Springs is likely to be the only time you'll put your skills to use." He looked over at Kayla. "Both of you, wasting your talents here. I hope you don't grow to regret it."

Kayla linked arms with her. "I think coming back to Sawmill Springs was the best decision I ever made."

Murphy smiled at her. "I have to agree."

Earl took a step away from them. "God…let me get out of here before you start kissing or something."

* * *

Kayla took a bite of her pizza slice, then leaned over and kissed Murphy, nibbling the sauce away from the corner of her mouth.

"I can't believe he did that," Murphy said for the second time.

Kayla scooted closer to her, moving the sheet aside. Murphy had a beautiful body, and she didn't want anything to hide it from her gaze.

"The guys are going to be pissed."

"No, they won't," she said. "They like you. They respect you. They won't be pissed."

"I hope you're right." Murphy leaned back against the pillow. "What do you think they'll do when they find out that we're sleeping together?"

"I'm not sure. Lori will be the biggest gossip, of course. Part of me wants to tell her and get it over with." She smiled. "But then it'll be so much fun trying to hide it from them and have them speculate and guess what's going on. Remember, they all think I'm straight."

Murphy laughed. "Yeah, I know the feeling!"

"There is probably *someone* we should tell though."

Murphy raised her eyebrows.

"Gloria."

"Oh, yeah? Should I tell her I'm seeing someone?"

"You should tell her you're seeing someone and that someone is quite enamored with you."

"Enamored, huh?"

"Very."

Murphy tossed her pizza slice into the box, then took her own as well. She closed the lid and slid the box aside.

"Show me."

Kayla smiled. "Show you what?"

"Show me how *enamored* you are."

Kayla laughed delightfully. "Again?"

"Again."

Bella Books, Inc.

Women. Books. Even Better Together.

P.O. Box 10543
Tallahassee, FL 32302

Phone: 800-729-4992
www.bellabooks.com